A QUESTION OF MURDER

"Miss Stewart, I have to talk to you."

Teal cracked the door ajar. She didn't know what he meant. She didn't know what he wanted her to do.

He raised his shoulders and let them fall. "Please. The police at Shell Bay laughed at my confession, but I told them the truth. I killed your friend."

The hairs tingled on Teal's arms. Albert Fontane hadn't meant accident when he said killed. She jerked the door wide.

Albert grabbed Teal's arm. "The sand messed me up. The car skidded and I hit her bad. The contract'd been specific. An accident, see. But the sand screwed me up."

"What do you mean, contract? Someone paid you?" Teal couldn't feel the step beneath her feet. "Mr. Fontane, the Cape investigation concluded Nancy's death was the result of an accident. You said accident just now. Your wife's illness must be a terrible stress, but this new fiction won't help."

"Fiction? This isn't fiction lady." Albert backed away from Teal down the steps. "And it wasn't an accident. It was murder."

A QUESTION
OF PREFERENCE

J. DAYNE LAMB

ZEBRA BOOKS
KENSINGTON PUBLISHING CORP.

ZEBRA BOOKS are published by

Kensington Publishing Corp.
850 Third Avenue
New York, NY 10022

First Kensington Hardcover Printing: October, 1994
First Zebra Paperback Printing: October, 1995

Printed in the United States of America

❓ PREFACE

The End of June.

Nancy Vandenburg tightened her fist around her head. Thick blond hair, "blunt cut and stylish," bent in disarray while the "simple two-carat diamond studs, her sole ornamentation," drove against an "impish" nose. Finally, "candid, jade green eyes" collided with "bisque pale skin."

Before her square, clean fingernails gouged through "high, broad cheekbones touched with the blush of modesty," she bounced her face to the floor.

The mutilated page uncurled to wink the paper eyes of the photographic portrait in a mockery of her rage. Warm June sun flooded her artist's studio and shimmered the pink fluorescence highlights on the text. The marks showed a careful, even painstaking, application to selected letters.

laMode People in the News
–An Artist for a New Decade–

With Sotheby's going, going, gone at over 1.3 million for a canvas known as *FRIENDS* just last month (April) and another presidential commission behind her, Nancy Vandenburg would not be impertinent to say, "Make room Norman Rockwell, here I am." Of course, this charming artist follows the suggestion with a shake of her blunt cut and stylish blond hair. America's foremost living painter of family and societal conventions herself lives a conventional life in a suburb of Boston, Massachusetts, with husband Michael Britton and young daughter Libby. While social problems—Adultery, AIDS, homelessness and death—are also depicted in Ms. Vandenburg's work, her genius lies in an insightful reaffirmation of American values, mixing humor, pathos, compassion and belief on canvases which speak directly to our hearts. The truth of basic values, not their perversion, infuse Vandenburg's paintings. Viewing her current exhibit at the Barrette Gallery on East 26th Street, I confess certain pictures move me inexplicably. Felicia Barrette, Ms. Vandenburg's career-long champion (Barrette Gallery has been the sole New York representative of her work) gives a simple explanation. "Nancy let's us feel it's okay to want to come home to a simpler ethic, despite how complex that ethic—discerning right from wrong, good from bad—can be." Later I asked Ms. Vandenburg if her paintings more accurately could be said to parody than reflect an idealized reality. Her candid, jade green eyes . . .

Wrinkles obscured the balance of the text, but the uneven strokes of pink remained all too visible. Nancy's transcription filled the margin.

"p u n i s h m e n t follows Adultery death f o l l o w s perversion confess n o w come home to th e right w a y" inadvertently captioned the image of a serene Nancy in her own, frenzied print. Ink smudged the spot where she had squeezed the paper like a neck.

Now her hand beat the windowpane. The fields beyond lay furred with early summer's tender grass. Two horses frolicked in the field just past the barn. Red barn, green grass, white farmhouse, blue sky and little Libby with the collie by the leafing maple tree—this was a scene Nancy could have painted.

Her hand drew back in a jerk before it sailed forward, barn shattering, sky falling, blood running. A shock of pain snapped her to attention as her inked "Adultery" bled black beneath drips of red. She stamped her foot to the upturned face as if to conquer fear with anger.

Fear won. Nancy Vandenburg needed help. Teal Stewart's kind of help.

? One

The End of June.

Teal stared at the files in the middle of her desk. She scanned the stack to the right, then swiveled to regard the heap behind her on the credenza. Her blue eyes darkened. These Fruiers Construction Company audit papers threatened to take over her life.

She sighed. Audit papers, the record of analysis and testing performed on the financial records of a client company by a certified public accountant, a CPA like Teal, were pretty much her life.

The sigh threatened to become a scream. But senior managers at Clayborne Whittier, the prestigious international accounting firm, did not scream. They did not crack under pressure. They did not let the great firm down.

Especially not in this case. Not when she had raised the charge of embezzlement herself. Fruiers chief financial officer had turned out to be as much a thief as a jerk. Now she was expected to provide the accounting evidence of "financial malfeasance adequate to convict" according to her last discussion with the Clayborne Whittier partner on the account.

Easy for him to say. He'd already been admitted to the

partnership. The one time she prayed for Fruiers' CFO to act stupid, he went and hired the best defense, Boston's hottest white-collar crime lawyer, Renee Maxwell.

Teal stroked a file. The audit papers contained irrefutable proof. The trick lay in assembling the complex data to convince a jury. But she would. No embezzling jackass was going to end her career. Hadn't *The Boston Globe* once described her as a "financial Sherlock Holmes?"

But why Renee Maxwell? And why this year when she was up for admission to the Clayborne Whittier partnership?

Teal knew the unspoken price of failure. Goodbye Clayborne Whittier. Goodbye big corner office. Goodbye to "E. TEAL STEWART" spelled out under "PARTNERS" on the directory in the lobby. Her name could look nice, and whether or not she wanted it there was a separate issue. However she came down, she deserved the right to decide, not some felonious turkey.

E. Teal Stewart shook her head and opened a file. This CFO had been greedy, not clever. Greedy enough to get sloppy in his scheme of faked invoices and diverted payments. The proof lay in front of her. Let Fruiers' attorney worry about R. Maxwell, Esquire. The company's attorney, not Teal, would be the one to face Ms. Maxwell in court.

Teal would provide the evidence adequate to convict. She liked puzzles she could solve, questions she could answer. Forgetting the possible consequences, this assignment wasn't all bad.

She checked her watch. Why had she agreed to meet Nancy Vandenburg for lunch with so little time to prepare for the trial? But Nancy, friend and confidante of many years, had insisted.

"Carole will know what to do, Nancy, or Michael." Teal tried to filter impatience from her voice.

9

"Don't put me off. This isn't some little problem with a show. It isn't something for my sister or, God knows, my husband. Please," Nancy said as she jabbed Teal's peppermint tea aside, sloshing pale green across the white cloth.

She slapped the tattered magazine page to the table. Teal looked down to Nancy's ruined face and gasped. Then she read the strange legend aloud.

"Punishment follows adultery, death follows perversion. Confess now. Come home to the right way."

Teal didn't think Richard Avedon would be happy with the dried blood effect. She skimmed the laudatory profile. She had read it before. Nancy didn't have career worries. The thought made her feel small.

"It isn't true?" Teal asked, alert to the stab of tension between them.

"I hope not—I'd be in big trouble."

The golden flecked green eyes locked to Teal's smoky blue. Conversations hummed and murmured unabated around them.

"Threat aside, Nan, is this about adultery?"

Teal had never seen her friend so uncomfortable. Nancy dropped her gaze to the article.

"They don't understand. I am finally home," she said.

"What about Michael, Nan? Does he know?" Teal asked carefully, like Nancy, easing away from the friction.

Teal had never approved of Michael. She never discussed why with Nancy, fearing an exchange of knowledge too intimate for even the best of friends. One view of Michael had changed with the years, she knew. And it was not hers.

Nancy's mirthless laugh interrupted more thought.

"No. Michael—look, I'm going to sort this out with him, but not this way. Not because of some creepy emotional terrorist. Help me."

The complexities of self-interest stalled Teal's impulse to nod agreement. Fruiers' CFO held the monopoly on her time. He could jeopardize her future with his inept greed. It made her want to kill.

Teal stopped thinking about herself. *Want to kill.* Might some nut mean the threat of death to Nancy? No. No way.

Teal fingered the garish message.

"Death follows perversion," Teal repeated.

Could she gamble with Nancy? Teal shifted her focus from the blood-flecked page to Nancy's scabbed hand.

"Should you tell me about that?"

Nancy shifted uncomfortably, then extended her fingers in a fan. "Some dramatic presentation of my personalized junk mail. Please, say you'll help."

"I'll do what I can." Teal suppressed an internal sigh.

"You're wonderful! I knew you would!" Nancy arched her lanky frame above the table and hugged Teal.

The room rippled to silence. Covert glances flicked over Nancy's long body, vivid in a yellow angora sweater and black leggings. Nancy lowered into the seat, and the staring eyes dropped away.

Teal recaptured the strands of hair escaping her chignon and squared the shoulders of her dove gray Italian dress. Nancy must be upset to display public affection. Teal signaled for the check and placed the magazine page into its envelope.

"I'll need to know everything. Everything, Nan, and you can start on the walk back."

There was half a minute, getting their coats, when Nancy's radiance disturbed Teal.

Obvious stares had followed Nancy from the dining room to the foyer. Faces concentrated to search memory. Who was she? Someone in last week's *People?* Someone passing asked Nancy if she'd been on TV. It took all of

Teal's concentration to remember that long ago she accepted Nancy could eclipse the rising sun.

But Teal had her own moments, like the afternoon a man had stopped her in the street.

"I saw you on the front of *Boston Magazine!*" he'd said.

" 'Biased in Boston? Professional Women May Just Agree.' The cover story," Teal replied, pleased.

The man walked by with his companion. "Wish my CPA looked like that," he said.

Teal grinned at the memory. That she wore a chic linen dress and restrained hair for the Clayborne Whittier side of the day did not make her a little gosling. It didn't make Nancy any less a swan, either. Teal laughed.

"What are you finding funny about this?" Nancy asked as she tossed a fire-red baseball jacket over her shoulder.

They pushed through the revolving door.

"No. I was laughing at myself. The worm of envy, Nancy. It isn't always easy being your friend."

Nancy turned a blank face to Teal.

"Surely you haven't forgotten my attempt to put you in your place freshman year?" Teal asked. Even now, she recalled the messy, adolescent eruption with chagrin.

"Oh that. Over fifteen years ago! I hate thinking about those days. I didn't do anything to be blonde or tall—"

"Or beautiful and talented. That's what you said, Nan, but you are and there can be moments . . ." Teal stopped.

If she could be envious, what might a sibling be? Seething with jealousy? Driven to threats? A sibling might be Carole Vandenburg, of course, paired to Nancy in a sort of mutual adoration society. Teal deflated.

"Yes?" Nancy said. "And you forget there can be moments with a best friend, her hair the auburn of fall, her height a graceful, reasonable five seven and the most outspoken individual on campus. I could hardly say a word without blushing." Nancy stared at Teal. "How did we start?"

The hardest thing to forgive, Teal understood, was Nancy's innocence of her effect. Yet her grace and graciousness were unfeigned. Teal remembered spending freshman year looking for Nancy's clay feet and little, prehensile claws. Teal found her own smallness and that was all. They roomed together the four years, inseparable.

"The auburn of fall, indeed. Is that off a tube of paint? Brown paint?" Teal laughed and raised her eyebrows. "Now, tell me more about the magazine graffiti."

It seemed to Teal that Nancy did a little stutter step, a mere second's hesitation.

"I found it in the Lincoln post box yesterday. Most business mail, about shows or buying or interviews, comes to Carole here in Boston. Personal mail goes to the house, so I don't make much effort to clear the box." Nancy shrugged. "That trash could have been there for days."

Teal read New York off the postmark. The date was illegible. Nancy explained Avedon had shot the photo in March with the *laMode* interview in April. Very au courant for the May issue. Teal had bought it and expected every one of Nancy's friends had done the same.

The lobby of the First New England Bank building brought Teal's primary concern back in a surge. She'd lost over two hours on Fruiers to this lunch. Worse, Nancy hadn't given her a thing to go on, but Nancy still expected her help.

"I need more, Nan. Like, what's happening with Michael? What's up on the famous artist front, aside from this?" Teal shook the envelope and it hit her. Nancy's lover was unlikely to be just anyone. She chose her words. "Could this be meant to hurt the man you're seeing?"

"No."

Teal caught the shift of Nancy's eyes. People pushed past them in a commotion of comings and goings.

"Michael is busy with the retrospective. He's a good publicist for all his clients, including me," Nancy said.

"You're his biggest, aren't you? The most important?"

"Yes." Nancy shrugged. "If you're asking if Michael could have done this—maybe, but it's not his style. Anyway, he doesn't know anything, Teal. No one knows."

Teal watched Nancy absorbing the visual of the lobby. Light, distorted through a wall of glass cubes, fell on marble floor tiles arranged to tease the eye. Nancy did not ask Teal about Hunt, the architect who had designed the FNEB building and stopped living with Teal in the same year. Teal couldn't afford to show Nancy equal tact.

Impatience sharpened Teal's words. "How is Carole?"

"Consumed by the retrospective's opening this fall. San Diego, Chicago, Washington, Boston, and then Europe. Carole actually enjoys chaos. And no, I haven't told her about this . . . new aspect of my life. Not yet."

"Afraid she'll be worried about you?" Teal asked.

Nancy grinned back, nodding.

"Okay. Your husband doesn't know anything. Your sister doesn't know anything. You didn't confide in me until today—and from my point of view, not much. Which leaves who? Felicia?"

"No."

The silence crawled. Teal changed tack. "I always liked *FRIENDS.*"

The painting of two men on the Cote d'Azur beach had been Nancy's first critical triumph. One figure leaned into the side of the other as they sat by the water. The rectangles formed by their backs filled the canvas. Water and sand became splashes of color over shoulders and beside buttocks. The simple tenderness of posture spoke legions about the depth of relationship, man with man. Nancy's genius was evident and startling, her tacit understanding of friendship's dimension and vulnerability clear. She had been twenty-two.

"One point three million." Nancy shook her head. "I think I received two hundred when Felicia first sold it."

"The benefits are coming now, aren't they, for you and Barrette Gallery. This price for *FRIENDS* will push your current works into the stratosphere. And what's this I've read about the buyer. A 'prominent, adulterous, bisexual capitalist'? Not your usual collector. Maybe the sale inspired the nut. The *laMode* profile starts with *FRIENDS.*"

"The message is—don't let bisexuals own my work?" Nancy groaned. "As though I control my buyers or sellers."

"I'm out of bright ideas." Teal shrugged, but the question remained. Who stood to gain by scaring Nancy?

"Teal, I've been successful for years and never held responsible for the quirks of my collectors. A president who only traveled with the blessing of the stars just about made my reputation—and people voted for him." Nancy's voice rose.

"Leaving your friend. Who did he tell?" Teal asked.

"Don't you get it, Teal?" Nancy snapped. *"No one knows about us."*

For a second Teal wanted to snap back, don't you get it, Nancy, because somebody does.

"I've been looking all over for you," Kathy interrupted with a tap on Teal's arm. Teal's secretary nodded to Nancy. "Hi, Ms. Vandenburg. Teal, the PIC wants to see you ASAP. He's been calling every five minutes, and I've run out of stories."

Don Clarke, Clayborne Whittier's partner-in-charge in Boston, could want her for only one thing, that damned CFO. Teal took a deep breath.

"Tell him I'll be right up," she said.

"I should let you go, Teal."

Teal sensed relief in Nancy's voice. Guilt at her own desire to dismiss Nancy's fears prompted Teal's next words.

"Don't worry, I'll help."

Relief lifted Nancy's lips into a smile.

"But I'll need to talk to Michael, Carole, Felicia, your friend. Discreetly, of course." It was the only way to start.

Nancy grabbed Teal's arm. "No! I mean . . . not yet. They don't know anything so what could you learn? I know you can find a better way."

Nancy, vivid in black, yellow, and red—and jittery with apprehension—stood with her back to the street. Daylight illuminated a faint glow around her shadowed face. The years of friendship had survived a fair measure of ups and downs, but Nancy was as close to a sister as it came.

"The better way, Nan, is for you to tell me the truth."

? TWO

At one time Felicia Barrette might have been surprised at Nancy Vandenburg's out-of-hand dismissal of the suggestion she had confided in Felicia. Actually, she would have been crushed. She considered artists needy children and her role to listen, soothe, and cajole.

Nancy Vandenburg had been no different, asked no less. Felicia knew Nancy's career success sprang from the nurturing support of Barrette Gallery, and Felicia *was* Barrette Gallery.

Felicia conceded the artist's talent created art. However—the however that separated fame from obscurity— the gallery positioned the artist. Barrette Gallery had promoted the comparison of Nancy to Norman Rockwell. Barrette Gallery had created the excitement preceding the Sotheby's auction. Most important, Barrette Gallery had brokered Nancy's first presidential sale when Nancy was only twenty-five. The sale put Nancy Vandenburg on the map and the gallery in the black.

At one time Felicia believed friends told each other everything and she considered Nancy as a friend. That Nancy, or any of her artists, might characterize their relationship otherwise would have confused and upset Felicia. But Felicia had had less to hide.

She hadn't been sitting then, as she was now, the bathroom locked and dread mounting. This fourth visit of the day showed nothing, absolutely nothing. She squinted. No speck of reassurance marked the tissue. Washing up, the soap burned her hands. The sensation offered the absolution of a purification right. Whispering hot water became a call to prayer.

"Please God I've never believed in, scald the corruption of the flesh out. Make me all right."

Felicia couldn't believe herself. She pulled back from the sink and rubbed a thin towel over her red, chapped fingers. A mirror above the basin showed no distortion, no foxing of the silver. She stood as always. Not exactly petite, her breasts' curve too lush, but not unlovely.

The pleated trousers and black sweatshirt disguised the effects of missing her daily workout. Shoulder pads and baggy pants hid more than the change in routine. And for a few weeks more, they should hide the truth. She curved her hand over her hip. Maybe she should just get it over with and take an early vacation this year. Maybe go to the Ranch.

She turned sideways, pulling the sweatshirt flat, sucking in her abdomen. Looking, looking. Boring the glass with her anxious brown eyes. Henna muted the copper penny of her hair to warm rose. The exuberant tangle contrasted with the purple of her bitten and pinched lips, their natural generosity reduced to a tentative line. Even her freckles contracted to anxious dots.

She lifted her rib cage higher, held her sweatshirt above her bra and stared.

"Felicia, Felicia? You in there, girl?" The door rattled with the knock.

Adrenaline flooded her body and embarrassment burned her face to color-up the width of cheek and chin which a moment before glared back at her bony white. She dropped the fabric and clutched the sink.

"Be right out," she said too brightly.

Her assistant, close by her side, rushed to talk. The sentences mounted. First one, then another, now a third tumbled against her ears. Felicia didn't listen. She worried the curve of her lipstick had not disguised the rigidity of her lips. She prayed her posture dispelled doubt, her full breasts high and shoulders square. Still, sweat beaded on the surface of the deodorant under her arms. Moisture soaked her bra.

She became aware of a changed rhythm in her assistant's speech. His sentences broke into short pieces now, the slight pauses inviting intervention. The best she could do mimicked indistinct agreement. She realized she must ease the strain.

"I'll take those," she said.

She pulled the telephone messages from his hand. None from Nancy, thank God. Felicia tried to concentrate. So many artists needed a call back. So many demands.

"It's up to you. You at least heard me say they're upset?" John pursed thin lips thinner.

Felicia quashed a desire to turn and run. "Upset?"

"I just told you, dear. They think we've shorted them on the American Images show. As if we'd even know how to do such a dirty deed, let alone cut off our little nose to spite our little faces. I've asked the accountant to come in tomorrow. You wait to return those calls until we've combed the records."

"The accountant?" Felicia's voice rose, but she realized her error. "Let's wait. You remember that bank mistake last year when I overreacted and made everything worse."

"I guess I'm supposed to say okay." John made a moue.

"Really, it will be fine." Felicia waved her handful of paper and walked away.

Entering her office, she shut the door in haste. Now she read each message with care. One, from the installation artist who claimed to be an anarchist, had the notation, "legal action threatened." Ridiculous, Felicia thought. None of the messages was from *him,* the coward. Coward and deceiver, she amended, bitterness tightening to a knot in her stomach.

Felicia picked up the toy car he'd given her. Memento of their weekend in the Ferrari she had rented. Big fucking deal, she mouthed, hurt propelling her vehemence. She placed the car on the floor and kicked it across the room, a whirring silver streak, its little wheels turning, its hinged doors flying open.

Kicking again she cracked it against the crouching stone woman by the door. The tiny headlights shattered. Her heel crushed the hood, jamming each wheel to its well. She stared at the mini-wreck.

That was what it had become, a mini-wreck. Defeat turned down her shoulders.

Felicia straightened slowly, holding the bits of plastic, metal, and glass. She tightened her hand until the metal bit. She stared right through Nancy's painting hanging over the desk, then her eyes focused.

Eleven years earlier, she had recognized genius at her first sight of Nancy Vandenburg's work and felt the euphoria of an immigrant at the Statue of Liberty. Felicia was flooded with knowing *this* was the representation of all America could be. She had spent the year in Europe seeking this reaction and knew that day she had found the artist to resurrect Barrette Gallery.

The visionary space for art her parents had opened in their twenties to showcase American talent had become burdened by insupportable debt by the year of their early deaths. Felicia rented the valuable retail space on an at-will lease and flew to Europe, hoping there, on the "Continent," a new American energy would be made manifest. Then she could go home again.

Nancy Vandenburg exemplified that energy.

Felicia remembered their meeting.

"I can sell the canvas," Felicia had said. She pointed to the big one leaning against the right wall of the studio. "If I do, I want you to let me represent you. Standard terms, the gallery gets its percent, you take the rest."

Nancy's response lacked the enthusiasm Felicia expected, but brought the result she wanted. Later, knowing Nancy better, she understood Nancy's ambivalence. Mr. Vandenburg's college graduation gift of a year in Paris presumed an ultimate graduation, as well, from adolescence. "When you come back," he had insisted, "you'll be over this nonsense about painting."

Nancy, the good daughter, meant to comply. She worked to believe her creative energy could be satisfied through motherhood and writing poetry part-time even if her poetry wasn't good. Felicia met her right before the return home.

"You'll never be able to sell it here," Nancy had said.

"Title?" Felicia didn't need to be told selling an unknown American in France might be difficult.

"RIVIERA? That's where I painted it in September."

Felicia contemplated the painting. "I think rather something like *FRIENDS."*

Nancy shrugged. "I expect they are."

Felicia sold the painting to the cultural attaché at the U.S. Embassy the same day. A peer of her parents, he still collected with an infallible instinct for talent. More than anything, the sale reaffirmed Felicia's conviction about Nancy. On his part, he delighted in the addition to the private collection he kept American to irritate the French.

Late that spring, Nancy's father died suddenly. Nancy never returned to Holland, Michigan, but left Paris for

New York. Felicia knew Nancy continued to write poetry, but only for friends. Nancy's arrival put Barrette Gallery back in business.

Today threats to survival plagued the gallery again, and again Felicia recognized Nancy's genius. Things could get better, after all.

Felicia dropped pieces of smashed car one by one into the empty trash can. The sound they made hitting bottom rang hollow and cold.

❓ THREE

Sandra Jordan swiveled her chair. The hiss of the white-noise system, an office amenity intended to calm the daily din, seemed to amplify the silence and further tighten her nerves. She unconsciously bounced her leg, rippling shock waves of fat across her thighs. A jaundiced tan suit sliced into her waist at the folded band. Poor tailoring constricted her arms where the fabric pulled across her back.

The tails of her pink blouse's self-tie bow hung artlessly on her chest. Fidgeting, she fingered strands of the black hair curled against her head. Taupe nail polish looked puce beside her brown skin. It was chipped from her furtive, fretful picking.

Why had Renee Maxwell specifically requested her as the replacement for the third-year first assigned the Fruiers' CFO defense? The question still left her confused. She asked it over and over, trying to answer as often.

She was the premier hire in her class, the group of young lawyers who started with Stimpson, Grey and Minot the previous fall. Irrefutable evidence supported her assessment. She had been graduated summa cum laude from Northwestern University Law School. She had received an offer from every firm with which she interviewed and was the first African-American woman at

SGM, a firm not noted for altruism or affirmative action.

She knew she had not disappointed. After garnering the highest score, and gold medal, on the Massachusetts bar examination last July, she had logged the most chargeable hours in the firm. June statistics weren't available yet, but she expected to lead them, too.

Most of all, she knew she must maintain the performance. She brought no other attribute. Certainly not social connection. The mere idea provoked bitter laughter. Socially, she always did the wrong thing. How wrong was evident from the only slightly masked disdain with which her colleagues greeted her attempts to be like them.

She recognized that. But she could better them, almost effortlessly, in research, legal analysis, and writing. And she did. Her SGM internal rating, the critical measure by the evaluation committee, placed her at the top.

On her part, Renee Maxwell had provided the sole reason for Sandra's selection of SGM over more lucrative offers. The famous criminal defense attorney set the national standard for litigators, male and female. Be they rich or poor, black, white, or any other color, few of Renee Maxwell's clients ever faced a verdict of guilty.

Sandra wanted to understand everything about Renee Maxwell, understand how the litigator did it, understand why. Sandra even went so far as to house-sit Renee's apartment over Christmas. Nominally optional, any new associate stood to be recruited by SGM's personnel department for the annual chore. Sandra volunteered. Her colleagues might debate the brownnose aspect; she didn't care.

But even Renee's historic gratitude to the employee who watered her plants left unexplained the placing of Sandra in a role more appropriate to a senior associate. Inexplicable actions always made Sandra uncomfortable.

Her foot jiggled faster, tapping her knee against the bottom of a drawer. Sandra involuntarily jerked her knee hard to the desk. The contact popped her panty hose open and sent a run down her shin. Skin mushroomed from the large hole. Sandra stared at the five dollars wasted. The telephone spared a display of anger.

"Sandra Jordan," she said, stilling her foot, sitting straighter in the chair.

"This is Teal Stewart at Clayborne Whittier, Sandra. Returning your call."

Sandra tried to get a picture of the woman to go with the low, resonant voice. Her own was high and in her throat under stress, carrying hardly to the telephone's mouthpiece. Teal Stewart must be someone white. Someone successful. Someone comfortable with her life.

Long ago Sandra had trained the hostility out of her voice along with the cadence of Chicago's south side.

"I'm our associate on Fruiers. Renee Maxwell hoped I could collect your signed deposition today, then Mr. Clarke suggested I make arrangements with you. This afternoon suits my schedule." Sandra waited.

"How about after four?" Teal asked.

"That's fine, thank you. I'll be by then." Sandra hung up to an encore of restless and apprehensive bouncing.

Don Clarke had entered Teal's office directly on her heels as she returned from lunch.

"Some persistent woman from Stimpson managed to get through to me on your deposition."

The fact of Teal's two-hour lunch stood as an unspoken issue between them. Loyalty to the firm was counted in many small ways. And unweaning loyalty counted almost above all else in an admission year. Above the needs of self and, certainly, above the needs of a friend. Teal saw Don watching her. She offered no explanation, no apology.

"Are we comfortable with it?" Don asked without pausing for her answer. "Counsel's reviewed it, hasn't he? This puts us in a damned awkward position. Bob Fahey used to be with us, you know."

Indeed, Teal did know Fruiers' embezzling CFO, Robert Fahey, had started with Clayborne Whittier over ten years ago, before she joined the firm. Their tenure overlapped before Clayborne Whittier concluded he wasn't "suited to current needs." The firm had extended the usual courtesies to him as an alumnus, job referral and placement among them. Don Clarke avoided raising this more sensitive issue.

Clayborne Whittier had proposed Bob for the position of Fruiers Construction Company chief financial officer. The international accounting and auditing firm supported him with a recommendation and endorsement to hire. Now, three years later, Fruiers expected Clayborne Whittier's expertise to have Bob Fahey convicted as a thief. Don Clarke did not want to be humiliated a second time. A relationship with a client and the firm's self-image stood on the line.

"Damned bad luck for you, too." Don laid a heavy pat on Teal's shoulder.

She imagined he meant to be kind and restrained herself from patting back. She swallowed the caustic "there, there" off her tongue. Maybe that's why she asked the question out loud, instead of letting it remain between them, unspoken.

"Does my admission to the partnership depend on the outcome on Fruiers?"

Don's eyes drifted to some middle distance past her left shoulder.

"So many factors make up the decision, Teal. You understand. An individual's technical competence, their communication skills, grasp of business issues, ability—"

"To develop staff. I've read the form, Don. What about *my* performance in *this* lawsuit? Fruiers expects to win. They can't afford not to. You and I both know that their attorney considers the Clayborne Whittier evidence critical. I understand I'm on the line. My question is, is it also the admission line?"

"I'd be dishonest to say it won't matter." Don's eyes slid past Teal's face to inspect the middle distance of the other side.

"Then be honest. How much will it matter?"

A peculiar agitation held her today. Don Clarke had sent Kathy chasing all over the city because a law office associate needed her deposition. The caution worried Teal. Exactly what role was this suit going to play in her life?

"Teal. Teal, you don't need me to tell you actions are as important as the verdict. You've irritated a fair number of my partners over your career. Not everyone is on your side—use this chance to change a few minds. Take Frank Sweeney, the partner on Fruiers. He feels vulnerable, too. Pointing the finger at a former CW staff hurt. It doesn't do for you to call Frank names like obstructionist."

Teal opened her mouth to protest that the partner to whom she reported on the Fruiers account wasn't just an obstructionist, he was an idiot, and the work he brought in to the firm trash, but she snapped it shut.

"Let's get back to the main point. You feel sure the deposition records what you meant to say? Maxwell didn't create distortion with her questions? Our counsel has no problems with it?" Don said.

She knew what was coming next.

"Perhaps you should run it by him and read it yourself one more time."

Teal did not grind her teeth. Not in public.

Don didn't want any adverse associations for Clayborne Whittier and neither did she. Whether she considered his request reasonable or not, he would second-guess every step she took on the lawsuit. Why not give herself a break?

"Our counsel is happy, but you're right. I'll take another look, myself." She smiled away the irritation straining the muscles beneath her face.

Don Clarke nodded his contentment. Teal stared at the door after he left. She knew he considered outside interests a game of golf and following clients in *The Wall Street Journal*.

Why on earth would I want to be like that? Teal wondered, and not for the first time.

On her best days she believed she would be different. Beat the odds. Trouble was, today wasn't among her best.

Kathy tapped once and ushered Sandra Jordan through the door.

"It must be exciting to work with Renee Maxwell," Teal said after Sandra settled into the visitor chair.

The young woman looked uncomfortable.

"Do you have a background in finance or accounting?" Teal asked in the third prolonged silence.

Sandra Jordan turned the most perfectly shaped head and arresting profile Teal had ever seen balanced on so ungainly a body. Viewed straight on, Sandra's deep mahogany eyes appeared as uncommunicative as plastic marbles.

"My law degree is from Northwestern. My B.A. is in economics. I took one accounting course."

Teal was sure that if Sandra could have answered entirely in monosyllables, she would have. She visibly did not enjoy small talk. Teal gathered the deposition pages from her desk.

"Here it is, Sandra. We may have differing views of Mr. Fahey professionally, but, still, we will be seeing more of each other. It's nice to have chatted." Teal stood with Sandra. "Renee has a reputation as a brilliant lawyer. Did you know of her before joining Stimpson?"

Teal regretted the question immediately.

"Every lawyer knows about her," Sandra mumbled.

"Of course, I should have thought—she practiced in your backyard, Chicago, before coming here." Teal shook Sandra's surprisingly firm hand before the woman fled.

How tactless of me, Teal admonished herself. Renee Maxwell's stature first sprang from the innovative civil rights work she'd done in private practice in Chicago following a stint as a public defender just out of Harvard Law School.

The year she moved to Boston, local publications and *The New York Times* heralded her arrival in a series of profiles analyzing the move. They reported Stimpson lured her to their fledgling white-collar crime practice with a partnership and commitment to support her pro bono interests with staff and time. Seven years later, Teal agreed the bargain seemed of mutual benefit.

She shrugged in annoyance. Renee's reputed disdain for accountants wasn't going to be much help to her. Then Teal grinned to think Renee was defending one. He wouldn't change Renee's mind.

I will, Teal decided. *All accountants aren't fools, and I'll prove it.*

Prove it. Prove she should be admitted to the Clayborne Whittier partnership. Prove it to herself she wanted to be. Prove it to the smug lawyer that an accountant could trip up her case. Prove that Nancy's threat is the ranting of some pathetic creep.

Prove it.

Teal shook her head. Her hand hovered above the dark phone on her desk. Nancy had been adamant—don't talk to anyone about the *laMode* clip.

Teal dropped her fingers and punched in Carole's number at the dial tone. How else could she prove it?

Sandra Jordan's rushing steps faltered in front of Brigham's. Inside, the lunch crowd had long departed, and the after-shopping influx thinned to three individuals in one booth. She sat behind them.

"What'll it be, dearie?"

The waitress's speed signaled she was coming to the end of her shift. Sandra didn't care. She didn't need any extra time.

"Hot fudge sundae on vanilla with whipped cream and double nuts, please."

Sandra heard the words float from her mouth, but she remained divorced from their reality. They left her, weightless and disconnected.

"Sure thing. Water?" the waitress asked as she stuck the pencil behind her ear.

After Sandra's "No thank you," the waitress left. Sandra burned with the humiliation reserved for fat girls. No one in the desolate restaurant seemed to notice her, but she imagined their revulsion at her order. Her mouth salivated as her mind admonished. Stupid and loathsome and fat, that's what they must have thought, because she did.

The sundae, set down before her, dripped fudge and spilled nuts to the orange formica. Air crushed from the foamy whipped topping and filled her mouth with sweet. Cold ice cream melted against her lips. She tasted vanilla and walnut and chocolate. Then she set to business, crunching the nuts, scraping spillage up with her spoon, wolfing down the dessert until finished. Pure sensation receded, and thought returned.

Yes, she had known Renee Maxwell before joining SGM.

? Four

Carole stood by her office window and stared down at the Old Granary Burying Ground. Across it, through the foliage of maple trees, she watched a back up of traffic on Tremont Street.

Tourists walked among the headstones and bent to read inscriptions. Some posed for the family camera to memorialize the moment. Children flattened new paths across the grass. Three little girls, ineffectually stilled by a weary mother, yelled up a racket as they skipped around the grave rumored to be Mary "Mother" Goose's. Blurred by distance, Carole saw the eldest, with hair a sun-bleached white, as much like Libby as a twin.

She smiled at the fondness she felt for her niece. She liked the position of aunt. The role fit. And Nancy shared her daughter—perhaps to keep Carole off her back to have more. Carole chuckled. Surely life was good.

She did not hear the reception door open. A sudden urban eruption of honks and sirens drowned the knock on her office door. She lingered within her daydream, remembering Nancy as a child, easily prettier and more charming than any other, even Libby. So much excitement had surrounded the advent of a new baby into the family, one Carole had been promised she could hold and feed and love more than her doll, Tiny Tears.

She understood Mummy preferred the sanctuary of her room to the commotion of two children. One had been struggle enough. Carole didn't mind. She was sure she didn't mind. She remembered Mummy's soft voice on her fourth birthday. "This year you'll receive a very special gift."

The gift, pink-faced and helpless, arrived in the form of Nancy.

A second, sharper rap brought Carole to the present. She straightened the jacket of her Yves St. Laurent as she turned from the window. The suit draped perfectly across her front, and Carole knew it. She presented a poised and polished face to the world and worked to maximize her every attribute, not like Nancy with her natural, radiant beauty. Carole enjoyed their differences. She did just fine.

"Yes? Teal?" Carole opened the door as she asked. Gold bracelets banged together in a soft clatter.

Teal set her briefcase to the floor. Carole touched her cheek to Teal's, leaving the meticulous curve of her pageboy undisturbed. For a second she smelled the rich mixture of perfumes, Teal's light and elusive, her own a denser spice.

"You can't come to Libby's birthday? Clayborne Whittier is that compelling?"

Carole didn't say what she felt—that Libby wouldn't understand a plea of too much work. What child could? Hadn't "Mummy's too tired" confused Nancy?

"Work is a lousy excuse," Teal said.

She did not say she'd come, Carole noticed. Carole pinched a smile from disapproving lips.

"Don't listen to me. I missed my share of family gatherings when I worked in New York. Anyway, Nancy tells me this may be your year. Admission to the 'sacred partnership' and all that," Carole mimicked Teal. "But you didn't stop by to discuss your odds of joining the ruling class, did you?"

She waved Teal into an overstuffed, chintz-covered chair.

"No, but I could use your gift of tact at work about now." Teal shrugged at the likelihood of that transformation. "But work isn't why I came. I ate lunch with Nancy today—"

"And you're worried about her." Carole's statement wasn't a question.

"Um. A little. Have you noticed something bothering her?" Teal asked.

"She didn't tell you?" Carole watched Teal's face. "No? I had hoped Nancy would be forthcoming with someone. She hasn't been with me lately."

"I could use a sister like you." Teal grinned.

Carole leaned forward.

"Help me with Nancy. She isn't talking to me, and, well, I can't ask flat out. I made that mistake with Michael. She forgave your objections, I'm not sure she ever forgave me. We didn't intrude in each other's private lives growing up. The difference in age, maybe, or Mother's illness. I gave her a love she couldn't get from Mummy and only the occasional unsolicited advice," Carole said.

"You took a risk with Michael." Teal bobbed her head.

"Yes. Well, Michael—I really thought I could protect her. She didn't see it my way. Sometimes I think she married in rebellion. Well, that's history." Carole lifted her shoulders and dropped them.

History was also far more complex, she knew, in a childhood where their mother daily lost ground against a mortal illness. The battle left little for her two girls. Nothing in the end.

Carole took charge of Nancy in the void. When Nancy grew up to be more lovely if less vivacious, more talented if less ambitious, Carole realized the adulation she had commanded at home salved her ego for later blows. She never begrudged her sister's success, and Nancy never stopped looking up to her big sister even after Carole stood a few inches shorter. And Carole never stopped feeling responsible for Nancy.

"This could have to do with Michael, of course," Carole concluded.

Teal snorted. "I can't imagine it doesn't—"

Carole broke in. "But she's put up with him for years, right? So what caused her to change her will?"

The hum of traffic underscored Carole's clear voice. Threads of sunlight burnished her hair to a molten gold. She pushed it from tickling her face.

"She's done what?" Teal asked.

Carole recognized surprise in Teal's voice. She, too, had been surprised.

"Made changes to her will. I don't know what. I expected she'd told you as the family tax and estate advisor."

"Not a word," Teal said.

"So we're both in the dark." Carole laughed, confounded.

Teal gave Nancy advice on many things, including the disposition of her assets. Why leave Teal out now? But Nancy had, Carole could see. Teal's irritation meant she really didn't know a thing.

A cacophony of honks erupted in the humid air. The sudden moment of quiet that followed held all the pent-up nervous energy of a hot summer evening. Carole glanced down. Five past seven.

"I have to run. Drinks with an old beau." Carole flashed a smile. "I haven't been much use, have I? Maybe she'll talk at the Ranch. Isn't that annual week at the spa with my little sister coming up?"

"In two weeks, thank God. I'm ready." Teal rose. "Oh, did you see the May *laMode?*"

"Of course. And I admit, Michael isn't worthless even if he is, well, Michael. The publicity took full advantage of the *FRIENDS* sale. *laMode* promised an extended profile during the retrospective. He's damned good at public relations, if nothing else."

"How are the plans?"

"Better than I should expect. This show should secure Nancy as *the* American artist of our time. It's nonsense only abrasive art can be profound. The critics just don't get it—Nan's celebration of a world dismissed by the avant-garde has returned buyers to contemporary art. She's finally about to get her due. It'll be quite a franchise," Carole said.

"You're a pretty great artist's manager, yourself," Teal said.

"I'm proud of her, Teal. She doesn't deserve more hurt. Please, let me know what you find out. Will it be year nine at the Ranch with Nancy?"

Carole laughed at the eight fingers Teal raised.

"Libby, right? Well, eighth year since you took the one time out."

Carole walked around switching off the lights. She turned back to Teal in the dark room.

"Can I persuade you to lend *IN BUSINESS* to the show? I promise the best handling and insurance. It's an important work."

Teal did not appear to hear.

"Carole, do you think anyone could want to hurt Nancy?"

"Intentionally? Who?" Carole rubbed a palm against her bracelets, working to control the surge of fear. "Okay, maybe Michael, if something threatened the good life. But you love her, Felicia fawns on the gallery's best pay check and, who knows, cares as well. I can't judge. Face it, most of us benefit from Nancy's work, which begrudges even Michael the benefit of the doubt. No. No one."

"Professional enemies, then?" Teal said.

Carole smiled. "Sure. Art's like any business, humans being human. Everyone isn't exactly pulling for her, but virulent enemies, no. You remember college. Even her rivals usually came to like her."

"True. Well, has anyone paid particular attention to Nan over the past year? Maybe a new collector Nancy found interesting?" Teal asked.

"How interesting?" Inexplicable resentment flashed through Carole at the implication. "Don't answer. The truth is, people always pay a good deal of attention to Nan and buyers expect as much fuss in return. But whoever she might meet, betraying family isn't Nancy."

Carole regarded Teal with open concern. Teal suspected an affair.

"Carole, if Nancy did act indiscreet, would disclosure hurt her reputation?"

"Nan's America's hometown girl; she sells to presidents," Carole snapped.

"So it could hurt."

Carole moved her head a fraction of an inch.

"Behind the art is the artist. Nancy's fame is as much in her life as her brush stroke. Felicia recognized that truth years ago, and it's made Nancy famous. Fortunately, Nan's values suit her art. Michael as husband has his uses, I've come to accept that. So, unless you can prove Nancy's involved, name the person—"

"Carole." Teal reached out. "I'm sure I'm wrong. I'll consider your request. Thanks for putting up with my grasp at straws."

They exited together to part in front of the State House. The gilt dome flamed in the setting sun. Air pollution made the sky glow orange. Carole stood to watch

Teal's progress along Beacon Street. Nancy might permit her best friend liberties barred a sister. And if she didn't?

Carole bit her lip. She'd been less than honest. For one thing, she agreed with Teal's guess.

? FIVE

The painting Carole mentioned had been Nancy's specially rendered gift of gratitude for Teal's hand during Libby's birth, Michael being absent. The canvas dominated Teal's office, arresting and holding a visitor's eye. *IN BUSINESS,* a portrait of loneliness.

Well, loneliness and avoidance, Teal conceded. She looked at the painting as she had each time, anew.

The partially obscured woman still gazed from an office window at all the imagined life below. She saw a world of couples arm-in-arm, children playing, and friends sharing confidences over coffee. Each store on the painted block, each square on the composed sidewalk, vibrated with life. Nothing gave detail to the office behind the woman. This peek outside reflected a stolen moment.

Teal leaned back in her chair and considered the overt propaganda in Nancy's scene, the long debate between them. Teal was vulnerable to the accusation she hid from life behind the excuse of work. Further inspection would hurt, Teal decided.

She thought about calling Dan Malley, instead.

Dan brought to mind someone else, someone who might have changed the picture, emptied Teal's office at a decent hour, given alternative purpose to her weekends. The memory was but weeks old and already blurring. But the pain persisted, sharp and acute, the question unanswered. What might have been?

Just thinking about calling Dan brought her heart to a race and her palms to a sweat. Silly reaction, she knew. As though it was Detective Lt. Daniel Malley's fault that her someone had been all wrong for her at the end.

She explored the hurt as though testing a bruise with a finger. He'd seemed to be everything Hunt could never be. Fooled you, honey, she thought, the pain fresh with each jab. Now even reliable Huntington Erin Huston was gone, off to design some corporate giant's signature building in Chicago.

Just when she could use him most—wasn't that the perfect summation of their relationship.

The knots at her jaw softened. To give credit where it was due, their three years together after she'd moved East fresh from an MBA at Stanford University had been pretty good. But not good enough for who knew what reasons. The rub of daily life. His obsession with his rocketing architectural career. Her willingness to compromise to survive Clayborne Whittier.

All of the above and none.

She left first, but he got to keep Argyle. Their handsome Scottish deerhound still didn't understand. He accepted Teal as his co-owner even after the years of separation.

The overwhelming emptiness of her love life choked her throat.

"Just received this by messenger."

Kathy's voice shattered Teal's self-indulgent thoughts. Teal reached for the envelope. Kathy hesitated in the doorway.

"Do you have a minute for something personal?"

Teal liked her secretary. She smiled, this request was easy to grant and a diversion.

"Personal is good for more than a minute, Kath. Do sit."

Kathy took the chair.

"Dan will kill me if he thinks I've told. He wants us to do it together, so promise to act surprised when we do."

"Promise," Teal said.

Her heart jerked. She was the woman in the picture looking out. She hadn't thought, asking Kathy to stay, but of course it would be Kathy and Dan. Other people's happiness.

"Dan asked me to marry him!" Kathy spread her hands in the joy of disbelief. "I'm so excited, Teal. He's the best, and we met because of you. We're both so grateful."

Emotion made Kathy mute for the moment.

"Wait," Teal said, and her angst dissolved. "Let's be a tad more accurate. I didn't play the cupid, but I guess better me than that corpse."

Kathy giggled. They both remembered that a body falling to Teal's feet brought Detective Malley into their lives last September.

"I'm hardly surprised, but I'll act the innocent with Dan. Kathy, how wonderful! Please accept my best wishes for your every happiness. He's a lucky fellow to marry you."

Teal embraced her friend.

"That's the good news," Kathy said as they moved apart.

Trouble strained the gleam from her heart-shaped face and her emerald eyes filled with tears. She rested her chin in her hand and mumbled against its impediment.

"The bad news is his mom. I want to love her, Teal. I really do. I'd take like. But right now I can't stand the sight of the woman. Dan won't admit she hates me. She thinks I'm taking away her Danny boy. Selfish old b—"

"Don't get so mad you forget Dan loves you. Remember, he asked you to marry him, Kath, despite Mom," Teal cautioned.

"But she's trying to destroy us, Teal. Oh, she said how nice it is and how happy she hopes Dan will be with me, but she doesn't mean a word of it. She talks with phony, quivering lips to make Dan too guilty to marry me. She calls him her 'precious baby' and 'little mistake.' She makes me want to scream."

"Have you picked the date?" Teal asked.

"We were going to choose Thanksgiving to make life easy for everyone. Both families come here—Dan's older brother and family from San Diego and my sisters up from Portland and most of our friends will be around. But *noo,* this year his mother is going out to San Diego, she says, after she's made his brother's family come here for years."

"Perhaps," Teal ventured hoping to suggest a truce, but Kathy continued, unheeding.

"Trust me, she's impossible to please. Anyway, Dan's going out to his brother's the last week of July, the week you're on vacation, actually." Her bright smile flashed. "He's going for help. It's about time Dan spread the load. His brother's dodged it long enough, though no wonder."

Distress reddened Kathy's otherwise milk-white face, turning her skin blotchy. She raised her hands to cover her tears.

Teal wasn't looking for shared misery anymore. Kathy and Dan were her friends.

"Kath, let it sort out. His mother's just scared and, okay, a problem, a first-class problem. But this will pass. Don't compound the problem by fighting with Dan. He'll only feel attacked from both sides."

Kathy's glum nod admitted to that very sin. Teal kept talking.

"Look, I was about to call him for professional advice.

That should cheer him up. And I won't say a word about the two of you although I can't wait to tell him he's marrying one of the best people I know!"

Teal's exchange with Dan lacked the intimacy of the former, but held equal regard. It didn't, however, promise Teal the help she wanted. Dan answered with as flat a voice as hers had been animated.

"You give me an unnamed friend receiving a message I can't see about punishment, death, and infidelity. You won't call it blackmail. Uh, of course, I s-s-suspect an affair. My advice off the record? Send your friend to the police."

"She won't," Teal said.

"Fine, then tell her to end the affair or end the marriage."

"That's a fat lot of help," Teal said, stung by his tone.

"Yes, it is. Take away the leverage. And common sense tells me you shouldn't expect to be much help, unless you convince her to call us."

"I have to help, Dan."

Teal could imagine the slow nod at her statement, a small duck of the head for which she once dismissed him as young and inattentive. She'd been wrong on the inattentive. In his middling twenties, he was among the youngest detectives on the force. A veteran father, now retired, and his own incisive, disciplined mind had seen to that.

"I understand." Dan paused a beat. "The best you can do is ask the questions you've thought of. Who would want to frighten your friend? Who would benefit? How? But stay out of trouble. Out of trouble, Teal, not like the last time. Most likely the matter will go away on its own. Malicious pranks aren't rare, u-un-unfortunately. Still, your friend can't feel sure."

They closed on talk about the outlook for Boston's long, hot summer. Teal gave not a hint of Kathy's news and hung up feeling better now that Dan all but dismissed the threat. She didn't want to take the time to worry about Nancy.

Fruiers' more pressing crime occupied the next morning. Nancy would understand the stakes. And what could Teal do for her friend with the information at hand? Nothing.

Fruiers Construction Company was Teal's hot client, or hot until the CFO wormed his hands around the stream of corporate cash. Unlike Nancy's situation, Teal could name the accused in this case. Bob Fahey. Teal didn't waste sympathy on him.

She'd been at it since 6:00 A.M. when the office was quiet and dark and her concentration sharp. Now, at 11:00 A.M., every footfall acted as a distraction. Her attention to the stack of Fruiers' workpapers snapped and she closed her eyes, unable to bear the thought of looking at one more page.

She could already demonstrate the case for embezzlement from the checks altered by erasure and the authorization of wire transfers into dummy accounts. So pedestrian a system with its erasable ink and fake payees, so lucrative at $600,000 in only the last eleven months, so stupid for greed to exceed his cover, it set Teal's head shaking.

Manipulation of inventory records could bury only so much. The inventory accounting system gave Teal the first warning. Teal had reviewed it with Bob Fahey herself, not an ordinary task for the senior manager on an audit. Nor had his explanations been ordinary.

Teal sighed. Would they had been, sparing her this tangle of accusations. She didn't mind the effort but the timing. Her year to keep her head down and spirits up had turned to one of high visibility and sinking morale.

Teal pulled a lined pad to the center of her desk. Nancy

deserved a minute. Maybe a miracle of insight would occur, maybe not. Teal wrote slowly and carefully, and sat back to enjoy the tidy list.

WHO BENEFITS NOW—THE STATUS QUO?
Michael
Carole
Felicia
Sotheby's
San Diego Museum
the lover? maybe

HOW DO THEY BENEFIT?
Michael–money, prestige, work
Carole–prestige, perhaps money but she'd inherited a bundle like Nan, work
Felicia–money, prestige, image
Sotheby's–commissions, publicity
San Diego–reputation
the lover–Nancy w/o scandal

WHO WOULD BENEFIT?
no one–Nan's worth equalled her reputation
the lover–to possess all of Nancy—it was a thought

WHO WOULD BE HURT?
everyone above plus Libby

WHY THREATEN?
force Nancy to end the affair
force Nancy to show her hand
force Nancy to run to the lover—or force her away?

It didn't give her much. Revelation of Nancy's extramarital liaison could hurt everyone, but "punishment" and "death" as the consequence seemed overblown. Teal realized she lacked a clue to either the lover or the creep.

By noon she had returned to Fruiers' ordeal, by half-past she ate the sandwich Kathy brought in with a deli-frigid carton of milk. Kathy had her own notion of duty, and bringing Teal a lunch on a busy day was one. She ignored Teal's protests as she did in every one of these exchanges.

Teal considered Nancy's dilemma while picking chunks of brownie from its cellophane wrap.

Michael Britton stood to lose face as much as money. Not a small toll on a man's ego and, as Nancy's husband, he was in the best position to suspect an affair. His own active lust would sensitize him to another's. Teal didn't know what he'd make of Nancy changing her will.

Teal cleared the sticky crumbs from her desk. She stared at the list again, stuck on Michael's name. She would call him before the week's end. Then, with good conscience, she could tell Nancy she'd done what she could. She wouldn't mention pushing the boundary of Nancy's rules.

No. Why risk alienating her friend? Teal crossed Michael off the call list. But she'd learned so little from Carole, Teal realized. She penciled him back in.

Then she reconsidered and struck him out.

 **Six**

Michael Britton changed her mind when he strolled uninvited into her office just past two o'clock.

Teal slid her list under a file and turned to her visitor with a wary smile.

Michael grinned. "Lovely as always, Teal."

She did not offer him a seat.

"I thought I'd drop by before your annual week with my wife. Take me this year. Or would a husband inhibit the exchange of girlish secrets?" Michael paused before he laughed. His white teeth gleamed.

Caps, Teal concluded as she always did. She fought a desire to say something snappy in retort. Actually, she couldn't think of anything on point, irritating her all the more. She hated her visceral response to his bullying vitality.

He ignored her confusion.

"Don't look so worried. There are some things a husband shouldn't know and a few places a husband shouldn't go. I really came to beg you to loan *IN BUSINESS* to the show."

So that's how lovely I'm looking, Teal thought. *How flattering.*

Michael's hand cupped her chin and rotated her face to the picture. He knelt by her chair.

All the mix of attraction and revulsion Michael could arouse swept through her. All the mix that had held her captive years ago after Nancy introduced them. He remained the same Michael—glib and suave, limber enough to rise smoothly from the crouch, his suit without a crease, his soul without a scruple. Well, maybe *a* scruple. Teal struggled to uncross her legs and push up from her chair.

"Sit, sit. Don't let me disturb you."

Michael leaned against the edge of her desk. Socks of an inky navy and mottled red showed above his hand-sewn, black calf shoes, below his custom suit's crisp cuff.

"It's a great painting, Teal. Nancy understands what matters, doesn't she? What's out the window? What's life about? What do women want? Look at those couples, happy and complete. She's achieved a dynamic of tension and longing with paint! It captures the essence of her women today theme. Say yes."

He stood as though unaware her appraisal was of him, not the canvas. All these years, and she still couldn't decide. Was he hero or villain or neither? She didn't vote for neither.

"Well? Come on, Teal. One word. Yes."

What did she want to say? She wanted to say, you prick. She wanted to say what she finally had said that night years before. She wanted to say get lost.

She hardly felt proud to have resisted the force of his appeal. Not when she had considered, however briefly, acting otherwise with Nancy's fiancé. The awful moment brought Teal to understand Nancy's thrill at his proposal even if Nancy now regretted her surrender. Teal's compassion was for both herself and her friend.

Teal let the past go. She took a deep breath and dropped her voice to slide like silk from her mouth to his ear. Two could play the seduction game.

"I'm considering the request." She studied the canvas.

"Nancy's insight is moving, isn't it? If she painted a picture about marriage, what do you imagine it would say?" Teal faced him, a teasing smile on her face.

Michael shook his head. "You're my wife's best friend, ask her."

Not exactly "our marriage is in trouble right now, that's why I'm threatening my cheating wife."

The telephone disrupted Teal's search for a reply. The third ring faded into a fourth. She turned an aggravated eye to the instrument. Who persuaded Kathy to let the call through?

"Go ahead. Pick it up," Michael said. "It won't bother me."

With Teal's back to him as she took the call, the amicable expression peeled from his face. Transparent, transparent Teal. "If she painted a picture about marriage these days . . ." Did Teal think him a fool?

He narrowed his mouth. She still managed to irritate him, remind him of her rebuff to his advance before his marriage. The memory stiffened the small muscles around his eyes. Well that was history, he reminded himself. The future was the thing. Strategy and careful execution would keep it bright. His wife was America's foremost painter, anointed "Norma Rockwell." If there was a glitch, and he couldn't decide for sure, he would control that, too. Family togetherness—that's what this long weekend was about.

" 'You filth atone or die.' "

Nancy's hysteria triggered Teal's heart. Her awareness of Michael, no more than three feet to her back, became acute. Surely he heard each word of Nancy's tirade.

"A Boston postmark four days ago—can you believe it? First that coloring job from New York, now this on plain paper. God, nothing can help."

The silence relieved Teal, but lasted only long enough for Nancy to breathe.

"You have to do something before the Fourth. I can't go to the Cape with this over my head."

Nancy stopped. Teal waited, but Nancy remained still.

"I understand your reason for urgency and your concern," Teal said in her professional voice. Nancy would get the message. "As I am tied up right now, may I call you back?"

Tap. The finger hit her shoulder like a cattle prod. Nervous energy exploded down her spine. She spun clockwise to face Michael's moving mouth.

"I can leave if I'm a problem," he pantomimed.

Teal shook her head. She wanted him now, more than he could know.

"Would five be convenient?" she asked Nancy, refocusing.

"Five, sure. I'll come to your office if I haven't gone crazy. Get to the bottom of this."

"Terrific. And with the new document, yes?" Teal watched Michael turn away to inspect *IN BUSINESS*.

"I'm not that distraught, Teal. I'll bring it." Nancy hung up.

Teal replaced the receiver on the cradle with care. "Sorry for the interruption. Where were we?"

"Negotiating the loan of this painting. You will let us use it, won't you? For Nan?"

Michael's good humor dulled Teal's suspicion. Thinking he had heard his wife was simple paranoia. Whether handsome or hideous, she supposed he was as vulnerable as any spouse. Nancy's affair would hurt. She almost felt compassion.

"I keep thinking of how I'll miss seeing it everyday. The threat of loss has made me more possessive than I expected. Human nature, I guess. What do you think?"

"I think you're agreeing to put it in the show," Michael said.

Had he ignored, or not recognized, the bait? Teal couldn't believe herself. Michael had every reason to stop by for the picture.

"Okay, yes." Her hand touched his arm, a calculated gesture of intimacy. "I don't mean to intrude, Michael, but when I saw Nancy last week, she seemed . . . I don't know. Are things all right between you?"

Michael shrugged her away. He ran a finger down his red-and-blue-silk tie as though considering his next words.

"Since you know us so well, I'll tell you. I have an abiding faith in such human institutions. The marriage has its moments, but I'd never let it end. Surprised?"

He grinned when embarrassment flooded Teal's face.

"I didn't mean to pry." Teal opened her door.

Michael chuckled. "False offense, Teal. You were fishing today. And feel free to pass my comments on to my wife."

If he'd a hat, Teal thought, he would be tipping it to her with that sardonic gleam in his dark eyes. As it was, he gave a mock salute. Her stab at compassion died.

Kathy nodded to him as she came into Teal's office. He winked as he passed her.

"Don Clarke wants you ASAP of course. Renee Maxwell's with him," Kathy said. "And who was that?"

"Michael Britton, Nancy Vandenburg's too, too clever husband."

But Teal was forgetting him. The immediate problem of Renee Maxwell represented a personal threat.

Don's secretary motioned Teal inside.

Renee Maxwell stood by the window. She did not look down to enjoy the view from the forty-eighth floor. If she had, she would have seen a sweep of Boston from the retail activity of Downtown Crossing to the grass of Boston Common, an urban scene in model-train scale. Distance made the city appear almost tidy.

Don fidgeted behind his desk. Renee and Don wore identical pin-striped suits, Teal noticed, sober and expensive summer-weight wools.

She had registered the similarity in dress and difference in demeanor at once. Renee Maxwell embodied collected power. Don, an old boy's old boy, affected a bluff joviality until it counted. Then he, too, played for the gold. And he expected to win handily with a woman, Teal could see. This encounter might be fun.

"You asked me to join you?"

"Yes, yes. Teal, you've met Renee Maxwell from Stimpson. Renee has a concern about something and I thought you should be a part of the discussion. I can't find Frank."

Don Clarke plunged a finger at his intercom. "Keep after him, will you?" he instructed his secretary.

Teal bet his real instruction had been closer to "Find him and you're fired." If Don underestimated Renee, he did not underestimate her capacity to make mincemeat of the inept partner on the Fruiers account. Teal didn't expect to see Frank anytime soon.

Renee moved to the big conference table opposite Don's massive desk. In a room of oversized furniture, she . should have been dwarfed, Teal decided, but force of character made Renee's presence more dominant than physical stature.

"Perhaps we should get started." Renee glanced at her opponents with a litigator's reflex. "This is an informal meeting. And Teal, it's nice to see you again."

She extended a perfectly groomed hand, no rings, no jewelry except the Tiffany tank watch and larger than expected gold ear clips. They were roundly sensuous and reflected miniature distortions of the room.

The lawyer was an interesting combination. In a snapshot, Teal realized, one might see Renee Maxwell as plain. Certainly her style roused no male sexual anxieties. Sensibly low-heeled shoes contrasted with Teal's vanity for added inches. Renee's dark hair capped her head as though cut under a bowl. Green-stippled brown eyes gazed with a canny, penetrating intellect. A formidable wolf in sheep's clothing, Teal concluded. Even Don began acting nervous.

"Get started, indeed." Don joined the table and turned to Renee. "It's your show."

"I did think it important to meet after I reviewed our notes and copies from your audit files. You see, I'm confused. Maybe you can help me understand why you didn't question Mr. Fahey's alleged activities three years ago? It's a puzzle to me, considering Clayborne Whittier audited Fruiers then."

Don set off to explain the professional standards governing certified public accounting. None required the CPA to uncover fraud, blah, blah, blah. He finished with pompous unction.

"When the red flags are up, we look further, of course. In this case, red flags led us to advise Fruiers something appeared out of line."

Renee didn't miss the opening. "But your client claims you informed them *this year* of something out of line *starting* three years ago. If you'd spoken up earlier, you'd have spared them the alleged losses of each subsequent year."

Teal began to think. Not about why Clayborne Whittier failed to identify the problem earlier—three years ago the dollars were too diminutive to be evident, the following year when she joined the audit, Frank refused to believe it of Bob Fahey. Frank accepted the CFO's explanations and tagged Teal the troublesome one. Frank was the partner and she wasn't. Teal had been furious.

No, Teal began to think about why Renee Maxwell chose to air her confusion now rather than try to discredit Clayborne Whittier in court. Teal snapped off her speculation at the sound of her name.

"Teal, can you help me out here?" Renee asked.

Hand me the shovel, will you, and hope I fall into the hole? Teal respected Renee, but she didn't have to like her or her methods. Teal suspected the feeling to be mutual.

"Hindsight can simplify most anything. I wouldn't be distracted by what Clayborne Whittier did or didn't do when your worry is Bob Fahey's behavior." Teal smiled brightly, feeling Don's anxious and angry eye upon her.

But Renee took the point.

"I see. Perhaps this isn't the forum. Well," Renee continued as she rose, "I appreciate your time out of a busy day. The trial starts in less than a week, after the Fourth. I imagine I'll see you both when Teal testifies. May I use a telephone?"

"My secretary is there." Don Clarke pointed through to a smaller office. "Shut the door for privacy, and Teal can show you back to the elevator when you're done."

Don and Teal continued to stand after Renee departed.

"What do you make of that?" Don asked.

"I think she's working to soften Fruiers to plea-bargain or drop the charges with reparation out of court. Bobby Fahey's been caught dead-to-rights and she knows it. She wants us on her side encouraging Fruiers to agree, that's what this was about. Renee just alerted us to her willingness to question our competence in court, hoping we'd rather avoid the embarrassment. You wait, there'll be an offer from Fahey to Fruiers by the end of the week." Teal's confidence made her grin.

"Women's intuition, eh, Teal?" Don Clarke patted her on the back and looked a good deal less sure.

"Intuition, Don, gender neutral."

Her grin faded. No sense trying to be one of the boys, they made sure to point out the differences. Suddenly she liked her fashionable dress and high-heeled shoes all the more, liked turning heads when introduced to clients. Unlike Renee Maxwell, she wasn't going to neuter herself on behalf of a bunch of uncomfortable men.

"Sorry to keep you waiting." Renee leaned around the doorjamb.

They exchanged little other than pleasantries on the way to the elevator, and stood in near silence in the wait for a car. At its bell, both extended a hand.

"Thank you for sharing your concerns," Teal said, the irony screened from her voice.

"Oh, don't thank me. Thank you for your help," Renee replied without inflection.

If it ever came to poker with this woman, wisdom dictated Teal fold.

Renee turned to enter the elevator and stepped into Nancy Vandenburg as Nancy stepped out.

"Teal, I couldn't wait. Oh—"

Nancy stumbled in the confusion of impact. Renee nodded politely. The elevator doors closed.

"Do you know her?" Nancy asked, her head craned around.

"Would that I didn't," Teal groaned. "But forget her, your problems interest me more."

That's when, in the middle of the hall, the decorous hush of Clayborne Whittier about them, Nancy Vandenburg-Britton began to cry.

❓ SEVEN

Crying at Clayborne Whittier? The disapproving glances of passing professionals said it simply wasn't done. Teal knew of tears shed, of course, at news of promotions missed, resignations requested, clients lost, but discreetly and behind closed doors.

No one walking the hall saw anything discreet in Nancy.

A woman over six feet in gold-hued shoes and a black silk jumpsuit shot with silver thread did not recede into the woodwork. Earrings bigger than a baby's fist were clipped to her ears while an orange band pushed back thick, blond hair. If onlookers managed to miss all that, the cascade of water she smeared across her face with one hand while waving the other and moaning, "I feel so damned vulnerable," would surely catch their attention.

Rumor of Teal's embezzling CFO had made the rounds of speculation on who was up and who was out in the run for partner. The appearance of her berserk, bedecked, and bedazzling friend guaranteed to refuel the whisper fire. Teal piloted Nancy from reception. By the time they passed Don Clarke's door, Nancy regained a near normal composure.

"Bet you didn't expect that."

Nancy's laugh sounded bitter. Teal shook her head obligingly.

"Oh well, neither did I," Nancy continued. "What a rotten damned day, Teal. Another stupid threat, and Felicia called. She's selling *SELF!*"

Teal slid her eyes to Nancy. Felicia represented Nan's work. Selling paintings seemed the thing for her to do.

"*SELF,* Teal!" Nancy motioned as though to make Teal understand. "I *gave* her that painting. I can't believe she'd sell. She's been in a fog all spring, forgetting appointments, screwing up payments—and I never said a word. Never agreed with Carole because I owed Felicia my loyalty. Boy, she sure fooled me. What a lousy day. The threats, this betrayal, bum—" Nancy bit the word in half with a snap of her teeth. "Make it better, okay?"

Teal had to laugh. Every heartbreak in college, every critical professorial comment on a canvas, every poem rejected by the college literary magazine and Nancy would ask Teal to "Make it better, okay?" The refrain became shorthand jargon for deeper communication. Nancy's request meant more than "help."

Kathy followed them into Teal's office.

"Should I hold your calls until I leave?" she asked.

"Yes. Thanks," Teal replied, grateful her secretary read things right.

"Oh, and Ms. Vandenburg's husband called. He'll send over the agreement by the end of next week."

Kathy shut the door as she left.

Nancy turned to Teal. "What agreement?"

"He and Carole have persuaded me to loan *IN BUSINESS* for your retrospective. I agreed," Teal said.

Nancy hit her forehead with her hand and groaned. "Damn, I didn't think of that. If Felicia sells now, it's going to be harder than hell getting *SELF* for the show. What is wrong with her?"

Nancy's anger was better than her despair beside the elevator.

"Perhaps she needs the money," Teal suggested.

"Why didn't she ask me for a loan? At least call? I heard this from a goddamned New York critic. 'Was *SELF* really on the market? And how do you feel about all this interest in your early works?' " Nancy mimicked. "As though my later stuff is junk. Damn it, Teal, she should have come to me."

Tears returned. Teal understood the ebb and flows of emotion. She'd masked her own often enough at work and with Hunt where maybe candor would have helped. Well, not a worry now. Hunt was in Chicago. Gone.

"Today's communication?" Teal asked.

Focusing on the mistakes Nancy had made with Felicia or her own with Hunt seemed pointless.

Nancy reached for her purple canvas bag and withdrew another large envelope. She held it a second before she handed it to Teal.

No address, stamp, nor postmark. Inside a single white sheet showed deep creases. Nancy's anxious twisting, most likely. An inch from the top, the message started:

YOU FILTH ATONE OR DIE
you filth atone or die
YoU fIlTh AtOnE oR dIe

repeated over and over in a mad graffiti art. Only, Teal saw, it wasn't art but sick and cruel. She held the page between forefinger and thumb. Her concentration wiped good humor from her face.

"So where's the real envelope, Nan?" she asked.

Teal hoped for evidence of chagrin. It did not come. Teal worried the word betrayal around her mind in the silence.

"In teeny, tiny pieces. In shreds. My therapy." Nancy's voice offered no apology.

"You destroyed evidence?" Teal spaced the words, her hands rolled tight to fists in her lap.

"Yes. And don't tell me I shouldn't have, I know I shouldn't have. But I wanted to and I did," Nancy said.

Nancy's own hands had raised to her hips, and she challenged Teal's disapproval with her tone of voice. Teal did nothing to acknowledge the tension.

"You saved the pieces, right?" she asked.

"Wrong."

Teal grasped Nancy's dilemma in that moment.

"The envelope wasn't addressed to you. Nan, how can I make it go away when you refuse to cooperate?" Teal restrained the urge to shake her friend.

"I am. It—"

"Don't lie, whatever you do, don't lie to me. . . ." Teal swallowed her next words.

She realized she was more out-of-control than appropriate. Bob Fahey was the liar in her life, not Nancy.

Nancy's eyes chilled. "You're right. It wasn't addressed to me. I was stupid to think I could fool you."

"Your friend, it was addressed to him." Teal nodded as she spoke. Nancy did not need to agree. "The creep isn't guessing, he knows the information you refuse me. I can't say I get it."

"If you can't forgive me, Teal, at least understand. Everything about this," Nancy gestured inarticulate pain, "is complex. I'm not ready to tell you, and you must believe I'd tell you first. It's more than confusion about my marriage. My very being is at risk. I need time to think, time alone. It's not that I'm not telling you. I can't tell you. *I* need to be sure first."

Boundaries, Teal recognized. Boundaries. Who am I and who are you, and whose is the right to know? And an affair for Nancy Vandenburg-Britton must put her very being at risk. Teal understood that, too.

"Dad stayed with Mummy all those awful years, Teal. He never for a minute abandoned the sick wife, whose sickness had turned her from him. Maybe if I hadn't had it easy, Carole taking Mummy's place for me, I'd appreciate how much desertion hurts. Some nights I go to bed hating myself. Some nights I'd do anything to be in a different bed. It's crazy." Nancy put her head in her hands, her voice cracking to a whisper. "But I feel alive."

A thread of envy pierced Teal's heart. Nancy dared to risk love.

"What can you tell me?" Teal asked. She wouldn't push the limits.

"I can tell you I still believe no one could know. Really—no one. We are never seen together. We take great care in our arrangements. Neither of us has confided to anyone. So it is not possible anyone knows." Nancy's lips fluttered with a smile. "This is denial, isn't it?"

"Is it?"

"Yes," Nancy whispered.

"Then help yourself. Tell me how you met your friend. How long you've been seeing him. Do you write letters to each other? Have anything in writing? Because someone does know, Nan, someone who isn't happy with you. He's not married, too, is he?"

Nancy looked up, genuine and unexpected humor lightening her face. "No, thank God. It's hard enough that I am."

Her smile faded and she sat for a moment in thought, as she unclipped and repositioned her earrings three times.

"Okay. We met at one of my openings about a year ago. Remember how you always looked for trouble in early spring? You said it was the weather. Well, last spring brought me a love so sudden and remarkable I can't pass judgment on whether it's trouble. I discovered myself, Teal. I thought it might be infatuation, pass, but . . . I was wrong. Anyway, I wrote a few letters from Italy last summer, that's it. Now Italy seems like ancient history."

Teal scanned Nancy's face.

"Did he reply? Or visit?"

"No letters. I couldn't take that kind of risk when Michael came to stay between trips to Paris for the retrospective. Felicia joined Michael and me for a week. But, yes, I saw my friend, briefly, in Italy."

Teal hesitated to break the reverie as Nancy retreated to memories of the happier past, but she had to.

"Was he there to see you or did business take him to Europe?" she asked.

Nancy shrugged. "Both arguably, but I guess mainly me."

"And after the summer? What did it become—a stolen hour here and there? What did you plan, Nan? Where could it possibly lead?"

"In the beginning there was nothing to think about. It simply was. God, the feeling of falling in love! I never experienced such passion. Now?" Nancy lifted tawny eyebrows. "Now I'm not sure. We're at the messy stage of needs not so easily met. So, with or without these—communications—I have to confront this, don't I?"

Teal inclined her head but did not speak.

"I'm thinking unimaginable thoughts. People call my life an American dream. It's ironic, isn't it, that I've set a deadline of the Fourth of July to decide? I don't want to be influenced by threats. That's why I want them to stop. Please."

Nancy's values were rooted in middle-America. Teal learned that the year they met and never changed her assessment. Despite heady success, Nancy still harbored her Holland, Michigan, naivete.

"Abracadabra, Nancy?" Teal considered shaking her friend. What good would that do? "I wish it were that easy. Someone knows, Nancy, whatever you want to think. And it's either someone intimate or an utter stranger who happened across the affair and is crazy or wants to score some kind of point. But, Nan, there *is* someone, and I need your trust to find them, and you aren't trusting me with much."

"I'm sorry," Nancy said.

I'm sorry. That was all Nancy said. Teal realized she had to let it go.

"Michael actually stopped in to see me about loaning the painting," she said instead.

Alarm straightened Nancy's posture and jutted out her chin. Teal had seen the response before.

"You didn't say anything about this?" Nancy said.

"Of course not! I made an unsuccessful attempt to get him on the subject of your marriage. He did say something rather odd for someone who you say doesn't know. Something like 'every marriage has its moments but nothing could bring ours to end . . .' " Teal's eyebrows rose to invite a comment.

Nancy raised her hands. "No. He'd go crazy if he suspected, absolutely crazy. He can't possibly know. Trust me."

"And no one else knows either. Fine. Look. Take my advice. Try the police. I'm out of ideas," Teal said.

Nancy bent to hug Teal after she stood. Teal did not rise to reciprocate. She meant what she had said, and the lack of response from Nancy had made her tired. No. Depressed and tired. Nancy must have caught on.

"I asked the impossible," Nancy said. "I guess wanting a miracle from you seemed easier than the introspection I need to do. You can forget my request for help because I have to face this alone, don't I? The real issue, not who sent a few pieces of junk in the mail. What I want. Once I have the answer, the nut won't matter."

Teal grabbed for the telephone when she entered her office from escorting Nancy out. At half past six it had to be a Fruiers call.

"Teal Stewart," Teal said.

"Renee Maxwell, Teal. I hoped I'd catch you before you left."

Teal tried not to feel challenged into an "I work longer, harder, more than you" contest.

"Your lucky day," she said.

"I'll get to the point. This is difficult for me to say, but Mr. Fahey thinks you harbor a personal vendetta against him. I will need to raise your motives for making the accusations at the trial. There is a legitimate question of whether you reacted with depression when your social relationship with him did not work out."

Anger tightened Teal's grip on the telephone and made her glare at the wall. Yes, she'd accepted Bob Fahey's invitation to dinner. She had been tired of going home to an empty house.

Bob Fahey had seemed a reasonable alternative to a meal standing at the black granite counter of her place on the top two floors of the town house she owned at the flat of Beacon Hill. The building had been a purchase of independence after the breakup with Hunt. Independence didn't make life less lonely.

By the third dinner, Teal realized her mistake. Professionals and their clients often socialized, but intimacies such as Bob desired fell out of bounds. Besides, he wasn't very interesting. She tried to be kind and clear, but he reacted with anger. The experience strained their professional relationship, but Teal never expected this.

Renee Maxwell certainly knew how to pull out the stops.

Teal didn't care if her voice sounded sharp. "Renee, Bob Fahey embezzled from Fruiers for three years, and I think the trial will prove he violated the law. My only motive is to adhere to the standards of my profession and fulfill my responsibilities to my client. Were I you, I'd look to your client's motive."

"I am sorry, Teal. I didn't intend to upset, but rather forewarn you."

Oh, didn't you? Teal thought, too angry to listen.

". . . Vandenburg, the artist, wasn't it, coming off the elevator? I've seen her works. Quite amazing. Well, I guess we will see you in court after the Fourth."

They hung up at the same time.

Teal sighed. So much promised to follow the Fourth. Nancy promised her life would be in order. The Fruiers case would be over. And Teal's admission to the partnership would be decided by a secret vote of the U.S. partners. Clayborne Whittier would share the outcome with her, privately, in late July, one day before making a public announcement. The firm considered the action a courtesy.

She pushed back the hairs tickling her face. She took a deep breath. The partnership. Well, she had decided to be rested and prepared, whatever the decision. Her calendar showed bold red letters across the third week of July.

ESCAPE—VACATION—THE RANCH—BAJA, CALIFORNIA

Her week with Nancy wasn't long away. In Baja they could forget it all—husband, creeps, trials, and partnership admissions. Teal circled the week in blue.

After the Fourth couldn't come soon enough.

? EIGHT

Felicia felt simply murderous. All her explaining, all her nervous justifying and abject begging came to an abrupt stop. Life was too short, she thought. Better still, life could be shortened. That was a nice, new idea.

She indulged further, imagining a push, tumble, and fall. She imagined the body, soaring in flight, hesitate before hitting earth, bits of being bouncing on the ground. Annihilation.

She envisioned the streak of the wooden bat as it arced, the crack softened to a thud as the head splattered apart—hair blowing, eyes rolling, brain exploding. She wasn't listening to the disembodied voice yell, "Are you still there?" from the perforations of the telephone.

She indulged in a craving to kill.

Her breath hissed between the narrow spaces separating her front teeth. Animosity stiffened her body and curled her fingers around the telephone. They turned frostbite-white, a color left off the Windsor Newton chart. The voice still rose as though to interrupt her thoughts.

She didn't want to be interrupted.

Felicia loosened her arm and firmed her grip. Her swing cut smooth and wide.

The black handset held none of the weight of a bat.

The rotund, fertile shape of her little American art pottery vase had none of the resonance of a head, but on impact it spun just as out of control as her imagination. The stubby, clay neck cracked straight off. Other pieces scattered across the carpet.

She was on her knees, deep in fury, when her assistant came to the door.

"Oh, dear, Felicia, let me help. How simply awful! Your delightful Teco." John knelt to pluck debris from the floor.

"Don't worry about it."

Felicia pushed against her hands and rocked to her feet to stand. She dropped the curved shards into the trash. The trembling of her fingers betrayed her agitated state.

"Well . . ." He let the word peter out.

"Well," John resumed. "Sotheby's called. Our Ms. Vandenburg is *very* upset at the proposed auction of her precious painting."

Both of them flicked their eyes to the empty spot on the office wall.

"They assure me their contract with you is unaffected, courtesy call was all. Very sweet. They didn't exactly want to tell it all to me, but you'd been on the telephone for the longest time. Oh, Felicia, do let me help," he insisted.

John's offer brought the swell of fury back to her throat. She'd been on the telephone, all right. The terrible conversations jammed to static in her mind.

". . . not a chance, Felicia, darling, at least not now. You understood . . ." Understood? Hardly—not for a minute, not for the last three months, certainly not in this hour to suit him.

". . . this is payment for friendship? You could have asked me. You still . . ." Easy for you to say, Felicia wanted to scream. Instead she had listened to Nancy's offer, tense and mute.

". . . I can't judge your decision, but you are the one making it so hard. What's really wrong, Felicia? Perhaps I can help you solve the cash-flow problem . . ." Teal's pragmatic sympathy made Felicia crazy.

Petty friction turned to threats in each exchange. ". . . drop you . . ." ". . . drop the gallery . . ." ". . . terminate . . ." ". . . terminate our association . . ." ". . . destroy your reputation . . ."

Memory whirred the words around her head. Who did they think they were talking to? Nausea came with the anger, then determination. She would not let the gallery fall to ruin. The first step in the remedy couldn't be avoided, not any longer.

Felicia finished picking up the pieces. Red hair stuck in the sweat at her temples, but she didn't mind. Buoyant with false energy, she faced her assistant.

"Really, nothing's wrong. We should cut the payment checks tomorrow to get them out before the holiday. If any of our artists wants express delivery, agree." She caught his expression. "You've been great, John. Better than great, honestly. I can't believe how close my mistake brought us to disaster. I'm even upset at myself for losing our installation artist."

"The work was shit. So banal. So messy. Frankly, so impossible to sell." John pursed his lips into a smirk. "I think you've been loyal beyond the call when it's not exactly hot. The gallery is better off. Forget your troubles because it is too divine, a long weekend! So indulge."

She waved until he was gone.

Indulge? What an irrelevant thought. She knew the price of independence.

Carole hummed and smiled and fiddled with her charm bracelet. A finger slid over her gold toe shoe, a memento of her ballet period at twelve. The sharp tail of a silver rocking horse had come from Daddy. The silver disk inscribed "Aunts are a Mother's best friend" curved like Nancy's smile. Miscellaneous lover's trinkets from her past didn't receive much attention.

Carole began to sing as she got down to business and pulled the mail to the center of the desk. People told her she had a lovely voice. She didn't miss a note as she flipped through the pile.

The retrospective plans continued ahead of schedule, and the attentions of her old beau last night proved life didn't end at forty. As if she'd wondered. Carole stopped mid-verse to smile. But there was her secretive sister. Carole didn't pick up the song she'd left off.

She hated the hurt of Nancy's withdrawal. As children, Carole could cajole her subject, Princess Nan, to tell all. Less able to perform the trick as an adult, Carole found Nancy's recent retreat disturbing. Things would work out, she reminded herself. They always did. Even Michael, the worst storm, had been weathered. He no longer interfered with the sisters. Carole relaxed and resumed the aria as she slit open the next envelope.

Her voice faltered and her smile dissolved as she regarded the torn page. Nancy looked back through large, wide eyes. Carole made herself read the message spelled out in marks of fluorescent green.

The emotion erupted so suddenly she hadn't time to consider. She whacked the paper to the floor and danced a sharp heel over the offending words.

Michael Britton did not knock, but pushed through the office door.

"Sorry to disturb you in the act of ceremonial dancing or radical pest control." Michael slid a hand down his tie and looked amused.

"You're hardly funny, Michael."

Carole set her foot across Nancy's head, the lime green unidentifiable as highlights to the text. Michael must not recognize the *laMode* with its picture of his wife and rude message. She bent, snatching the sheet from the floor, moving to the offensive.

"San Diego confirmed the visit and expects to see you in three weeks. You may be amused to hear you'll be out there while Nancy is a few miles to the south at the Ranch. Actually, it will help if you need her support in negotiations with the museum. That's my news. What brings you to me?"

Carole slipped the page in the basket behind her desk.

Michael leaned back in the stuffed chair to settle in. "Nancy says she wants to quit Barrette. What do you know about this?"

Carole faced Michael, astounded. Was Nancy talking to her about anything these days? She managed to recover.

"Not much. I suggested the move a couple of months ago. Felicia's let the gallery go to hell. Nan said no. She has to be the only one of Felicia's artists to have stayed loyal. I'm not happy to hear this now, though. The timing could hurt the show."

"Felicia's selling *SELF,*" Michael said.

Carole pressed a sharp, gold heart to her skin. "*SELF?* No!"

Michael nodded dissent.

"I don't believe it! Felicia must be in much worse trouble than I imagined," Carole concluded.

"She's a big girl. I expect she can take care of herself. I just wondered if there was anything else behind Nancy's decision and thought you'd know." Michael stood.

"When did Nancy tell you?"

Carole stumbled on the question. Asking Michael about her sister distressed Carole. She laid a smile on her face.

"She didn't, exactly. I overheard her on the telephone yesterday. She hung up and said, 'I'm not in the mood to discuss the show.' " Michael shrugged. "So, I didn't push her. That's your job, sister-in-law. I'm off. Don't miss me too much."

Carole heard him laugh all the way to the elevator. Panic joined hurt. She pulled the magazine page from the trash. The message still looked ugly. It could not be true. *Could not be true.* She would have known. The paper rattled as her hand shook. Her charms tinkled. There was one good result. The torn paper gave her an excuse to pry, despite Nancy's denial.

Carole studied Nancy's calm face. She would confront her sister after little Libby's birthday party over the Fourth. Carole trusted ties that bind. Family above all. She recovered the envelope and put it in her briefcase to show Nancy. Then Carole started on "The Star-Spangled Banner" off-key.

Michael heard the lawyer say no.

"I'm sorry, Mr. Britton, your wife's personal affairs are her own. You must ask your questions of Nancy. Now I'm afraid I'm off to probate court. I won't mention this to Nancy and I suggest neither should you."

The dismissal grated Michael's veneer of goodwill, or maybe the lawyer himself bothered Michael. He'd seen Nancy's appointment book, that's why he'd come for a little discreet research. Michael saw two of Nancy's paintings on the office wall. The lawyer collected his wife. This was news.

Michael wondered if the man's professional manner veiled personal scorn. The prick advised his wife on issues as intimate as any in life. And other intimacies? Michael shrugged. Seeing the will the lawyer had refused to discuss was more important.

The lawyer's secretary, a temp on a vacation rotation, didn't object at all.

"Sure," she said. "I made the changes yesterday after

your wife left. She's beautiful. She'll probably want you to see the new trusts, too."

The girl busied about the banks of drawers. She was clumsy and slow, but displayed a useful, if pathetic, yearning to please. Michael tried uncharacteristic patience and characteristic charm. Trusts? He wanted to see them very badly indeed.

"I can't imagine where they are. God, I hope I haven't lost the file. At least I sent the originals out in today's mail for her review and signature, but our copies have to be here." She sounded distressed.

"Don't worry, I could come back," Michael said, gauging his effect on the girl.

He tugged on his French cuffs and turned until the emerald cuff links caught the light. He smoothed his pink-and-yellow tie, the yellow band almost invisible to the eye, the pinks a bold rose and paler coral hue. He was better than this little secretary would ever do. She'd give him what he wanted on a platter if only she'd find the damn file.

"No, no. Please. I'm sure they're here somewhere." She looked stricken.

"Perhaps still on your desk?" he suggested.

She paused in the pulling-out and pushing-in of drawers, the scrambling through jammed files, and turned back to look at the chaos on her desk.

"Ooh, yes. I hadn't got to file them yet. This office is crazy. He makes me take his dictation, says he can't talk to a machine. He's a great lawyer, I'm sure, but really! Clients are calling or in and out all the time. The tape's so much easier, but he won't . . ."

Michael stopped listening. Then she found what he waited for.

"Here you go. Should I make a copy?"

"No need to trouble with that. You've been wonderfully persistent finding them for me. I'll just sit here if I may and look them over."

"I'll get you a coffee, then," she suggested and shot out the door.

Michael smiled until she'd gone. Then he skimmed each page. The trusts placed Nancy's wealth—her real property in Lincoln and on the Cape, her shares of inherited stock, her paintings and drawings—out of reach. Carole was named trustee, Libby the beneficiary. The codicil newly amending his wife's will conformed to the minimum due him under Massachusetts law. The surviving spouse stood to receive half of her probate estate, but the trusts put everything of value outside of probate, out of reach. Clever, clever lawyer.

He need read no more. Nancy had protected Libby's future from *any* mate. He realized with a shock she was preparing for a separation. And just like Nancy, first addressing the division of spoils in death, before she faced the division among the living. Divorce.

He stood to be replaced! All his suspicions jelled. He wasn't intended to be Nancy Vandenburg's spouse, surviving or otherwise. His hand shook as he slipped the documents into his briefcase. The happy temp returned with coffee.

"I hope you take cream. I had to look the world over to find it. Such a mess! I brought sugar, too. You're not done, are you?" she asked, her voice rising and her face falling.

He saw her in a series of minute details. Chunks of blue mascara dusted the rise of her cheeks, dark roots showed at the part in her lank hair. Foundation caked in the pores of her nose. He needed time to readjust the world back into a larger whole. He nodded slowly.

"I'll stay a minute, you've been so kind to bring the coffee. Oh, where should we file this?" he asked and held up the long folder.

"Not for you to worry." She patted her desk.

"No, no, at least let me thank you by making life easier. Really, I'm quite good with the alphabet, so point to the drawer." He smiled his boyish grin to reveal white teeth. It had worked on better women.

She giggled and squirmed a shy showing of delight and indicated the metal cabinets on his right.

He didn't let himself think of what he'd read, that it had gone this far, Nancy providing for Libby with no concern for him. He put the empty file in place, drank the coffee with its clumps of dairy-free tropical oil "cream," and took his leave as fast as he could. Before starting down the hall, he stuck his head back round the door.

"Does he handle divorce?" Michael asked.

"Oh, no. He's estates and trusts and tax things. His partner does the divorces. Your wife stopped in to see him yesterday. Ooh—" The secretary clasped a hand to her gaping mouth.

"Would it be too impossible to ask that you not mention my reading to him?" Michael asked.

He tilted his head toward the lawyer's empty office. He didn't react to her revelation or her smile, pathetic with hope.

"Sure." Her eyes begged for affection. "You have a great weekend."

"Thanks, you kick up your heels a little, too, over the holiday."

He beat a quick retreat. Rage propelled him, anger blinded him. By the time he reached the edge of the Boston Common, stunned and faint, he needed a seat. The wino at the other end of the bench spit in disgust.

"Fancy pleated pants sits with no concern for my privacy. You in piss, man." The drunk lurched away.

Michael heard none of it. He replayed his visit to the lawyer. Then he imagined the variations of Nancy's confession and his revenge. She'd have fireworks on the Fourth.

By the time he stood, vertigo and disbelief were behind him. He flipped quarters to begging men and smiled at small children. The sun warmed his back, shade trees cooled his path. Topping the hill, the golden dome of state authority shone brilliant against the cerulean sky.

Surely this, too, like all things, must pass, he thought, but instinct made him hold back his last dime.

? NINE

Early July.

Nancy knew what she knew.

She'd sorted her emotions into self-knowledge, poised her art to plumb life's depths, and ordered her material affairs to take care of the interim until the transition was finished. She could manage. Courage would sustain her through the weekend. After that, whatever unpleasantness transpired, whoever she disappointed, her new life would begin.

The Fourth of July would be freedom's day indeed.

"Teal, I've decided. I'm leaving him. The threats don't matter." Nancy's voice caught. "Not anymore."

"Leaving Michael?" Teal repeated like she hadn't heard the words.

She bent over the telephone, turning from her desk. The move let her concentrate unprovoked by her stack of unreturned call slips. Renee Maxwell, Sandra Jordan, Fruiers' president, Don Clarke. They could wait. She waited for Nancy, but Nancy remained silent.

"It may be harder than you realize," Teal prompted. "He could—"

"Go for custody of Libby, I know. He won't win."

Nancy's tension carried over the line.

"Anyway, we're off to the Cape for Libby's birthday. She's all excited about staying up for the fireworks and quite impressed with the idea of turning six. She gives me perspective, Teal, she really does. Even in the face of this. You should consider a kid."

"Let's not start on my life just now, okay?"

The argument over the meaning of life was as old as their friendship and as unresolved. Nancy married Michael because marriage was a thing good girls should do. Babies came next. Who could say who chose right?

"What about those threats, Nan? Waiting might be more prudent. The author isn't happy with you or your friend. Word of a separation could set the nut in gear. Higher gear. Give me information and time to find the culprit."

Teal crossed her fingers like she had as a child. Despite Fruiers' call on her time, she wanted Nancy to agree.

"No, but thanks. I don't care about any sicko. I'm ready, that's all that matters, and believe me, after this weekend, I'll have nothing to hide. I expect to tell Michael on Sunday evening. He can clear out his things in Lincoln while Libby and I stay on the Cape. This will be it, Teal. I haven't even told—"

The sentence pulled up short. "Anyway, wish me courage. You heard it first."

"Then courage, Nan. Call me anytime day or night, night or day," Teal said.

The innocent pledge returned her to a time no secrets stood between them, no career worries came first. Life was simple then. Teal sighed, embarrassed by her relief to have the Nancy project end.

"What next, Nan? After the Cape is it into your lover's arms?"

Teal meant to tease, but heard the sharp intake of breath before Nancy laughed.

"Well, there is some sorting out to be done. Look, you're the greatest of friends. You've never let me down. Thanks," Nancy said.

"I love you, Nan," Teal threw out.

And I have let you down, we both know it, Teal thought but did not say aloud. She straightened the draft financial statements lying beside the phone, her long fingers tapping upon the square edges. They were tidy and neat. Not like anonymous threats, Teal concluded.

No, she censured herself. She was being too dour, the Scottish legacy. Nancy wasn't worried anymore, and it was foolish for Teal to be worried for Nancy. Teal lifted the balance sheet.

She couldn't concentrate. Nancy Vandenburg had been wrong before.

? TEN

Sunday, July Fourth.

Nancy's first doubt came on the ride down.

Friday traffic stuttered along the Southeast Expressway, an undigested lump, a rat in the python, the gas fumes rising and tempers flaming. Libby, wriggling and excited in the backseat, asked too many questions. Michael never once made eye contact with Nancy. That's when she began to worry. She had counted on surprise in her court.

Saturday morning she was sure she'd imagined the friction. The family played tag on the beach, Libby shrieking with delight. Over dinner, they talked about renovation plans for the summer house like any husband and wife. The hypocrisy troubled her, but good sense forestalled blurting out the truth. She would preserve peace through Libby's birthday.

Carole joined them Sunday morning for brunch on the porch. The ocean kicked up spindrift and a haze of salty air while Libby kicked up a fuss to rush the party. Michael surprised everyone when he left for a quick trip into town. Carole's offered to take Libby for a swim gave Nancy a chance to make her call.

"I'll talk to Michael tonight, after the party. I am leaving him, love, don't worry," Nancy said.

The static crackled the line.

"You have to understand." Nancy could sense anger at the other end, but it would be pointless to argue. "By Wednesday I can come straight to you, and we'll make plans—"

"Wednesday won't work. You forget, I'm due in court. We should talk. I'm coming down tomorrow morning."

"No," Nancy contradicted her lover.

She watched Carole through the screen door. Another few seconds and her sister and daughter would be in the house. She swung around.

"Really, I have to do this my way. I'll call tomorrow morning instead, when I go out for a run."

Neither of them liked the solution, but she didn't have any more time. Nancy hung up.

"Who was that?" Carole asked.

"My lawyer," Nancy replied, her caution unraveled.

"On Sunday? Boy, that's professional dedication. What are you doing with him?"

Nancy returned to the moment, struck by the danger in her response. But Carole questioned only the obvious, no more than mildly attentive. Nancy swallowed hard.

"My will, remember? I told you I finally got to it."

Carole snorted and her eyes narrowed. "Are you sure that lawyer isn't interested in more than your will? Buying *two* of your paintings this year *and* making weekend calls—should you tell me more?"

This felt as familiar as growing up when Carole liked to think she never pried and did. Nancy made herself laugh and shake her head. Then she changed the subject.

Felicia turned into the drive well after Michael. The adults were sitting on the porch, relaxing in the lull of the day. Libby played on the grass in the shade. Felicia watched surprise rearrange every face.

"Hey, folks! Guess what? Personal business brought me to Boston, and I couldn't fly back to New York without greeting the birthday girl."

Felicia decided not to say the stop in Boston had been an unmitigated disaster, that this detour was an effort to make sense of her impulsive decision.

She stopped to hug Libby. Maybe it was foolish, Felicia worried again, walking like this into the lion's den. But maybe it was the only way to settle her life.

Felicia considered what she would say. Maybe something like, "Nancy, I'm pregnant. I'm going to have your husband's child."

She could imagine Nancy's stricken face. Or maybe not. Maybe Nancy would be happy. It was the maybes that were driving Felicia crazy. She needed something in her life to be sure about. Confronting Nancy had to help.

Felicia gave Libby an extra squeeze, and she arranged her social face. She would confront Nancy tonight.

Libby liked Victoria best. The baby doll lay all dimpled and pudgy in booties and bonnet just waiting for love. And Libby yearned to give it, holding the plastic infant so tenderly, afraid she might break. Nothing was too good for Victoria, who stayed by Libby the rest of the day.

Mummy gave her a bicycle with red streamers and big wheels. Daddy gave her a giant stuffed dinosaur named Dino. Felicia gave her the party dress she now wore. Teal's quizzical, mohair German bear looked to be a special, if prickly, friend. The delivery, made by a singing bumblebee, had everyone laughing. But Carole's gift of Victoria, the beautiful Madame Alexander doll in her nest of pink tissue tucked in a box of blue, remained the best.

After presents, the circus cake with seven candles and ice cream shaped like a clown came out. Everybody sang "Happy Birthday" to her. Victoria clapped with them at the end, too.

Much later, when the first fireworks started, Libby could hardly keep her eyes open.

Sandra Jordan hated the group joviality. She'd hated it on the ride down in a car overcrowded with associates, and she didn't like it any better now, after two hot and humid nights. Nor did she understand why the invitation had been extended.

The revival of the SGM associates' traditional group rental on the Cape started with one of the more popular, if less brilliant, hires in her year. Almost everyone in the class bought a share in the house. She refused, but the group pushed hard to get her to join them for this weekend which stretched over the Fourth.

She hated that part of herself, the part that had said yes, the part that wanted to be like them. Like how, she wondered with scorn. She touched the hair she'd straightened two nights before and picked at her thumb.

The cover of *Sports Illustrated*'s swimsuit issue adorned the refrigerator door. "Our goal" someone had captioned across the top. The white model lay blonde and provocative, a golden tan against dark lava rock. Your goal, Sandra thought angrily, feeling the helpless confusion of her desire. She reached into the freezer for a Mars Bar and pushed hard against the svelte beauty as she shut the door.

The house stood quiet and empty, everyone else having left for touch football on the beach.

Sandra sat at the kitchen table, staring at the wall. She ate the frozen candy methodically—chomping, chewing, swallowing fast and furiously, the taste little more than a cloying afterthought. Shards of brittle milk chocolate melted off the slick caramel as nougat sucked at the fillings in her teeth. Her anguish mollified, but too soon the last almond crunched and the bar was gone. She wadded the wrapper and cardboard to a ball.

Sandra squirmed on the pitted chrome tubing of the dinette-set chair. A frosted turquoise plastic seat stuck to her thighs, bare and tanned a deeper brown where they emerged from her shorts. Fat sagged over the edge of the seat. She gave herself a sudden and hostile poke before rising to raid the freezer again. The squeaking boards and footsteps on the porch stairs stopped her dead, caught like a rabbit in the headlights.

"Need a few more brewskis and chips. Come on down, Sandra, the sun is tan-fastic." Her fellow associate loaded up, looked a second at Sandra and left.

Sandra shut the door. Shouts of laughter drifted up the path from the beach. She'd been told it was a lucky rental, on the water and the only visible neighbor some famous artist. That family was down. Sandra could see three cars under a big shade tree.

Why had she come to Cape Cod? It never worked, running away. Renee Maxwell still filled her mind, that voice challenging her conclusions, editing her statements, correcting her research.

Everyone said Renee thought she was about the best associate in the firm. They said constant correction was Renee's style. But what did anyone really know? Sandra didn't want to hear that voice, see that face in her mind every night. She didn't want to need to say ". . . and if I die before I wake, I pray the Lord her soul to take . . ." for one more day.

A woman, as lovely as the *Sports Illustrated*'s paper doll, crossed the neighboring yard. A little girl ran after her, clutching a baby doll and shrieking her delight. Sandra's eyes held onto the woman as she considered her desire for revenge against an unfair world. When her mouth began to salivate, she turned to the freezer and opened the door. The last Mars Bar cooled her hand.

Swinging wide, she shattered the sweet to bite-sized pieces against the radiant smile of the sex and swimsuit hustler.

"Take that, you bitch," Sandra said.

Carole watched her niece with an indulgent eye. Over-stimulation showed in the little face, a cross between angel and angler for her own way. When Libby lost, much cajoling and whining could ensue. That's where aunts were so useful, Carole decided. Aunts had more latitude. Like now, with Libby insisting they drive to town hours before the fireworks.

"Why don't I take Libby, and you all can meet us?" Carole suggested.

Libby brightened. Everyone else sighed in relief.

The plan bestowed first-choice seats for the big display, and Carole settled them at the end of the pier. Later, when Nancy arrived, she handed around sweaters for the cool night, and they all ate Popsicles. Libby and Victoria dozed beside Carole. Someone threw a firecracker across the water. Its sharp boom left the child undisturbed.

Felicia found them last. "I got lost," was what she said.

She would, Carole thought. She considered Nancy's attachment to the woman inexplicable. But perhaps that was changing before her eyes. Carole leaned forward to listen.

"I'm sorry about *SELF,* Nancy," Felicia said.

An uncharitable glee surged through Carole. How dumb could the woman be? How heedless of the day as a family gathering? Nancy sat, unresponsive and mute while Michael looked astonished.

"There are a lot of things I need to say, but that's first.

You see, I thought it would be the best way out. I didn't know what to do, and you had saved the gallery before. I thought if you could do it again . . . with *SELF—*"

Michael jumped in. "Felicia, it's my daughter's birthday. Maybe this isn't the time or the place to discuss adult business."

"No, do let her finish," Nancy said.

Carole could have warned Felicia about the third-person approach. Felicia continued, oblivious to the group.

"I never meant to hurt you. I never meant to get in this deep—"

BA-BOOM! The first barrage rocketed color above the harbor. Libby jolted upright. Felicia leaned into Nancy, mouthing soundless words. For the next half hour, Carole watched the pantomime illuminated in shades of red, white, and blue. Michael made frustrated, angry motions to pull Felicia away, but Nancy always intervened.

At the finale, Felicia stood, anguish twisting her face. Nancy no longer appeared willing to give her agent the time of day. She stared at the burning sky until Felicia fled.

"So, want to tell me what that was all about?" Carole asked on the way to the cars.

Michael walked in front, Libby asleep on his shoulder. Victoria swung from his hand. Carole slowed to pull Nancy farther behind.

Nancy didn't break stride, forcing Carole to catch up.

"Not right now," Nancy said. "Felicia will spend the night with us, but I think she'll be gone by the time we're up in the morning."

Nancy gave Michael a long look.

"I'd guess that suits you fine, doesn't it, dear?"

Libby curled tight with worry that the noise would wake the white witches and black warlock under the bed. She could hear the guttural rhythm of the alligator's snore. Her quick, fretful turn toward the wall left Victoria vulnerable on the far edge. Surfacing to semiconsciousness, Libby realized her baby's exposure. Horrible voices rose, angry and shrill.

". . . you ruin my life . . ."

". . . gallery? Are you telling me . . ."

". . . over my dead body . . ."

". . . without warning? Just like that? You silly . . ."

". . . stop it, both of you . . ."

". . . you're dead . . ."

". . . I could kill you . . ."

A crash sent her grabbing for the doll. Damp hair tangled wet threads to her eyelids. She pushed the nightsnarls aside to see the shadows of moonlight. A car revved in the drive. Doors banged and slammed, words distorted on the wind and got lost in the slap of a rising tide.

Libby hugged Victoria to her side. A pillow slid to the floor and ended up balanced against the bed. Libby tried not to breathe as she willed the witches away, but the fallen pillow bridged the domains. Libby could not move for fear. The witches screamed bitter words until, in an instant, the alligator gave a snort and they scuttled away. With a bang of his tail, even the alligator was gone.

Libby waited for the vibrations to fade. The silence grew thick and dank. She pulled the sheet over her head and laid Victoria to her cheek. Nose whistles punctuated her breathing, joining other murmurs throughout the house. The refrigerator's distant hum, the wind under the gables, and the whine and click of each rotation of the old telephone dial filled the night.

She thought of calling out for Mummy, but it seemed less urgent. Mummy would tell her that the witches and alligator were her imagination. She hated that, even when said with Mummy's loving smile. Victoria could reassure her.

84

———

At the top of the landing, beside the table with the old telephone, the caller's urgent whispers did not reach Libby's now sleeping ears.

"I've made up my mind. I want to go through with our deal."

? ELEVEN

Monday.

Nancy sat on the back steps to lace orange-and-purple running shoes and double-tied the bow. A night dew of fog and sea salt soaked through her old rip-stop nylon shorts. She tucked two bills in her shoe to make change in town for the call. She rubbed her stiff fingers warm against the soft fabric of her favorite T-shirt. Libby's free-form art decorated the front in clotted streaks of fabric paint. The familiar outfit gave her no comfort this morning.

The sun had yet to break the horizon, leaving dawn damp and chill. She sat a minute longer, shivering and dull, her fingers wound in the fabric at her front, her eyes staring without seeing the paint peeling from the step beneath her feet. Nothing worked out as expected in life. She should have known this would be no different.

Her thoughts scanned through memory, the small building blocks of circumstance and event which brought her to today. The trauma of her mother's illness and death had been eclipsed by a longer history with a loving father and sister. Her charmed life—a talent recognized and rewarded, an indulged childhood, financial security—gave background to the confusion she felt now.

Even her mistaken marriage to Michael brought the joy of Libby to her life. So maybe she wasn't foolish to have hoped Michael would accept her decision without a fight. She tried to cheer herself with the thought that things had worked out before. She had time.

The whine of door hinges jolted her alert. Then she saw his foot and looked up to his shorts and on to his face as he bent over.

"I'd like to join you," he said.

"Michael, don't start again."

Nancy heard worn hostility in her voice. So must he, but he grinned. The optimism she had worked to revive died. Why hadn't he left her life last night?

"Give up the fight, lovely wife. I'm running with you. Surely you can accept a desperate man's need to make a last plea. Throwing everything over isn't as simple as you think. We have a child, Nancy, and a history. You mean a great deal to me," Michael said.

He reached out a hand.

"What gall," she spit back, but resignation deadened each word.

She ignored his offer and stood on her own. Michael shrugged. He danced his feet on the ground.

"You set the pace, I'll call the route. Last request of the condemned man." He grinned. "Let's do the salt marsh."

His teeth bared, white and predatory in the tanned face. Nancy wanted to slap him. How could he suggest the salt marsh, her special spot? The arc around the pond had been her discovery on her first run after Libby's birth. They'd just bought the Cape house.

The route lay a good distance in from open water, and reeds and marsh made closer access impossible. But the land's slope, down and away from the street, presented an unequaled view of three seas—the tall grass, the trapped salt pond, and the ocean. Like a kid after finding the road, she held the route secret even from her husband for the first week.

Nancy knew she would have picked it herself, today. The pond had become her habitual course, but perhaps Michael didn't know that anymore. Still, his making the choice felt like an invasion.

The run started from their house to the pond road and wound a good two miles beside the marsh before a stretch through developed streets took them home. The longest section had no dogs, no houses, no intersecting streets, only an occasional twist of estate driveway behind a high gate punctuated the land side. The line of box hedges hid these summer cottages of the rich and more famous from view. One time Michael had collided with a bicycle on a blind curve.

He survived. And she would survive this run with him, she reminded herself. Present circumstance couldn't change the beauty of the scenery. But he pissed her off with his false sentimentality.

Nancy set out at a slow jog. Past their drive, the street's shoulder lay soft and sandy, sucking at each footfall, making her quadriceps exert extra effort to move forward. A slight breeze pressed her back with a counterbalancing boost.

They didn't talk. Michael paced at her left side, just out of sight unless she tilted her head. At least he wasn't going to renew last night's fight, or beg, she thought, but she felt his weight hold her back. He knew she hated the sensation of someone breathing down her back. It made her erratic, veering between hedge and road. Quarreling about it had ended the shared runs right after she found the pond.

At the turn, she dropped back and motioned him forward. He laughed and moved by. She saw him through a dispassionate eye, last night's storm of rage exhausted.

She couldn't guess why he had joined her this morning. He had promised to be out of the house by mid-morning. The promise was enough. She could make her call later.

Scrub pine gave way to the trim of the first tall hedge. Across the pavement, a bank of wild rose bordered the marsh edge. When the blooms fell off, their hips would flatten and pinken to a tart fruit. Late in the summer, she would pick them with Libby. Together they would make the "sumber jam" Libby loved in the cold of winter.

Nancy relaxed as her movement became more limber. Warm sweat beaded her neck, dampened her hair and soaked the T-shirt limp. Her joints and ligaments coordinated to a smooth, relaxed motion and she should have felt fine.

The beauty of sun on the far water's edge turning blue to a reflective gold escaped her eye. She didn't hear the gulls caw or see them dive for breakfast from the sky. Last night had returned to occupy her mind.

He had reacted as if stunned. Betrayed. He swore he couldn't leave and pressed her hand to his heart. He forgave her. He pleaded. How could she give significance to an affair against their years of marriage? Their child? They had both transgressed, he said. They should forgive and start over. Renew their vows.

Nancy shuddered and nearly went down, but she regained her footing. Last night she refused to discuss her future. The point was, it wouldn't be with him. She hadn't said more, even to Carole. Carole let her cry and weep into the night. No one had prepared her for how hard it would be.

No one had warned her about the guilt, the humiliation of failure. Had she made a mess of the marriage? Nancy didn't know. Michael said her indifference had pushed him into Felicia's arms. The funny thing was, Felicia had said about the same thing at the fireworks.

Nancy didn't care about Felicia. Nancy cared about herself and Libby.

Until last night when she told Michael it was over, she had thought only of the future, a new life with a new love. The prospect offered freedom and growth and opportunity, her art matured, her daughter secure, herself at peace.

It remained the truth. She ran faster, manic with a need to believe, and veered into Michael. The contact bounced her into the road, deaf to the automobile coming up behind.

The jerk was sudden and swift as Michael's fingers pinched and left bruising throbs in her arm. Her stride propelled her off balance. She teetered farther forward into the street. The car screeched past on locked wheels that spit pebbles at her knees.

"You silly goose, you came damned close to being hit!"

Michael's eyes glittered with rage. A horrible suspicion surged fear through Nancy's veins. Panic made her stumble.

"You pushed me, Michael!"

Imagination accelerated the thick beat of her heart. She didn't wait for his response, but thrust her legs against the ground as hard as pistons. The advantage of surprise and a concentration of effort should take her beyond his reach. In a hundred yards lay the turn for home on a street ordinary with families. A street on which the actions of strangers would be noticed. She ran for that street.

Her flight gained speed and he had yet to react. Each second as she moved more away, he remained immobile. She was not afraid. She lifted her arms to embrace the future.

She did not see the battered Skylark lying in wait. She did not hear the engine rev or see it nose from the estate driveway into the street. She did not sense it follow her turn, the turn to take her home.

I am so lucky, was all she thought, confident with a euphoria of hope.

The left front fender caught her calf almost at the knee. She spun a crazy half circle before she suspected something was not right. The Skylark skidded on the sand blown across the road. It sideslipped after her spin, moving farther, moving faster until it was plowing through her skin.

? TWELVE

Monday.

Sandra Jordan saw it all.

First she noticed the BMW 318i convertible idling in the dense shade at the side of the road. Lacquered a sharp red, nothing could have kept it from catching her eye. The tan fabric top looked like an insufficient barrier to the 6:30 A.M. coastal cool. She slowed to rubberneck, frustrated by the tinted windows that obscured the driver.

Sandra choked on a surge of dread.

Chicago. Sandra's palms began to sweat. This was like Chicago. Fancy cars cruised her childhood streets, the window glass dark and mean. Chicago. She had to let herself remember. Chicago. The name stirred the hate coiled in her soul.

"Girl, watch yourself," she said.

She bit a fingernail and concentrated on the present. Renee Maxwell would not accept excuses. Her command to meet in the office by ten held no hint of apology for ruining Sandra's long weekend and no capacity for compassion if Sandra should be distracted on the way.

Blind anger replaced dread. Sandra kicked her foot to the accelerator. The car surged toward the soft edge. She yanked the wheel hard around and found herself aimed at the woman running in the middle of the road.

This is all wrong, Sandra realized. She pumped the brakes and pulled right. The car's front wheel started to catch on the unstable shoulder. Sandra jerked her hands and the car lurched to the asphalt. The woman jogger continued by without swerving.

Sandra hardly registered the faded green Skylark that passed as she tried to regain her composure. She returned to the proper position on the road and glanced in the rearview mirror. In that instant, reflected in the distortion of the cheap glass, Sandra Jordan saw it all at the apex of the bend before her turn cut the Skylark and the woman's flying body from view.

Sandra rationalized the decision again. She would have been stupid to stop. Stupid and dangerous. The guy running behind the Skylark had a better position to see the accident. He would be the best witness.

Sandra trembled when the BMW roared by on the right. Another person who did not bother to stop, she realized. She felt sick.

Past Plymouth, "America's Hometown," a sign with Golden Arches drew her from the road. At 7:45 A.M., no lines backed from the counter, no kids slid around her legs. Arctic blasts from the air-conditioning system increased her shivers. Ordering, Sandra looked down to see her hands with their fingernails chewed to the quick. She shifted her eyes away, shamed, and dodged the smile of the thin girl behind the counter.

"Two hotcakes with sausage, large coffee, cream and sugar. Here you go!" the girl chirped as she loaded the plastic tray set with a paper mat. "You have a nice day!"

Sandra raised the plastic fork and regarded the three uniform hotcakes beside a disk of sausage. Whipped margarine buttons, liberated from their plastic cups, melted into an oily blur. Sandra squeezed the brown, viscous syrup from a plastic boat. It soaked into the cakes and pooled on the plate.

Sandra cut and speared and shoveled.

Wedges of hotcakes and sausage moved from plate to mouth with a mechanical efficiency. She gulped coffee nearly too hot to drink and felt the burn of liquid and the compulsion of greed. Her universe contracted to a mouthful, each disappearing sooner than the last, each swallow anxious for another.

Afterward, the haze cleared and her senses returned. She loaded plates and cutlery and condiments into the bin by the door. Outside, the morning sun struck passing cars. One reflected back brilliant red and Sandra saw it all again, the woman arcing into space and the BMW flying by. Sandra recognized her shame.

Teal's discomfort intensified with each hour.

Light bore into her office through drawn blinds until the heat fairly shimmered the air. Sweat threatened her hairline. Her contact lenses gummed to her eyes. The *Diamonds and Dirt* on her T-shirt stuck to her back. What she wouldn't give to be at a Rodney Crowell concert right now. Good ol' country pathos exploring the cheatin' heart, not slick city ambition obsessing on a lawsuit.

Friday morning she had assured Don Clarke that the Fruiers case would settle out-of-court well before her scheduled testimony Wednesday.

"Enjoy a long weekend of golf," she had said then, smiling with confidence. "I hope every hole is under par."

Remembering the awkward exchange, she could kick herself. But she had to be correct on the suit. Fruiers' attorneys all but guaranteed as much. Bob Fahey left a trail of damning evidence. Smart lawyers understood cutting a loss, and Renee Maxwell was one smart lawyer. Teal couldn't understand why she hadn't received the call on Friday.

She willed the offer to come today, despite its being a Monday holiday. She waited in her airless office beside her silent telephone and wanted to believe a commitment to client service inspired her devotion. She knew that was not so. The suit threatened her future at Clayborne Whittier. Fruiers' attorney simply had to call.

Teal swiveled to look at Nancy's painting opposite her desk. She wondered if Nancy's weekend had gone well. When the Fruiers' suit came to a close, Teal decided, she'd get to the bottom of the threats, whatever Nancy said.

Teal preferred to blame her halfhearted pursuit of Nancy's tormentor on Nan's restrictive rules, but the justification stank. It was as self-serving as the truth. Teal knew in the grip of her ambition, Nancy's dilemma fell second. She vowed to help the minute the lawsuit ended.

The telephone rang. Finally, Teal thought. She raised the instrument with relief.

Carole's jaw seized shut and the strain tensed her tongue, immobile, against the roof of her mouth. She squeezed out a mutilated sound.

"Teal . . . the doctors say Nan's . . . dead."

If all the king's horses and all the king's men . . . then Teal must be the one able to put Nancy back together again. Teal had to.

Carole's polished nails clicked against the receiver clutched to her ear. Her palm sweat. Up until right now she had managed to appear in control. She had talked to the police, waited with Michael for a doctor to exit intensive care, made it down the hall to this telephone. Calm, even composed, doing what needed to be done.

When they told her Nancy was dead, reduced to a

corpse, she didn't scream. She gave them the instructions for disposal and she nodded as if she understood. Sweet deception.

Her tongue stuck on each word.

"I am at the hospital."

Tears dripped from her nose. Saliva bubbled over her lip. She banged her head on the side of the booth. Understanding was coming.

Earlier, in the hush of the tiny chapel, she'd sat with her back erect and head bent. God simply had to be reminded of her sister's need for His grace. That was all. She would help Him bring Nancy to full health. She would fix it all. She never considered the failure of all the king's horses and all the king's men in surgical scrubs.

"Carole? Carole, are you there?"

Teal's careful voice brought her back, brought her at least close enough to respond.

"I love her so much, Teal. *This can not be happening to Nancy!*"

Visitors on the way to sit by relatives averted their eyes. Carole did not care that she despised public displays of grief. She pressed her head against the wall and pressed a finger to loosen the clench of her jaw.

"Nancy was hit by a car out . . . with . . . Michael . . . out running. The ambulance got to her but . . . at the hospital they said she . . . God, Teal, I can't." Carole sobbed out the last words. "Come down, Teal. We need you."

Every time Teal couldn't see to drive, she'd pull off the road. Despite frequent stops, she made it from Boston in an hour and forty-five minutes flat. She remembered dodging the traffic in the rotary at the Sagamore Bridge. Nothing else registered before her last turn took her up Nancy's drive.

Libby ran out to meet her at the car.

"Auntie Teal, did you bring Mummy back?"

Teal looked at her goddaughter, hair as tousled as dandelion fluff, face screwed into a knot of childhood fears.

"No, honey. I came to see you and Carole and to say I love you." She scooped the girl up in her arms to walk to the house.

"Will the witches let Mummy come back?"

"What witches, darling?" Teal asked, careful not to dismiss Libby's fear.

"The ones under my bed. I jumped to the big chair to get out this morning. I never touched the floor." Libby's proud face dropped. "They yelled and scared me last night."

Teal remembered her familiar terrors as a child, her own black bear in the bedroom closet. She had hated the raised voices of parental fights. She held tightly to her favorite child.

"The witches have nothing to do with your mummy, honey. She got hurt out running."

"Auntie Carole says Mummy's gone." Libby's face screwed-up in fear.

"She died, Libby, in the accident. She never wanted to leave us. Most of all, she didn't want to leave you."

Teal considered telling Michael about Libby's witches. She respected childhood fears. They deserved to be taken seriously. Later, she'd try.

Carole's question was as direct as Libby's, if more mature. She appeared wan and worn, but in greater control than on the telephone. Her greeting held the familiarity of those joined more closely yet in sorrow. Teal clung to Carole.

"Nancy said she'd told you she planned to leave Michael," Carole said in a voice which cracked.

Teal considered her response as Carole paused to regain composure. Her voice remained shrill when she started to talk.

"She said she'd finally found true love. And now this.

Who was she seeing, Teal?" Carole's fingers dug into Teal's shoulder. "He should learn from family about . . . Nancy."

There was something different from pure compassion in Carole's request. Teal understood. She, too, wanted to order the chaos around Nancy's death.

"I don't know who, Carole. Nancy never said. I think she hoped to protect him until things were settled. This is horrible."

Carole nodded, as though shared grief brought a certain solace. Carole had raised a serious question. Who would be there for Nan's friend?

"She told me she met him about a year ago in the spring at one of her openings. And he collects her paintings," Teal said.

Carole stared as the shock widened her bloodshot eyes. Teal realized Carole was not seeing a thing. Carole pulled away from the comforting embrace.

"No." Carole shook her head and choked. "No. God, not her lawyer. When he called yesterday, I stood right here teasing her about him."

Carole jammed a knuckle in her mouth.

"There's nothing you could have done." Teal reached for Carole's clenched fist. "Would it help if I called him now? Told him about the accident?"

"Accident?" Carole jerked her head forward. "This wasn't an accident. Someone did this to her! Someone murdered Nancy."

"Murder? No!" Teal's denial spit out the word.

She couldn't contemplate murder. Had her neglect of the threats killed her friend? No. Please no, she prayed. In this, she understood Carole's desire to assign blame.

Carole left the room and returned as quickly.

"Look. I wanted it to be a joke," Carole said and pushed the envelope at Teal.

The postmark spelled a blurry New York. Inside, the

page Teal unfolded looked too familiar. Nancy remained radiant in the May *laMode.*

" 'The adulteress will die,' " Teal said aloud as she decoded the bright marks.

"It arrived at the beginning of the week. I showed it to her last night. I didn't know what else to do after she told me she planned to leave Michael. She laughed. She said ending the marriage would solve everything. She told *me* not to worry! She refused to listen, Teal."

Carole's misery held a familiar assumption of her own guilt. Teal decided not to tell Carole about the other mail. That discussion could not ease her pain right now.

Teal's own remorse flushed her face, bright and hot. If she had come to the Cape for Libby's birthday, if Nancy hadn't been alone with Michael on that road. If . . . Teal dropped the magazine page and hugged Carole's sagging shoulders.

"I'll call the lawyer right now. Come sit by me."

Teal tried not to think any further. Certainly not about murder.

? THIRTEEN

Monday.

Albert Fontane stuck to the literal truth. He switched
his answers between the young male cop with all the
questions to the dispirited woman taking notes.

Albert didn't say nothing, but Tina woulda been
squawking about that if she was here. "Feminist?" she'd
complain. "I don't know about that, but I'd like to know
why the girl's taking the notes. Isn't fair giving the glory
to you boys!" And she'd shake her head a tsk-tsk. God,
he loved her.

He nodded at both cops. "Sure I saw the lady passing
the drive, and I waited to pull inta the road. No problem.
You know what I mean? I couldn't see around that blind
bend, so I crept, and Jesus, the crazy woman takes the
turn wide. There she is, and no time to stop. Ask the gen-
tleman was with her. He saw me swerve. Then the sand
blowed all over the road catches me in a slide. I tell you
officers, wasn't nothing to do."

"And your speed at the time, sir?" the policeman
asked.

Albert liked the nice, respectful tone, but knew it
didn't mean a thing. He answered like it took thought.

"Under the limit, maybe thirty-five. I wished I'd known she was there, poor lady."

"Mr. Fontane, what brought you to Shell Bay?"

Now this was the question, wasn't it. Albert shrugged. He wouldn't budge from the truth.

"Business in Hyannis tomorra morning. The Slip-Inn Motel near the marina. I do uniforms for the Cape. Hotels, motels, restaurants, nursing homes, you name them and I make'm and all custom, if they want. You know what I mean? 'Dick' and 'The Slip-Inn Motel' on a three color breast patch cursive or block, your choice. Very distinguishing, gives a friendly look with class. I do rent or sell plus maintenance contract, your choice with competitive pricing."

The woman was smiling. Albert smiled back.

"So, anyways, I'm down a day early, maybe scout out a few prospects, maybe take the scenic route through Shell Bay."

"Where did you plan to spend the night, Mr. Fontane?" the male cop asked.

"The Slip-Inn. Customers on the hospitality side make travel easy. A nursing home now, I would take a day trip. You know what I mean?"

"How long have you been in uniforms?"

Albert looked up. A kid, wet behind his ears. Stood like a poker tickled his tender parts, wanted to be State but had to settle for starting in the minors. Probably end there, too, and damned lucky though he'd never agree.

Albert sighed. Didn't these kids understand an accident like this shook up an old man. Three years to retirement. He and his brother agreed. Sixty-five years old was enough.

Albert fingered his plain breast pocket and wished he could go back to the days when he smoked, before everything was dangerous to some part of your health. His brother wanted air bags for the next car. Air bags! Sam'd gone soft!

He continued with a truth exact to the end. The lady cop suggested he be available for further questions. She never looked him in the eye. What did she think? He was scum? Funny thing to get to him.

He had taken their breathalizer test and pissed in the cup. Why not? He was clean. It was a terrible world when they suspected a man his age abused drugs. Alcohol, sometimes, but at crack-of-dawn in the morning? He didn't look like that. He ran a hand down the golf pants Tina'd just brought home, rubbing up the nice green.

"Sharp as a tack," she'd said when she made him model the matching golf shirt, the little thread clubs crossed on his breast. He didn't remark on the cheap embroidery, she was too proud. Maybe she still saw the slender, muscular, teenaged boy in the round old man. Maybe love didn't see the gray hair combed in strings across his balding head or how he shrank more each year.

Tina, he whispered to himself.

Albert thought of the dead woman's husband then. He'd been calm as could be, not hysterical like the sister. Maybe he'd been the one made the contract. Who could tell these days, one outta two marriages ending kaput? Not everyone had the blessing of a Tina. Albert shrugged. He made a point of never trying to guess. Husband, sister, lover, parent, best friend—what did it matter?

The male cop nodded at him with courtesy before he pointed him out the door. The woman flipped to the next page in her notebook, prepared for the next problem, next notes. She lifted her dark eyes once to his face. The outside hugged him, bright and still.

He couldn't get the bitch of it out of his head. The mistake. Not that he blamed himself. The thing was, when he clipped her, very soft like he'd been told, *she spun right for him* just as the old 'Lark hit the sand. So, bang, now she's dead. First royal screwup in a long time.

Squeamish had nothing to do with it. Client wanted death, he'd do death. Client wanted maim, well, he maimed. He understood the difference!

This was not good. This was not good at all. Sam would not be happy taking the heat. Albert didn't blame him, but luck of the draw gave his brother the problem.

The rotation put up Sam to answer the call, Albert to complete the assignment. Next job, they'd switch. Albert talk. Sam work. The system worked nice to leave them clean. Even a crazy client couldn't prove a thing. The client was reminded of the fact. Albert liked it like that.

When he did it, he never knew who hired him, never would. Next time he'd screen for his brother. Kept it business. No worrying why or judging. And he never, ever involved himself wondering who. That was his rule. Life itself was a loser's game, some just lost early. No accounting for fate.

Chatty customers with guts to spill were turned away. Albert once suggested a priest to one. Sam's disgust ended the counseling. On the other hand, if a client got cold feet after the fact, Sam and Albert's being brothers kept the trust. On this job, if they ran into a problem with payment, Sam could collect without getting all emotional and involved.

Still, Sam'd be pissed, no escaping that. Hell, Albert was pissed.

He liked the basic setup okay. Only a couple of projects a year, plenty of rest between and only accidents. No mob hits, no kids, no filthy methods. Their ad in the paramilitary magazines made their skill plain without setting up a legal fuss. He could repeat the text by heart.

"Daring, creative individual available for adventures, help with the accident-prone. Boating, hunting, driving, etc. Your objective realized without inconvenience to you. Reasonable, confidential."

They'd done the lot, even an electrical "malfunction." Albert hadn't liked that one, and, afterward, Sam agreed. Stick to the basics—they never got you caught. No record. Albert and Sam stayed clean, not one case in court.

Mosta the time, Albert stuck with uniforms, Tina, and the kids, but the sideline kept him on his toes, helped with college and retirement. Hell of a world with college costing more than their first home and no end in sight. And now little Al the Third saying he had to have an another degree to get a job. Albert sighed.

He remembered when he and Sam cried at little Al going to Harvard University. First in the family at college and it was this Ivy League. They were so proud. Little Al was a good boy. It humbled Albert to recognize he was grandfather to a talent like that. Tina deserved the credit, how she raised Al, Jr., and both girls. The sideline paid for the education of the grandchildren, Albert never forgot that.

Most days, Albert wouldn't let himself think about retirement, but he never could help it at this point on a job. Right after the accident, before the feelings faded, before he forgot what they looked like or the cries of the next of kin. Retirement dreams helped.

Big-game fishing—he couldn't wait. Tina sure to play bingo with the girls and complain about men all day, and he'd be out on the boat. They had the house down on Marco Island, Florida, and he couldn't wait to stay the winter. He knew Sam didn't feel the same, but he and Sam'd work it out.

Shit, the mistake better not queer the deal. Five thousand collected, more to come. Never ceased to amaze Albert, either, people came through. Of course, they were smart to honor the contract. Sam and Albert made the consequences clear. Still, this one looked a royal mess.

Sam thought the deal'd gone south when the up front money lay around for a month and not a word. The call over a week ago looked to prove him wrong and Albert got set. Friday and it was off again, Sam saying the buyer canceled.

But no, last night, Sam in a sweat, the word was go. At once was the instruction. This Monday morning. Fine, Albert rejiggered his plan and wouldn't you know but a real screw-up.

He didn't like it, such a nice-looking girl all legs and blonde hair. Mother, too, the police said. He needed to get to a bottle of Maalox. Goddamned! How could the husband take it calm? If he ever lost his Tina, he'd about go crazy.

❓FOURTEEN

Monday.

Felicia tried to smooth back her hair, repeating the gesture over and over. She shifted against the airport lounge's molded plastic chair. When she couldn't stand the tension a moment longer, she got up from her seat.

A line stood in front of the counter at the gate. Felicia crowded at the end.

"How long until we board?" Felicia asked when she made it to the desk.

The shuttle attendant looked up with a pert smile. "Any minute now, miss. I'd say no more than five. Enjoy your flight."

Felicia didn't hesitate. She had time to call Michael. How many false starts preceded the final decision? Maybe even preceded the first yes, before cold feet reversed the decision to no? She couldn't remember who decided what until the last time.

She'd let Michael push her along until Friday. She thought it could make everything come right between them, but on the flight to Boston she hesitated. Reneged and canceled after landing. The about-face left her wanting to look Nancy in the eye. Beg if she must. But under the artillery of the fireworks, Nancy shot Felicia's hope to hell.

Casually, with a shrug.

Nancy worried only about the damned picture. *SELF*. She wasn't interested in Felicia's empty life and laughed at the money Felicia had squandered on the affair. "Bill Michael," Nancy had said. The threat to Barrette Gallery, the potential ruin of Nancy's reputation, these moved the artist not at all.

Abject with shame and a terrible fear, Felicia had cast aside pride. She wanted to explain she hated herself more than Nancy could and began with the painting.

"Auctioning *SELF* looked like the chance for me to make money. I owe my artists, my assistant, the gallery, everyone. Nan, please, I've been foolish—"

"I'm not sure I need to know. This is hard on us both," Nancy broke in. "I'm about to make a few changes myself. Please understand I don't care about you and my husband. I plan to leave Barrette this week, along with him."

Felicia tried to see Nancy's face, read a different message than what she'd heard. She wanted to take Nancy's shoulders and shake her and scream no! Her investment in creating Nancy could not be shrugged away. NO! Felicia had hoped for a catharsis by telling Nancy and expected Nancy's anger. She never had considered such a dismissal.

The fantasy of Nancy's forgiveness and her excitement at a half sibling for Libby came down to that. Fantasy. Felicia's month-long fog lifted.

"Go ahead, leave! Oh, one more thing. I'm expecting Michael's baby."

Amazement lifted Nancy's brows. "You were silly," she had said before she turned away.

Felicia couldn't recollect how she came to her feet or walked the length of the pier under the bursting sky or when the full fury of rage hit. Maybe it was the indignation of the guilty. She didn't ask herself.

She made the final call from Nancy's house. It wasn't for Michael, it was for herself. He had smiled his crocodile smile and never asked about the change of heart.

Felicia hurried to find a telephone along the airport corridor. Two rings and Teal answered. Michael was not in.

"I'll try later," Felicia said and started to hang up.

"Felicia? Felicia?" Teal's voice carried from the phone.

Felicia put the instrument back to her ear. "Yes?"

"I hate telling you like this, but you should know."

Teal's voice sounded cracked and too low. Felicia tensed for what came next.

"Nancy was killed this morning, Felicia. You know how she ran every morning. She was out running, and a car . . . anyway, it skidded. The doctors said she didn't suffer."

Felicia slumped on the airport wall and gagged the words of sympathy she managed to whisper.

Over Connecticut, she entered the lavatory to double-over the metal bowl. Sodden bagel heaved from her stomach and out her mouth to catch the ends of her tangled hair. Bile burned her nose.

No end should be like that, was all she could think.

The New York bound plane began its descent.

Teal dialed Nancy's lawyer. He answered on the third ring. Five minutes later, she hung up.

"He's not Nancy's friend."

"But yesterday Nancy acted as flustered as any married woman with a lover," Carole insisted.

"I believe him," Teal said.

Carole wavered between disappointment and bitter relief. She tried to smile at Teal.

"I'll be fine," she said and could not take the next breath. *"Why is my sister dead?"*

Carole sensed a slip over the edge. She heard her voice vibrate through the room, strained and shrill. She wasn't fine or in control. She scared herself. If only she could find the lover to make sense of Nancy's death. The lover was at the heart of the equation.

Carole hated the anxiety seizing her lungs closed. She remembered the summer of her mother's death, the asthma she had developed in trying to do everything right. She worked so hard to be Mummy's perfect little girl. Everyday she prayed to get Mummy's attention. In the end, Mummy turned away dead.

Carole rubbed a finger along the curve of the rocking chair dangling from her bracelet. She pressed the thin edge. She'd loved to sit on Mummy's lap, gentled by the motion, lulled to a deep sleep. After Mummy's death, Carole knew how to provide the same comfort for Nancy.

Thoughts of childhood faded as Carole loosened her hold on the little chair. She must face the terrible truth that Nancy, beloved sister, would never rock in her arms again.

Teal never expected to see Michael looking anything but his best, and she didn't, even now. He sprawled across the porch chair, almost natty in bright turquoise shorts and a designer T-shirt. Heat forced him to wipe sweat across his sleeve, rub his face against hands covered by the fabric of his shirt. So male a gesture, Teal thought, and felt a flash of pity for his inarticulate pain.

"They let him go. Nothing to hold him on, what else could they do." Michael telegraphed a reluctance to judge. "Poor bastard, driving down to Hyannis and ending up with this. What was Nan thinking, running down the middle of that road? She acted crazy this morning."

Carole fairly shimmied with rage. "She 'acted crazy'? *She? He* killed my sister. I told Nancy not to let you go."

A vein pulsed over Michael's right eye. Teal realized everyone on the porch would have done anything to remake the day. But the hell of the fact lay in its persistence. The fact was, Nancy was dead.

Later, when Carole found Teal sitting in the lee of a dune, watching the ebbing tide with eyes seared dry, Teal didn't want to talk or listen. She wanted to watch the gull dive at the water. A streak of silver flapped in its beak as the bird swallowed.

"I heard the fight last night, Teal. Nancy screamed, 'You watch me file for divorce,' while Michael yelled. I was scared for Libby up in bed. Do you think she heard?"

But Carole did not wait for an answer.

"I asked Michael this morning to leave Nancy alone. He didn't listen. I was interfering with his agenda." Carole twisted the last word from her lips.

"You are saying what? Michael pushed Nancy? Come on!" Teal wished the bird would return.

"You think I'm being ridiculous? Then you tell me why Nancy died in the middle of the road!" Carole rubbed tears into her skin. "Please. Just talk to the police. And help me find her lover."

Carole's unadorned face and windblown hair gave her more charm, if less glamour than usual, Teal realized. Teal gazed past the sea grass and sand to the far horizon. Distant sails filled with distant wind. A spinnaker billowed open, bright with color in the blazing sunshine.

Teal accepted everyone reacted in a different way to grief. She could afford to assist Carole.

"I'll talk to the police, but that's all I can promise," she said.

She wondered if she could have done more for Nancy

before. Before, when death seemed only a paper threat. Before, when Nancy lived. Teal's heart ached.

Teal entered the station and met with the police.

No question, the Shell Bay police regarded her inquiries as ridiculous. They hardly muted their snickers of disbelief and stared without embarrassment at her long legs before attending to her words. She hoped the irritated spark in her blue eyes caused shame. It didn't. They acted more amused as anger marked her oval face and twisted her lips. The station hung with machismo.

The responding officer, barely out of his teens, called her an exaggerated and irksome ma'am. He shifted his attention from her to the chief to the door. The chief, a man facing his mid-fifties trim and tanned, acted tickled by the encounter. The one female officer stared at the floor.

"You think this colored mail relates to her death?" the chief asked. "Why would Fontane be interested in a young woman's affair? Was she a nurse or in the motel industry? You know, having to wear a uniform?"

The responding officer couldn't keep the smirk from his face. At least it wasn't mirrored by the chief. He listened with polite disinterest.

"I told you, she was an artist, a famous artist. Lots of people knew of her. She's been featured in every weekly magazine this year. These letters used the words 'perversion,' 'death,' and 'atone.' A fanatic could as easily be a stranger as a friend," Teal said.

She willed herself to remain cordial, act as though the police cared. She suddenly very much wanted them to care.

"Are you proposing Mr. Fontane has fundamentalist leanings? Might have gone over the edge? Is that what you're saying?" The chief sighed as though he considered her another crime-crazed city person. "A good many here in Shell Bay might be candidates, then, and none of us is dead. Of course, she was a summer resident."

That brought the house down in shrieks of laughter. Teal relaxed her fixed smile. She wanted to scream.

"Tell you what, little lady. You bring in those letters and we'll take a good look at them and go from there," the chief said as he reached to shake her hand.

The arresting officer followed suit, then the deputy and the chief's assistant. Hard and calloused, soft and clammy, tough and dry, sticky with lunch—Teal wanted to wash.

"You were kind to see me." She didn't say what she thought.

The policewoman shadowed her to the door. The woman shifted and glanced back to the room before she spoke.

"I'm sorry, but we're not exactly used to requests like this. The guys can be pretty difficult."

"If you're really sorry," Teal said, "then call me if you learn anything."

Teal laid her card in the woman's passive hand.

Michael watched Carole and Libby diminish to bouncing dots. In the late heat of the July day, fog sweat off the ocean to cloud the beach air to a haze. Libby held Carole's hand and he sighed with relief. They should be gone for a while.

He stood from the chair, surprised he still wore his running shorts. They made the morning real. Death hadn't exactly been in his plans, but he wasn't going to think about that or about Felicia. He was going to find Nancy's copy of the revised will and those damnable trusts. If Nancy could die with no will and no trusts, Massachusetts would award him a minimum of half the entire estate.

He hesitated at the second floor. Unlikely they'd be in

the bedroom. Nancy had no desire to share the documents with him. Her natural habitat and most private place was her studio, either the big one in Lincoln or the converted shed here on the Cape. He backed down the stairs and ran through the door.

The building across the yard was locked. Not a problem, Michael thought, grinning an adolescent's grin. The window popped with ease and he flipped in.

Blinds drawn across the skylights shadowed the room, though it remained light enough for him to see. Both easels stood empty. Not one sketch pad littered the floor. A new canvas had been half stretched across a frame on the worktable. Nancy would never finish the task.

Michael rocked back on his heels with the force of his disbelief. It wasn't possible Nancy lay in some human storage drawer. Really, not possible, not at all what he'd meant to be. But since she did, he had to find the will.

Sandra pulled down the drive, dumb with heat and angry that she had returned to the Cape. But she knew leaving early wouldn't be right. She was her mother's daughter, raised to be polite even when she remained an outsider.

A man walked across the neighboring yard. She watched him jimmy the window lock of the toolhouse and hurdle the sill. Exiting the car, she peeled her dress from the back of her legs. Sweat ran a network of rivers down her right thigh. Maybe she should call the police or maybe it was just another prank, like Renee Maxwell's. Sandra didn't laugh.

"Hey Sand-man, I hear you got the ol' Maxwell commitment test. You really rate these days. It's the first time she's pulled it on anyone at our lowly level. Scuttlebutt is she does it to her favorite senior associates, a test of their mettle for the old partnership. So, in your absence, we voted you comer of the decade." Sandra's housemate grinned.

Sandra squirmed as he continued.

"Actually, we think Renee outdid herself in being a jerk to pull the joke on a long weekend. Or, excuse me, 'a test of willingness to serve clients at any personal cost.' Well, she's paid a high price, the old witch, but you shouldn't—not like today. So, in honor of your composure under stress, and we all agreed you were great when you called to figure out what to do, the gang is getting lobsters and beer. I'm the greeting committee. Later we'll cruise for ice cream in town. Welcome home, buddy."

He extended a hand for her briefcase and Sandra tightened with the urge to cry. He hadn't looked at her funny, not once, not even knowing, as he would, that her ugly print dress cost too much. Offering ice cream hadn't been a mock. She had to change the subject.

"Did you see that man go through the window of the shed next door? More what I'd expect from where I come from. Chicago." Sandra cracked her first collegiate smile as she confessed to what had shamed her before.

Her fellow associate smiled back, a pleasant sight. "I didn't see him, but some woman is using a key on it right now."

? FIFTEEN

Monday.

Teal pulled the key from the studio door and shoved her sunglasses up on her head. Her hair spiked out around the grip of the plastic earpiece, but she could see into the dim room. She hesitated, then stepped inside Nancy's sanctuary. She blinked and saw the figure crouched beside an open drawer across the room.

"What are you do—"

"How did you? . . ."

The questions slapped together to create an abrupt and immediate din. They ended to leave the room silent. Teal took a step back, away from the rage on Michael's face. Shivers ruffled goose bumps on her skin.

"I wanted to be with Nancy—so much of her is here."

Teal's voice matched the gesture of supplication she made with her arm. What is wrong with me? she wondered.

Michael straightened with a sorrowful smile, his earlier expression imagined or dissolved. Teal squinted, the better to see, but his smile remained.

"I think I felt the same way." He ran a hand along the top of the old oak flat file. "She put herself into every picture, every sketch. I thought looking would bring her back. Well. Not to be."

His voice wavered. Teal didn't know what to believe.

"You came in the window," she said.

The observation was void of inflection, yet remained an accusation.

"I haven't your privileges, my dear. No extra keys for me." Michael's face said many other things.

Teal heard the irritation, the old jealousy butt against his posture of melancholy. She did have copies of all Nancy's keys. The practice had started in college when Nancy locked herself out of the dorm, her car, her home. She would call Teal to the rescue.

Senior year, Nancy handed Teal a silver ring engraved with "make it better" and holding all her keys. The pattern, lasting long past need, became a talisman of their friendship. That was all. Yet it was, really, everything, Teal knew. Maybe Michael recognized the truth.

He came toward her from across the room until she shrank back on instinct. But he swerved around her to stop at the open door.

"There isn't room for both of us, is there? Not right now," he said in a voice vibrating with emotion.

Teal, surprised and touched, watched him stride across the lawn.

Michael worked to keep his foot light, his heaving shoulders square. He wanted to stomp the ground, grind out the image of Teal. The interfering bitch. But he'd fooled her, his wife's so smart friend. She believed the anger cramped in his throat was sorrow. He'd seen her stricken face. Michael laughed without joy.

Still, he'd only started. What he had seen turned up nothing, just paints and brushes. No will, no trusts—no good. He began to sweat. He hated sweat with its smell of poverty and fear. It took him back to the boxing ring.

Michael pulled his soaking shirt over his head in the middle of the yard.

Carole and Libby rounded the path from the beach. The fit, adult blonde and the small, childish girl were caught backlit in the burning, melon sun. His daughter tugged free of her aunt's hand and ran to him.

"Daddy, Daddy, look at my star. See?" Libby bounced her outstretched arm, her hand held in a special fist.

"Yes Libby-Libs, I do," he said and gave up hope of a quick rifle through the house.

Teal hooked the skylight shade and gave a gentle pull. Light opened the room. Teal inhaled air filled with the memory of Nancy surrounded by charcoal dust, the aroma of oil paint and turpentine. Nothing but a half-prepared canvas lay in view. No works in-progress graced the easels; no alternatives leaned to the walls at the edge of the floor. Suddenly the studio did not evoke Nancy at all.

Teal crossed the room to shut the flat file where Michael had stood. The unusual piece dominated much of the area with its large, shallow drawers designed to accommodate blueprints.

Teal hesitated at the waiting canvas. Holding the loose, puckered end, she pulled the cloth straight and taut. The fabric became a blank square, inviting imagination to fill it in. For an instant, Teal marveled at Nancy's genius to make empty space communicate.

Perhaps this canvas was to be the beginning of the break from the past Nancy had suggested. The preparations for change could explain the studio's empty state. Her past swept aside, the future on the verge of being realized.

In other circumstances, Teal might have been amused

117

at her thoughts. In these circumstances, she was not. Teal released the canvas.

Nancy considered her sketches private, an artist's most intimate diary. Only when an idea was transformed to pure line, sentimentality removed, did she take up a brush and expose her vision to review. Some ideas never graduated. Some she trashed. None was ever shared too early.

Teal drew a finger along the file. She curved her fingers around the first set of pulls and tugged until the drawer slid open. Forgive me, Nancy, she prayed.

Hundreds of clean brushes, of every conceivable size and bristle, lay side by side. No revelation resided here. Teal's tension abated.

The second drawer displayed tubes of paint, some plump, some squeezed, and two curled near dry.

Opening the third, Teal's heart resumed pounding when she saw the sketch pad. After a long second, she wrestled it free of the drawer.

She bent her knees to the floor and rested her back against the file's side. She flipped the tablet open. The first drawings seemed more abstract than Nancy's realism. The second set explored details of the first. Teal appreciated the composition and the form, but could not find the Nancy she knew in these works. Then Teal turned to the next page and stopped breathing.

"Nancy," she murmured between pleasure and pain.

"I don't see smoke, do you?"

Sandra shook her head. "Nope and he's out the door."

Her companion stared for what seemed a minute longer than necessary.

"I don't believe it! That's her husband, Mr. Britton. Oh, Christ, I forgot. You don't know. You missed our excitement. Not quite the thing to say, is it? Sorry. Anyway our neighbor, that artist Nancy Vandenburg? She was hit by a car this morning. Not a good show. She died."

Died. He said died. Damnation, Sandra thought, she *died.*

Sandra stiffened at his onslaught of eager words. No one should be excited by death. Old memories of the titillation of other strangers came to mind. No! Now was now. Now she was a lawyer, an officer of the court and now, whatever she had thought to do, she'd screwed up.

"I heard the family didn't come down last summer. Some life! She was in Italy." The young lawyer twisted his mouth. "Of course, her summers just ended. Goodbye fame. One misstep running and you're dead. . . ."

He rattled on, the woman no more than a celebrity name.

Sandra stood struck dumb. She'd never made the connection before. *That Nancy Vandenburg.* The artist responsible for giving a young black girl hope in a summer of despair.

That horrible, horrible August, the Chicago museum ran the controversial show, "African-Americans As Depicted Through Time." Nancy Vandenburg's painting hung in the area for "Honky Art."

Derisively tagged or not, Sandra had stood transfixed before the black family seen framed through a kitchen door. Dad bounced the baby on his knee. Mom in cornrows laughed by the stove. Their teenage son teased a sibling hidden out of view. Sandra didn't judge the work. She loved the artist for painting hope. Until today, she had forgotten the name.

The name of the woman in the middle of the road. Damn.

Libby didn't want to say she was afraid. Daddy and Aunt Carole might get more sad. She didn't want them sad anymore today. She wanted Mummy. She held out the starfish for her father's review.

"I think it lost a leg," she said, not sure how bad that was. "Does Mummy have her legs?"

There, she'd asked. Finding the dead starfish made her have to know.

"Auntie Carole says I can't see her. I want to, Daddy, please?" No one liked a whiner, Mummy once said, so Libby tried not to plead. She sensed the adults exchanging *those* looks over her head.

"We'll see, honey. Now let's have a look at that starfish again."

Libby loved the smell of her dad like this, all sweaty and sharp. She loved the long, silky black hair growing out of his legs. She loved that he didn't say a flat no. She could save her special secret for another time. If she remembered. That was the hard part. Last night with the witches under the bed, Libby heard their scary talk. Or was it outside her room? She counted off in her head.

First, "No, don't you dare come down. Wait until I call tomorrow."

Later yelling. Libby wondered if yells broke bones or starfish legs. "So you think the plan is stupid now. Well, you came up with something fucking swell . . ."

Libby knew saying "fucking" was wrong.

Then someone crying. "I don't know what to do."

Or maybe it was Mummy or Felicia, then Daddy or Auntie Carole or Mummy. Already memory began to blur. Maybe it wasn't much of a secret anyway to have been listening and awake. Her shoulders curled in defeat and her face drooped. Last night was the night before her mother went away. Libby never wanted to forget.

Nancy gazed at Teal with a wide and loving eye. Held Teal spellbound with delight. Teal touched the smooth plane of Nancy's high cheek. The rub of flesh to paper jerked Teal to earth. She rocked the tablet Nancy to her chest and remembered.

Nancy standing in front of the dorm on the first day at school, more matched luggage than Teal had seen in her life.

Nancy sobbing her humiliation when her English professor commented "sophomoric at best," on her poetry.

Nancy challenging Teal to a bottle of the horrid Seagram's Seven. That episode ended their college drinking and only just spared their lives.

Nancy whooping when the fellowship came, "If I get only one year as an artist, I will have lived, and Daddy agreed!"

Nancy exhibiting with Barrette Gallery for her first New York show. Her works became the talk of the town.

Nancy walking down the aisle, Teal in front, Michael at the end. Nan's heel caught at the runner's edge and her "Oh, damn" echoed through the gothic arches.

Oh, damn, indeed.

Nancy holding newborn Libby in the crook of her arm, mother and child her next year's prolific theme.

Nancy. Teal stroked the line of paper hair, touched the dryness of a paper lip. How could Nancy be dead?

Teal's tears splattered Nancy's charcoal face. She caught her breath, her fingers shaking as she turned the page. Another Nancy drawing up a tub, her eyes on a dream far away. Looking felt like snooping and Teal blushed. These drawings bared Nancy like an act of unadulterated, uninhibited love. For whom were they intended? Teal wondered.

Teal spoke aloud to a Nancy poised to bathe. "Ah, my lovely friend, what secrets do you have in your heart?"

Teal listened until silence forced her to turn the page.

The figure dominating the rectangular space held a naked charcoal Nancy in the embrace of charcoal arms.

Teal gasped. The familiar black-and-white face radiated a sexual force. It could not be, Teal thought and stared down. It was.

Renee Maxwell.

? Sixteen

Tuesday.

Renee pressed the plastic bag of melting ice to her head. She ignored the rivulets of water which snaked down her forehead and slid beside her nose like glacial tears. The fifth of scotch she fished from the floor showed transparent when held to the light.

She'd never thought to see a bottle of liquor empty in her house. As a practical matter, she gifted out the better brands she received from clients as soon as they came in, and all the bottles she received were the better brands. But Nan liked an occasional jigger of this single-malt scotch, so it had stayed, opened and poured maybe twice until Renee attacked it today.

She redirected her free hand, skimming it along the floor until her fingers snagged the tooled-leather book. She raised it, wavering, to within an inch of her nose. Too close. The hand-penned words and line drawings blurred to erratic strokes. She thrust out her arm. Almost. Blinking brought the words to focus.

> Not Robert's place, that
> has to take you in . . .

No, not that one. She turned the pages with a drunk's exaggerated care and smelled Nan's perfume breeze back. She saw the quick watercolors of Italy's coast. She averted her eyes at the sketch of them arm-in-arm. She wanted to read just the one poem again, wanted to touch the pain like prodding a sore tooth with a restless tongue. But the book slipped from her grasp as she passed out, unable to read the lines lying on her chest.

> . . . and it's not easy
> Not easy to turn away
> tearing self from self
> (a joyless abandon, leaving)
> And it's not from lack of loving
> but for loving too much

"Dan, how should I know what to think? She was my best friend, we were closer than sisters. I might have said than lovers. I thought we were close, but she never told me *that.*"

Hurt burned at the edge of Teal's voice. Tension puckered her oval face. Her natural grace had turned clumsy today. His friend was troubled. He considered his response before he spoke.

"She never confided that she might be gay?"

"Lesbian, Dan, lesbian," Teal snapped.

"Hey, okay. I didn't realize—"

"Women prefer lesbian? Let's respect her that much."

"You've been suggesting murder. Because of her lifestyle?"

Dan watched Teal struggle to shrug as her eyes filled. He pretended not to see her surreptitiously rub the tears away. The anger only appeared directed at him, he understood. He'd taken worse from friends, spouses, next of kin. Yell, scream, rail at the police. Sometimes it was the best the bereaved could do, Dan the most accessible outlet for pain.

He also understood it best to bring attention back to the matter at hand. He sighed. He liked Teal. She'd helped him, taken him seriously on his first homicide. She'd introduced him to his future wife. He wanted to do what he could for the attractive CPA. He flipped open his notebook and pulled out his pen.

"The car hit her in another jurisdiction," Dan said.

The comment hung in the air until her silence unnerved him.

"Okay, I'll talk to the Shell Bay chief strictly because you are a friend, but it may make matters worse. I can do a *very* little poking around. Run a make on Fontane, run a check for homophobes. I'm not holding out hope."

Teal's eyes showed a flicker of light. "You'll find something," she said.

Dan shrugged. "I know you don't want to hear this, but it may be an accident, Fontane the poor soul he says he is. Her husband isn't complaining. Teal, you may not have liked the Shell Bay guys, but they did their job."

"Michael wouldn't complain if he gave her the push. Or set it up in advance," Teal said with set lips.

Dan missed her animation, the hands in constant motion and her face moving with expression.

"Let's say you're right. Fontane hit her on purpose or saw the husband give her a shove. Say Mr. Britton hired Fontane and lied. Why?"

"She planned to leave him."

"So? Wives walk every day."

Teal shook her head no. "It's not that simple."

Dan nodded. "I'll try to make it complex. The guy's unhappy, maybe even a little crazy if he thinks his wife prefers a woman to him. But you're suggesting murder, Teal. I need more."

While Teal studied the floor, Dan studied her office.

Fabric walls to muffle noise, expensive furniture, even real art, not Boston P.D. Homicide for sure. The weirdest truth was Kathy sitting outside the closed door. Kathy, who had been the one to call his office.

"Teal can be moody," Kathy had said. "And bossy as hell under pressure. But, Dan, she's never been like today. Like she thinks she's to blame. Come give her your kind of help."

So here he sat, for Kathy, for Teal, for himself. But his kind of help? How?

Teal leaned forward.

"More?" The word cracked from her mouth. "Here's more. Money's at stake in a divorce, and social status—and lots of both in this case. Michael Britton basked in being Mr. Big-Shot Artist. And leaving for a *woman?* He had to be furious."

Teal's enthusiasm was thin, but she'd gestured, Dan noticed. He hesitated to dampen her revived spirit. He didn't have a choice.

"*Did* he know?" Dan asked.

Teal sighed her doubt. "If Nancy didn't confide in me, I have a hard time believing she told anyone before this weekend. Carole claims she overheard everything Nancy and Michael said last night. Sounds carry in old cottages and Carole listened. She doesn't know the gender of Nan's lover, so if Michael does, he didn't learn on Sunday."

Teal struggled with this theoretical defeat, and won. Dan didn't know whether to be glad or sad.

"Let's say he did," Teal said. "Forget how. Imagine he sent the letters to force the affair to end. Scare Nancy, scare Renee, and, when nothing worked, get Carole into the act because she might find out more through sibling power. But Nancy responded all wrong. Michael had to get serious."

Teal's theory wasn't bad. Victims were most often

killed by the individuals they know, wives by husbands, girlfriends by boyfriends. Men driven to control.

"Uh, is there reason for Michael to believe Nancy's sister would disapprove? He took a risk sending a clue to her."

"Carole dislikes Michael, that's no secret. But Carole is practical and Nan's agent. Michael could expect her to put sense into Nancy's head. I imagine he didn't think even a tolerant sister could believe Norma Rockwell's kind of public would accept a lesbian affair."

"Would this, uh, lesbian affair trouble anyone else?" Dan asked.

While Teal's face smoothed in concentration, Dan stretched his legs and cracked a knuckle. Good thing Kathy wasn't in the room to get after him. He flexed his fingers, chagrined.

He and Kathy should tell Teal soon. The thought of marriage brought his mother to mind. Why couldn't she accept he loved her and always would? No one could change that, not even Kathy, and she wasn't trying. Dan understood, now, why his brother lived in California. Time for bro to share the maternal burden, that's what Dan expected to say in San Diego.

Teal tapped his knee. "You still here?"

Her voice carried a slight pique. Dan wanted to grin, she so matched Kathy's description, but he refrained.

"Yes ma'am," he responded, the policeman's servile defense.

"You asked—anyone else?" Teal said as she held up her hand and spread her fingers wide.

"Felicia."

She shook the pinkie.

"Carole."

She wriggled the ring finger.

"Michael—no surprise."

She held her middle finger as though by the neck.

"Renee Maxwell, the co-re-spon-dent."

Teal dragged the word through her lips and shook an index finger.

"And, perhaps, a person yet to be known."

Her thumb stuck up in front of his face. Teal dropped her hand and kept talking.

"Felicia and the gallery would lose if Nancy's behavior became public. Felicia couldn't afford a collapse in the Vandenburg market. She was about to sell a major one herself. It gave Felicia reason to wish her dead. Then there was Nancy's change in artistic direction. Nan didn't think Barrette was right for her new style, but Barrette couldn't afford to lose Nancy. Felicia's money problems are more than a rumor."

Dan struggled with the intricacies of art and money and death. Picasso changed his style countless times and lived to a fine old age. But Teal had dismissed the gallery to move on.

Teal waved her ring finger. "Carole. She left a brilliant job in New York to manage Nan's career. She denies it was a sacrifice and claims to hate New York. But Nancy ended up with the fame, the husband, and the child. Still, what do I know? Nancy says Carole loved her selflessly from the day she was born."

Teal swiveled her ring finger so-so. "The next one's better."

Dan laughed with her, pleased to see the depression lift. Teal raised her index finger.

"Renee Maxwell, my dark horse. Nationally prominent attorney, perhaps with aspirations to the Bench. The woman is pure ambition, believe me. Having her sex life exposed in the press—I don't think so. Nancy Vandenburg and Renee Maxwell is at least a quarter page with captioned photo fronting the Living section in *The Boston Globe*. And the *Herald*? Front page. 'THE LADIES

ARE LOVERS' in one-inch bold, with a blow-up of some otherwise innocent embrace."

Dan nodded. He wondered how the boys back in his office would react. They knew Renee Maxwell. She'd destroyed more than one case in court and dismissed his colleagues as fools along the way. Their most tasteful response would be to cheer damage to her career. Their least tasteful he didn't want to think about. Dan agreed, exposure stood to hurt Renee. Would it make her kill?

"You really believe that?" Dan asked.

Teal circled a finger on her desk.

"There's the reverse," she said. "Maybe Renee feared the affair was coming to an end. Nancy voiced confusion about the eternal conundrum, balancing love and independence. Maybe Nancy's caution surprised Renee. And hurt."

"But Felicia, Carole, and Renee didn't run with Nancy that morning," Dan said.

"No. We're back to Michael."

"Without enough—" Dan started.

The office intercom buzzed. Dan didn't listen when she took the call, but heard the residual quiet around her side of the conversation instead. Not like his office, if a battered desk and sprung chair qualified. Teal's space contained silence like a commodity, like something you could cut and wrap to take home.

The hush led him back to his mother and love. Why couldn't his dad see it, her need for attention, her constant turning to the boys? To Dan, really, the little one stuck at home. Now she was afraid to lose her baby. God, Dan hated the feeling her need aroused.

He sighed. He had chosen Kathy, but he wished she'd make it easier, maybe see his mother's point. No. Blaming Kathy wasn't right.

Teal hung up like the cat who ate the canary.

"Nancy's lawyer says she talked divorce and cut Michael out of her estate, or as much as she could through a transfer of assets to trust. He drafted the paperwork last week, and get this. Coincidence of coincidences, Michael visited the law office Friday, and today the lawyer discovered his copies of the documents have vanished. That must be what Michael wanted!"

Teal gestured like an impatient conductor when Dan remained confused.

"Nancy had the originals with her to review and sign on the Cape. I thought Michael wanted a private place to mourn when I found him in her studio down there. I bet I was wrong. He wanted the will and trust. I must have been a terrible inconvenience."

"Did you find what he was looking for?" Dan asked. She could have and decided not to tell.

Teal shook her head. "No. And I don't think he'll ever find what I saw either. I hid the sketches before I left. Nancy deserves some privacy in death."

"Leave the drawings where they are for now. I'll do what I can. Keep your theories to yourself and let me know if her will turns up." Dan stretched his legs and bunched them up. "There's something else I'd like to talk to you about."

Teal looked at him as he'd hoped she would, collected and calm. Jesus, he prayed Kathy never found out. He cleared his throat.

"I kind of need a woman's advice. Kathy and I will tell you together, and you have to act surprised, but my mother and Kathy . . ." and he told Teal everything.

Her advice was supportive and kind.

"Thanks, Teal," Dan said and stood.

"No, I should thank you. Your patience means a lot to me. If Nancy was murdered because I screwed up—" Teal's voice broke. "I have to know."

Dan understood guilt. Teal thought she'd failed

Nancy, and Nancy was dead. Teal was convinced she should blame herself.

"Look. Trust the system to work and stay out of it. Not like the last time, right?"

He didn't want to remind her last time her stubbornness almost left her dead. But Teal nodded assent. The thing was, Dan couldn't see the two fingers crossed behind her back.

? SEVENTEEN

Tuesday.

Humidity smothered Boston in a noon temperature over eighty-five degrees, but the air inside the building numbed Sandra's arms. Evaporation of the sweat worked up during her walk began to chill her scalp. She entered her small office and sat to unpack two pizzas-for-one and a double-chocolate frappe. She had learned the word frappe replaced Chicago's milk shake almost her first day in Boston.

Her foot tapped to the floor as she lifted the top pie from its box and caught a slide of sausage and double-cheese with her tongue. Oil splattered a dark ring on her blouse.

"Damn," she said staring down.

She looked up to see her friend from the weekend ease into the room.

"Sorry to interrupt lunch, but I have to say I can't believe Her Reneeness isn't here to reward you with a shower of praise today."

He openly scanned the mosaic of briefs and memos pushed to the perimeter of the desk.

"I'm not looking for her," Sandra mumbled, a sullen undercurrent depressing her voice.

He had intruded into her lunch, catching her as she most hated, a fat woman eating and feeling out-of-place. She imagined he wanted to distance himself from the familiarities of the weekend, wanted to reestablish her bad fit.

She watched him sink, at home, into a chair.

"Well, when you are, don't hold your breath," he said. "Her Reneeness's office is dark as a tomb, but her car is in its usual space. Thus I've deduced she's not at a client's and she's not here, Watson. So where is our regal friend? I propose so embarrassed by her wicked ways she stayed at home. Imagine living close enough to walk to work and have the firm pick up your garage costs. That's the life."

"You recognize her car?"

Sandra was impressed. She ignored his speculation. She didn't notice that in her curiosity she let down her guard.

"Her car, the managing partner's car, the newest partner's car, every partner's car. You don't? I admit to the occasional detour through the garage before coming up, but today's census is entirely legit. I happened to take an interminable and boring deposition out in some godforsaken town, necessitating the use of a car. Normally, I do the correct thing and take the T. Don't believe that," he said. "I really hate the exorbitant parking fee. Today a client pays."

"You know every partner's car?" Sandra couldn't let go.

He stood, but lingered at her door, prepped out in a pink shirt and bow tie. His suspenders matched his socks, his voice hummed with a genetically ordained nasal whine. He grew up on an estate he called home and, in those years, summered in Maine. He'd seemed an alien to Sandra, but now, under the skin, she saw him as he was, a first-year as insecure as she and less well-rated.

"Every one," he said. "Old Minot the Third drives a banged up diesel Mercedes, our woman tax partner with the new baby just bought a Volvo. Too stereotypical if you ask me. Here's the clue to Renee's buggy—precision engineered, makes tracks, draws attention to itself. And SGM's Ms. Maxwell is brilliant, can claim a meteoric career, and commands all eyes in court. Maybe her bright red BMW 318i convertible isn't all that odd. Do promise to tell what she says to you."

He waved as he backed out the door.

Sandra fingered the congealed cheese and pinched a rubbery piece into a larger ball. She sucked on the frappe's straw. The chocolate tasted only brown, the cheese like grease. The old trick had failed. Eating did not distract her at all.

Renee Maxwell had been on the Cape yesterday morning, hers the car beside the road. Renee had witnessed the artist's horrible death but did not wait around! Sandra smiled.

She stripped the pizza clean of sausage as she thought.

N. Vandenburg—Nancy Vandenburg must have been the Vandenburg who called the day Sandra waited in Renee's office. Answering the ringing telephone on the desk had seemed appropriate behavior.

"Ms. Maxwell's office," Sandra had said.

"Oh, my, who's this? I meant to call her private line," a voice responded.

It was the private line, Sandra realized, looking at the brightened button on the multiline phone. Each partner had one. Embarrassment stiffened her voice.

"May *I* ask who *this* is and take a message?"

Sandra swore she heard a chuckle.

"Of course. Tell her the painter called."

"And the painter's name, please?" Sandra asked, angry with humiliation.

The chuckle became a laugh. "N. Vandenburg. She knows the number."

Then the line clicked dead.

Sandra had pushed the call from her mind when Renee stormed through the door and never gave the message. Now she wondered if N. Vandenburg's call was the answer to fifteen years of daily prayer? Nancy Vandenburg a way to get at Renee?

Sandra began to strip the polish from her thumb nail and pushed away the pizza. She wanted to cry.

"Your intuition, Teal? Dead-on! The call came to Fruiers on Friday afternoon and counsel negotiated with Renee Maxwell through Sunday. Can you believe the woman? But Fahey pays back every dollar, plus interest, over five years and Fruiers drops the charge. You're off the hook. No court tomorrow."

Teal couldn't help it, she shook her head in disgust and watched Don Clarke avoid her eyes.

"Now don't be harsh. What's the company to do? Waste time and money that might not get them what they're getting now? Only a fool prefers a lawsuit to settlement these days. Fahey learned his lesson."

Don's hand pressed the back of her chair.

"I shouldn't say this, but I'd take it as good news if I were you. Oh, and Fruiers' CEO sends apologies for getting to us so late. Renee insisted we be kept out of it until they signed the deal. She's no fool. Anyway, the CEO tried us Monday afternoon but expected we'd be out. I'm happy to be the one to tell you."

Don turned for the door and reversed as fast.

"I almost forgot the best part. The CEO just called Stimpson, Minot, Grey. Renee Maxwell is unavailable." Don snorted. "Licking her wounds, no doubt. Why don't you take off the rest of the day? You deserve to, Teal."

Don gave her a bluff pat on the left shoulder and

smiled pleasure at himself. Teal wondered if he imagined they'd communicated. She didn't want to dwell too long on his "I'd take it as good news."

The partnership lure pulled both ways. Not making it would offend her ego; admission threatened her self. How much would she change? Even now, anxious to hear the partner-in-charge's comments, she had pushed aside grief like it wasn't there. How could she when her best friend was not dead two days? Teal's head began a pounding ache.

Don had a good idea. Why not take off the rest of the day?

Teal fingered Renee's card and read the home number marked on the back in dark blue pen. Writing it, Renee had said, "It's a Boston exchange, that dull, luxury high rise downtown, but convenient."

Teal had completed their fraternal exchange without confessing her love for her own time-consuming town house at the flat of Beacon Hill. Nor did she say she even loved her tenants, most of the time. She handed Renee an equally annotated business card. Professionals could be so civil. Neither ever found cause to call the other at home.

Lucky Renee had described the building, Teal realized. Only one truly dull luxury high rise stood in the middle of downtown Boston.

The doorman intercepted her. "You'll want to stop at the concierge desk to be announced."

"Why, of course." Teal tried to smile.

Concierge indeed. Teal walked across the gaudy lobby. The bored woman sitting behind an expanse of empty desk nodded recognition at Renee's name and grudgingly punched four digits on her control board. That action gave Teal what she needed to know.

"No, please."

Teal raised the paper cone of flowers. It was as much a decoy as her prop to deceive herself into believing this visit was one of sympathy. Surely she had no real intention of double-crossing Dan.

"I'd like to be a surprise. If you don't mind, I'll just scoot up to twelve-oh-two unannounced."

The woman clicked off the intercom, demonstrating the building's real concept of security.

The elevator opened to an empty hall. Twelve-oh-two's steel door stood down and across. Teal pressed the built-in bell, then knocked, then hit the bell longer. Silence held. She heard nothing, not a footfall. She twisted the knob, a stiff and unyielding globe of brass plate supported by at least one dead bolt. Renee's copy of *The Wall Street Journal* lay outside the door. She had to be inside.

The hall stayed empty as Teal slipped off a shoe. Empty as she hammered the sole against the steel. The old sneaker slapped the metal with a resounding racket.

On the eighth slap, Renee Maxwell opened the door.

Teal's impression was that Renee looked like hell and so did the apartment. Then Teal saw the painting on the far wall. Nancy first had refused to show the portrait of a mother and daughter, too much like offering Libby and herself for sale. Carole changed Nan's mind. The critics raved and called the canvas Nancy Vandenburg's coming of age.

"I found the drawing," Teal said as she focused on Renee.

Renee stared. It *was* Teal Stewart standing here.

"No one else has seen it, but at some point somebody will. I thought you should be prepared," Teal said.

Renee stared, a flicker of panic tapping against her heart. This Teal came not in her professional role, but as Nancy's best friend, best before the advent of Renee, of course. There was no room in Renee's mind for any Teal. Not now. Not here.

"I don't mean to intrude, but I came for another reason as well. The Shell Bay police say her death is an accident. I'm not sure. May I ask for your help?"

Renee narrowed her swollen lips. Teal Stewart offered no solace for a splitting head, no succor against a loss so painful Renee felt rent in two. Now the CPA intimated murder. Renee flashed back to Nancy's body arcing in the air.

She gagged and began to slam the door.

No. No, better to ask Teal in and listen.

Renee's knees shook. What exactly did the best friend know? She squeezed her bloodshot eyes closed. Could she trust herself, like this? Her eyes opened as the instincts of an attorney tilted her head to the side.

"Come in."

Renee, dressed in worn purple sweats, looked small and slight, as though grief and liquor had reduced her height, compacted her frame to that of old age. But even at her best, Teal registered for the first time, Renee stood shorter than Nancy. Much shorter than the Nancy who, in college, refused to date any but the tallest boys.

"She must have loved you very much," Teal blurted out.

Renee closed her eyes and tensed her lips for a second.

"Sit," she said and dropped, herself, into a chair.

Teal chose the maroon leather sofa. She edged the empty bottle underfoot to the side. Renee really did look like hell. Teal knew she must be gentle, for Nancy, and spent the next half hour getting nowhere.

Renee alternated between upset and polite. She swore she wanted to help and sidestepped Teal's probes.

Frustration forced Teal's voice to new, sharp notes. "Did you keep Nan's letters from Italy?"

Renee's leg kicked out as it crossed her knee and her foot clipped the coffee table. The glass clattered against the metal support.

"How did you know?"

? EIGHTEEN

Tuesday.

Teal's mind burned with the passions of the three letters she just read. What a bind for Nancy with her public face and private desire on so direct a collision course. That she ignored the inevitable until pressed by threats was clear. But pressed she had turned to Teal with half the tale, and Teal failed. Well, not again.

Teal glanced at Renee, hunched and diminished compared to the woman of memory, the famed lawyer of only days before. The ill effect of liquor mottled her skin. She looked to have a broken heart. Then again, who knew?

Teal's attempt at impartial assessment chilled to doubt. *The Globe*'s theatre critic once teamed with the paper's legal reporter to review a Renee Maxwell performance in court.

"In the ability to manipulate," he had written, "she bests Lady Macbeth. In theatrical talent, she rivals Sarah Bernhardt."

Renee motioned Teal to attention. "She promised to tell him this weekend. She promised to come to me."

Renee laid her face on trembling palms. She took a

sharp breath and straightened to turn dagger eyes on Teal.

"You knew? How could you? No one knew—"

"About the two of you? After I saw the drawing, Renee, not before. After the accident. She told me about writing these, but not to whom. I wish she'd told me the truth. Nancy was my friend."

Tension twisted Teal's throat. Why was she defensive about her relationship with Nancy? She had been Nan's best friend. Renee's indulgence in overt misery made Teal mad. Renee had shared the letters to prove her superior rights.

Teal dropped her gaze to the letter in hand. Death invaded privacy. Every privacy. She placed the paper on the table. Beneath the glass, a book lay askew on the carpet. Teal bent to retrieve it, but Renee moved faster.

"How careless of me," Renee said, snatching the volume away with her hand.

She set it between her hip and the arm of her fat green leather chair. The book sank out of sight.

The book had looked familiar to Teal. She could not think why. She turned back to the letter.

Seven simple lines caught the beauty of a rainstorm on Capri. Beside them, Nancy wrote:

> Please
> Don't hold me
> don't help me
> don't put your umbrella above me.
> You can suffocate me with your love.

The letter's text contrasted with the sentiment of the poem. The letter repeated graphic desire among the vignettes of Nancy's days. Teal blushed at Nancy's lush lust, admitted to so easily.

Teal chilled at the memory of her own penned indiscretions. No caution inhibited this writer. Nancy's signature showed prominently under the scrawled "love & lust & longing." Yet the poem's call for independence remained.

Teal wondered at her assurance to Renee, that hearing of the nature of the affair from Nan would have been fine. Teal couldn't know, not learning like this. Maybe there would have been a flicker of confusion, maybe jealousy. But not now. Or did she fool herself?

Surely not, she decided. She didn't begrudge Nancy's love of Renee, but perhaps mistrusted. This love *had* been different, had been the prelude to Nancy's death.

Teal considered her interpretation of reality.

"I am not the only one who knew, Renee. I tried to warn Nancy. Someone else, someone who sent ugly communications to Nancy, to you, to Carole—that person knew."

Renee raised her head. "Carole? Nancy never mentioned Carole. What did it say?"

"I don't think Carole took it seriously. She only told Nancy this weekend. It said something like 'the adulteress will die.' But my point is someone found out even when you swore they couldn't. Could it have been from reading these?"

The letters' intimacy disturbed Teal. She could not look on Renee as before. That impersonal distance, shaken by opening Nan's sketch pad, disappeared on the first reading.

"I keep them here. No one read them but me," Renee said with a stiff tongue.

Her reluctance mimicked Nancy's denial. Teal made herself sound patient.

"Something gave the affair away."

Renee turned a sullen face to the floor.

"Who visits? Who's been here alone?" Teal asked.

Something clouded Renee's face. Her eyes tightened into hard focus, but as quickly closed.

"Who? Who, Renee?" Teal's voice quickened.

Renee shrugged a no.

Teal tried to bite the irritation from her tongue.

"Let me run through the basics. Who visits you?"

"Hi. Is your boss in?"

Dan couldn't keep the happiness out of his voice. He loved any excuse for a brush with his fianceé. That professional necessity prompted this exchange made his pleasure greater, gave the interaction a certain zest. He and Kathy inhabited a daily world so foreign to the other.

"Nope. She left for the day hours ago. She needed it. Now, is there anything, perhaps, I can do for you?" Kathy asked.

Dan could imagine the sly gleam in her green eyes, that demure and devilish look he couldn't resist. God, he felt lucky. His mother be . . . well. He sighed.

"Anything wrong?"

"No. Yes, actually, for Teal. Sort of." Dan pushed ahead to safer ground. "My message is too long to take down. Just tell her I'm out until Friday, and she can call me then."

"Patience isn't Teal's strong suit. Take all the time you need, I'm ready."

Dan wondered if Kathy understood her effect on him. At her behest he snuck two hours out of a hectic week to go on her boss's wild-goose chase. Kathy's innocent power almost made him angry, almost scared him into running.

"Bad news," he said. "The word on Fontane is clean, no record. The guys down in Shell say his story checks out in every way. Family man, owns a business, makes ends meet and a little more. He's sixty-two years old and wears glasses thick as an old Coke bottle bottom. His wife has worried for years about him driving with those eyes. Tell Teal I'm having a hard time thinking this guy did a thing."

Dan couldn't really believe he had called the wife. His love for Kathy and her loyalty to Teal were the inspiration to do some foolish things. Talking to Tina Fontane about the length of her marriage for one. Talking to her at all. But he liked the warmth of the woman's voice when she sounded off about old Albert. Maybe Kathy would have that tone about him in thirty-five years. He hoped so.

"That's it?" Kathy broke in.

"He changed his name as a teen from Fontanez to Fontane. I guess his father was Puerto Rican, but I don't think that means anything more than his parents divorced."

"No good news?" Kathy asked.

"Will neutral do?"

"Not like good, but I'll take what I can. She's upset, Dan."

Kathy, pretty, lively, able, compassionate, did something melting to his insides. Dan hated his next thought. His own mother, now so needy and dour, started out that way. The vivacious woman in the pictures of thirty-odd years ago, where was she?

Marriage—he pushed back the panic attacking his throat.

"I'm not sure what this means." He paused. "Shell Bay is like any small Cape town, with maybe more money than most. So I mimicked Mom's approach the summer we didn't like our neighbors on Buzzards Bay. She got their life story from the local real estate agent. Shell Bay has three."

He could feel Kathy's attention.

"They said the market stayed quiet this year, most

rentals repeat, except for a few properties that won't sell. Shell Bay owners want rentals of a month or the season. The two-week crowd like the Malleys aren't welcome, so the community is a bit dif—"

Kathy laughed as she interrupted. "This has a point, right?"

"Right." Dan ducked his head, feeling foolish. "The p-p-point is a new group took the house next to the Vandenburg place. Young lawyers from Stimpson, Minot, Grey. Renee Maxwell's firm. A Tully C. Barrow, junior, signed the lease, wouldn't you know. Anyway, Teal might want to talk with him. Not much, I'm afraid."

The conversation moved to the kinds of things which occupy people who are engaged. For his part, Dan responded on cue. For her part, Kathy began to sound strained. They agreed on Wedgewood but deferred on the stainless. Still plenty of time to register at Jordan's. Still plenty of time to second-guess their decision remained unsaid. They hung up with mouthed kisses.

Teal hesitated in the middle of the lobby.

"Damn," she said, half turning to the elevator's closing doors. With the concierge watching, Teal acted like she was reconsidering.

"Maybe you can help," she said to the woman behind the desk. "My friend Renee Maxwell raved about her cleaning person, but we got on another subject. Now she's at the health club up top. Is there a chance you have the name?"

The woman broke into a smile.

"Everyone seems so happy with him. Management is not in the business of cleaning, of course, and we make no guarantee, but here's his card if you want to call directly."

Teal nodded thanks and pocketed the business card as she began to walk away. She wheeled back to the woman.

"Maybe you can help me with one more thing. I need someone to house-sit and I'm getting desperate."

The concierge shook a no. "People here seem to use friends. You might ask Ms. Maxwell about the black girl who stayed the holidays last year."

Teal couldn't hope the woman referred to was Sandra Jordan, but hope she did. "You don't mean a tall, handsome woman?"

"Tall? Yes, but handsome, I don't know. Large. Never said boo."

A hired cleaner and Sandra Jordan—not nobody—had been in Renee's home alone. Forgetting one or forgetting the other, maybe Teal could understand. Forgetting both—no.

Teal spun through the glass door and turned onto Washington Street.

Downtown Crossing, the city's old retail district, was a sea of ages and races. Men and women pushed home from work, young mothers toted infants out to shop for the first time, old men sat on benches in the sun. The importuning of the homeless, ill, and destitute joined the general din.

Litter bounced and flew along the brick sidewalks into the gutter. Gum stuck to Teal's left sole. Sunlight played off the roan police horse shifting foot to foot and chomping at the bit. The evening smelled of summer, the sour odor of fast food from pushcarts, and a damp wind from the harbor. The evening felt like summer, hot and humid and still.

Teal registered only blurred shapes and a slithering mass which she dodged through doggedly. All she could see was in her mind—Renee, stubborn in the apartment's door, unwilling to meet her eye. Teal hoped unwilling was all it was.

Earlier, Renee, forgetting caution, left the book while she took Teal's flowers to a vase. Teal seized the moment, memory nagging her on. Turning back the cover, Teal understood the familiar look. She had received a similar gift. A gift of Nan's verse and scattered drawings, a gift of friendship or, in Renee's case, love. Nancy wrote poetry for special friends. She never cared that she wasn't good. Like Teal's, this volume was beautiful.

Nancy appreciated the bookbinder's art. The gold-tooled leather gave pleasure to sight and touch. Teal skimmed the open page fast.

Dare I strike the match?
Light passion's flame to heart's
desire? Or shall cold despair . . .

Hearing Renee, she had snapped the cover shut and returned the book to the chair.

At the door, Teal had to ask, an odd pulse beating at her throat.

"What are you reading? You know, the book I saw under the table?"

"A novel," Renee had lied.

Remembering, Teal clenched her jaw and swung her arms, stiff with tension. Did Renee take her for a fool?

"Lady, watch your damned case!"

The furious words grabbed her attention. She relaxed her hold on the leather briefcase, a professional-looking ruse to transport her shoes. She never brought work, Clayborne Whittier work, home. Living so close to the office, she stayed late when required. She carried the shoes because she couldn't possibly walk any distance in them. Today her spikes were black slashed with red.

She dressed that morning as though nothing in the world had changed, selecting a short and vivid red dress. In her office, she had changed from sneakers to the crippling shoes, reviewed her calendar like any ordinary day, then shut the door to stare catatonic with pain at Nancy's painting.

Thank God for Dan.

She hoped Carole would agree.

Teal stopped to call Kathy from a pay phone then turned up Winter Street to Park and from Park took the right on Beacon. Home lay down the hill the other way.

Teal hesitated, the pressure of the question making her want to turn. What to tell Carole?

Nothing about Renee, Teal decided, not right now. She expected Carole loved her sister any way she came, but Teal hadn't answered her own questions about the lover. Why torture Carole with doubts? No. She'd tell Carole what Kathy said about Dan's research. An accident, a tragic accident. It didn't wash with Teal, but a policeman's word might comfort Nancy's sister when there was nothing else to tell.

Teal stood before the building, dread dragging her pace. She watched traffic tangle to a snarl. To further delay the inevitable, Teal walked the four flights. She thought of Nancy in the dance of love affecting Michael and Renee, planning to turn everyone's life upside down.

Teal pushed back her loosening hair, frustrated by the tickle of strands freed from her chignon's restraint. Why hadn't Nancy confided the truth? *Sure,* Teal thought pushing at the door, *like I'm about to be entirely candid with Carole.*

? NINETEEN

Tuesday.

The instant Carole said her goodbyes on one call, she was punching out the next number. Five hours and she had reached *L*. Michael had laughed at her for wanting to tell everyone herself.

"There won't be a newspaper in the world without Nancy's obituary on Wednesday. Give yourself a break," he said.

How like Michael, she thought. As though he understood. Everyone she talked to appreciated her call, and he told her she was crazy to be in the office at all today. What did Michael know about loss and pain?

Carole concentrated on the distant ring.

"Allo? Ici Claudette," a disembodied voice answered.

The story did not change in French. Nancy, beloved sister, remained dead. And beloved she had been from all accounts. Collectors, gallery owners, museum curators, and critics offered kind words and private memories of scenes from Nancy's life. Yet earlier, under *B*, Carole had sighed in relief to find Felicia out. Carole didn't need to hear Felicia recount *her* discovery of Nancy.

Carole completed *L* and started on *M*.

She'd taken frequent breaks to cry in the morning, but

now her tears were spent. Everyone asked, "Are you all right? Can I do anything? Are you sure?" Carole answered "yes, no, yes, I am" each time.

She didn't say, "I'm falling apart, can't you hear? Don't you see? I want to have died, it's all a horrid mistake. Can you understand? I can't. How did it come to this—my family dead? I relive the weekend again and again. Should I have made her confess? Could I have changed the outcome? Don't you realize I'm full of confusion and pity and misery? I've lost my sister, of course I'm not all right!"

The second *M* droned on with sympathetic talk.

"So brilliant a painter, so vibrant a legacy for those of us left behind."

Carole's throat tensed for a scream. Forget Nancy's paintings, Nancy's death left *her* behind. The prickle of loneliness pressed Carole's chest. It was all she could do to murmur, "How kind" before she hung up.

Her mind bumped about her skull like a dazed bird. The questions she worked to squelch rose to a crescendo. She needed to blame someone for this horrible result. But who?

She must enlist Teal's help.

Carole listened to Teal repeat herself for the third time. As though rearranging the words could change Carole's mind.

"Dan said Shell Bay has nothing. Albert Fontane is no more than an ordinary old man caught in a horrible event. Carole, I know this is hard to accept, but there's nothing more the police can do."

Carole leaned forward in the heavy chair, her eyes drilled into Teal.

"You don't know. No one knows—not one thing. Do you think I haven't been up all night wishing I'd done something different? Of course I have. I can't stop, even now, but I try. I tell myself there will be truth and justice out of this. I can't dismiss my sister's death as an accident when I look down on her grave this Friday. I don't give a damn what the police think."

The silence between stretched thin with the weight of insuperable grief. The Park Street Church chimed the hour, flooding the office with false and recorded sound. Carole sat, rigid and still.

Voices drifted in from the burial ground with the sound of children tired and overstimulated at the end of a summer's long day.

Carole pictured Father calling them to supper on evenings as hot as he stood on the wraparound porch. She helped wheel her mother in from watching the lake. Nancy tagged along underfoot, unhappy to stop their play, Carole superior in her show of obedience. The trailing end of the day, when they left the land of make-believe to enter the house, that moment held an intimation of all future loss though she did not know it then.

A child's voice rose from the graves, bossy and thin. "Come on!"

Carole submerged her anguish. She pushed up from the grasp of the chair.

"I have calls to make. The Coast, the Pacific, you understand. People are so shocked."

Teal did not rise.

"Carole, let me make some—"

"No, no!" Carole waved off the threat.

Teal stood and grasped Carole's hand before she left, unaware the gesture cut Carole's fingers against her sapphire ring. Carole did not flinch. She liked the sudden, specific pain.

"I'll be fine, Teal. Really." She accepted a hug, then pulled free. "I'm luckier than her lover, alone with pain. I wish I could at least share that grief."

"Can grief be shared?" Teal murmured.

Carole did not respond, though she agreed. She took Teal's hand.

"I can't accept an accident. Nancy should not be dead! Please, humor me, Teal. Find out everything you can. It's only fair to Nancy, her lover, and me."

The message light on Teal's answering machine blinked one. Teal stared for a long time. She wondered if it could be Hunt. Surely he'd call if he heard? He liked Nancy and had stayed her friend even after Teal left. Even in the awkward time between love and friendship, the time when Teal hated anyone to so much as say his name.

Did she want him to call?

She walked to a window triple hung with glass to mute the din of Storrow Drive below. Across the asphalt, the Charles River shimmered like polished silver. White triangles strained into curves as sailboats glided over the surface of the river. Trees obscured much of the bike path on the near bank. Teal discerned an occasional flash of wheels.

Yes, she hoped Hunt's voice would greet her from the machine. Maybe if he'd been in town she would have called him, would have stopped at his loft on South Street, would have taken comfort in Argyle's gray head laid across her knees. But Hunt was in Chicago with the dog, gone close to a year.

Teal could remember the turmoil of their breakup like yesterday. She had voiced the first doubts, but he agreed too readily, like an insult to what they shared. The day she moved out, he almost strangled her in his rage. She thought of that lesson now.

Lovers threatened with loss could be lovers who killed. Nancy and Renee had their own cycle of independence and dependency needs. Had Nancy's restlessness surprised Renee? Or was it the reverse?

Teal turned back to the desk and stabbed "play." A female voice ended dreams of Hunt.

"Hi, Teal, it's Kathy at about 4:30 P.M. I spoke with Tully C. Barrow, Jr., as you requested. Guess who was part of the SGM group this weekend? The associate on Fruiers, Sandra Jordan, is who. I left a list of all the names on your desk, but she may be the only one you know. Take it easy tonight, and I'll see you in the morning."

Sandra Jordan?

Sandra Jordan, associate, working for Renee. Sandra Jordan, house-sitting in Renee's home. Sandra Jordan, right next door when Nancy died. Teal began to wonder.

What did Sandra Jordan know?

? TWENTY

Wednesday.

Sandra wriggled in her bed. She smoothed flat the creases of a second photocopied page with a moist palm. As with each reading, the words made her feel dizzy and strange. The writer's abandon to carnal pleasure under a hot Italian sun agitated Sandra with each specific, descriptive phrase. Sandra hated the rising beat of her own heart, the confusing tickle of desire.

She'd found three letters in the table beside Renee Maxwell's bed, and copied each one. Sandra read them stimulated by a different appetite. The motive she only admitted to herself today choked her with humiliation.

She pushed mortification aside to finish the third letter. The disconcerting words could turn into opportunity, a point of leverage. Sandra knew she had reason. She remembered the sweltering Chicago courtroom where she had sat a confused and excited child at her father's side.

He wanted her memory to be clear on the day justice would be done. Her father pressed her to sit straighter before the judge gave the verdict. For an instant, the courtroom rustled. Then the judge spoke. Sandra could still hear each word echo against her father's scream.

"Not guilty!"

"How can you do this to my girl? To me?" her father cried.

Memory's eye saw the triumphant lawyer rise and shake the defendant's outstretched hand. Sandra twisted the copied letter to a rag.

She knew she should celebrate this turn of fate, the infamous lawyer crushed and devastated by Nancy Vandenburg's sudden death. But Sandra remembered standing in front of that painting and the joy it brought to a confused little girl. Where was the sweet in revenge?

Her foot beat a tattoo against the bed.

Right now. Say it. Right now. Say I read the letters, understand the meaning. I saw you in Shell Bay. I know what you did!

Sandra opened her mouth to begin. Spit bubbled from the right corner. Her hand shook as she wiped the saliva thread from her lip.

"I don't mean to put you on the spot," Renee said.

Sandra could not discern passion or sorrow in the crisp voice. Renee's court voice, the voice which said Renee expected the response to be yes. Assumed yes. Renee would.

Sandra wanted to see the composure crack, hear Renee's voice crack, scared and raw. She wanted to witness fear as the realization Sandra had read the letters dawned. Sandra knew something else. She had seen the strange message hidden under Renee's desk blotter.

"You filth atone or die."

Sandra began to understand. Filth referred to *them,* didn't it? The lawyer and the artist.

Would Renee beg for mercy? Sandra hoped so. Then Sandra could use Renee's words. "Mercy is never a substitute for justice." What justice had compelled a murderer to walk free? What justice? Sandra's justice did not intend to let Renee off as easily. So. *Say it.*

"I read . . . I really don't know."

"Sleep on it, Sandra. You're familiar with my practice. Think about the aspirations you spoke of when you joined SGM last year. Talk with the associates in the group. Then come back and say yes." Renee smiled.

Sandra shifted her attention from Renee to the desk, from the desk to the floor. She sat mute and restless. She raised her eyes as Renee gestured.

"Sandra, you have the stuff to be an outstanding lawyer. Brilliant even. Face the challenge. A civil matter like Fruiers is nothing compared to the thrill of criminal trials. Particularly the pro bono ones. You'll be able to do such good. We afford a hope of equal justice for the poor as much as serve the corporate world. I promise. Well." Renee stood.

Papal audience over, Sandra realized, and pushed against rubber legs. *Say it. Say I can ruin your life too. My equal justice.* Her knees began to buckle.

"Oh, Sandra." Renee raised her eyes over her reading glasses. "I'm not unaware of how hard you've worked to come to my attention. It amused me, but house-sitting didn't convince me to ask you here today. Your gift for the law did. Don't squander that gift."

Sandra hated being told she had a talent for law. And by Renee Maxwell? Sandra's bitter smile answered the question. No word of apology for Monday, no mention of Renee's absence yesterday. Even asking Sandra to join her group, the woman remained selfish and rude. Of course, the famous lawyer had other things on her mind. Sandra suppressed a cruel smile.

"I should also apologize about the other day," Renee said, breaking Sandra's trance. Tension squeezed Renee's voice. "A problem came up, I'm sorry. I hope I didn't cause too much inconvenience. Unfortunately, we still need the final Fruiers filing today."

Sandra gripped the back of her chair to brace her impotent legs. *Say it.*

"I'll have it on your desk by noon. As to the other, may I let you know?"

Renee nodded as she waved Sandra out the door.

Sandra didn't feel her feet walk across the deep carpet or hear the door shut. She was too busy reviling herself. She barged into her office and slammed the door.

"Scaredy-cat fool," she spit out.

"Will you consider joining me for lunch?" Teal asked, turning from the window's glare.

Sandra gasped as she jumped.

Renee bent her head to her hand, kneading knuckles into her brow. Today she contrived to do only simple, pleasant tasks. Inviting Sandra Jordan to join the criminal practice ranked first among them. She also planned to stay late, as late as she could fool herself into caring about work. Late enough to go home and take a pill and bury herself in bed.

She recognized her search to avoid consciousness during any unoccupied hour. So what? She couldn't bear the empty house which brought self-recrimination and guilt with each idle moment.

"No." Renee banged a palm flat to the desk. She refused to think about Nancy. "No."

She searched her desk for an escape and found Sandra Jordan's open file.

There was something about that girl, Renee decided. She concentrated until a finger tapped the data sheet. There was something about the young associate the statistics did not reveal. Even for a first-year, Sandra tried too hard to please. That's why her response today surprised Renee.

Renee admitted to being caught off-guard. She'd done no more preparation for their discussion than expect

Sandra's immediate assent. Renee shrugged, then grimaced at the emotion shooting through her heart. She'd judged a good deal wrong of late, assumed too much and made a terrible last mistake.

She forced her attention to the file. Sandra Jordan deserved a chance. The girl's legal ambitions were recorded under the section for goals: "I plan to do superior work and join R. Maxwell's criminal practice group."

Renee liked that.

She scanned the summary page. Sandra M. Jordan's LSAT result was the highest possible score; editor-in-chief of law review; top SGM rating. That this performance emerged out of a background of financial deprivation and personal loss was evident from the record of financial aid. Under parents was written "deceased."

Despite the roster of accomplishments, Renee suspected some more salient fact was missing, something to explain Sandra's behavior today. Renee sighed. She would have liked a simple yes.

Renee squeezed her fingers against her head, visions of Nancy floating through this crack in the mental door. Why hadn't Nancy answered yes? How did it get so confused?

Stop it.

Renee grabbed Sandra's file, bringing it to her nose, and forced herself to consider these facts.

"Sandra Jordan started her academic career in an inner-city parochial school. St. Mary's."

Renee stopped talking aloud for a moment, then realized it diverted her grief.

"I think I'll talk to St. Mary's. Maybe learn something useful from the formative years," she said to her wall.

It was unnecessary, of course, but why not? Renee buzzed her secretary to place the call.

The process of elimination, Teal decided in arbitrary fashion, might as well start with Renee. Well, not so arbitrary. Who better than the lover?

Renee Maxwell had the reputation as a woman without a private life, as a professional devoted to her work—not a woman devoted to another woman. Teal could understand Renee might prefer a lover encumbered with a husband while accessible to her arms. Renee might not thrill at the prospect of a Nancy divorced. How better to hold Nancy at bay than a scattershot of threats?

But threats did not work and Nancy planned to leave her former life for Renee.

Teal tried to imagine arranging a lover's death. It would be enough to turn an abstainer into a drunk.

Speculation, Teal admitted. But fueled by familiarity with women like Renee. Women secure in their careers, less adept with the confusion of love. And if the latter threatened the first, crazy behavior resulted. But murder?

No. Teal did not believe Renee committed murder. Attempt to control Nancy with an intimate threat? Maybe.

The need to answer the question placed Teal here at the Milk Street Cafe. Sandra Jordan led, tray in hand. A more expensive restaurant, Teal had reasoned, and Sandra might feel bribed. A richer menu than the Cafe's Kosher vegetarian and she might resent the implications juxtaposed by the act of eating and her weight. Milk Street seemed a neutral choice.

They unloaded upon a table for two. Windows flooded the room with noon sun. Noisy lunchtime chatter gave privacy. Teal smiled at Sandra.

"Thanks for agreeing to join me," Teal said as she tried to read a response in Sandra's impassive gaze. "I hoped you might be able to help."

Teal paused to fuss with her salad and shift a bowl of lentil soup. She broke off a piece of bread and chewed. Curiosity finally crossed Sandra's face.

"How?" Sandra mumbled.

Teal watched as Sandra rearranged a tomato across the tuna in Syrian bread. Sandra snapped a dill pickle into thirds.

"I understand you spent this weekend on the Cape. As it happens, Nancy Vandenburg, the woman living in the house next to you, the woman who, you may have heard, was killed . . ." Teal faltered. "Nancy is, was, a close friend. Did you ever meet her? Did you know her work?"

Sandra jiggled in her seat.

"Why ask me? Other people in the house go every weekend. I'd never been there before," Sandra said.

Teal nodded. "Nancy was a wonderful person. I think you would have liked her. Anyway, you didn't say if you knew her."

"No."

Silence followed. Sandra consumed the sandwich. Teal ate her soup. Had Teal thought about it, she would have judged it very good. Their silence was nothing, neither awkward nor companionable. Teal broke it on a gamble.

"Nancy was also a friend of Renee Maxwell's. You took care of Renee's condominium over Christmas, didn't you? Renee owns two of Nancy's paintings. Good ones."

Sandra's surprise gave her away, and Teal smiled.

"Renee had a couple of letters, too. They were filled with drawings from Nan's last summer in Italy—but I imagine Renee put her correspondence away."

Teal didn't expect an answer, but if Sandra had seen the letters something in her face might tell. And give Teal an opening to chat more about Renee.

Sandra jerked back her chair. Her voice was flat, her eyes narrow.

"What are you saying?" Sandra fought for control. "I'm sorry. Thank you for the meal."

Sandra rose to leave.

160

Teal wanted to kick herself. Some start to her investigation.

Damn it, damn it all. Sandra lurched through the restaurant. Teal Stewart had guessed right about the letters, about Sandra's illicit knowledge of Nancy and Renee. The thought expanded—Teal never said that.

Sandra hesitated to collect her will and wits before going back. She fixed a hesitant smile on her face, the smile of a supplicant she'd used year after year. Not threatening or self-assured, but penitent and grateful. It always fooled them. She mustn't talk fast, she reminded herself, but remain reluctant as before.

Sandra waited a beat and turned.

"I did hear the name, once, when I answered Renee's office phone," Sandra said slowly.

"When? Last month?" Teal asked.

Sandra shook her disagreement. "No. December maybe. What makes me feel badly now I know she was your friend, I'll always connect N. Vandenburg with the weird message on Renee Maxwell's desk."

Sandra didn't admit her snooping had been to find Renee's confidential evaluation of Sandra's performance.

"What did it say?"

Teal followed Sandra through the restaurant. The crowded room impeded their progress. Sandra liked the impatience in Teal's voice. She held the information the CPA wanted.

"It said 'You filth atone or die' typed over and over on the paper."

Sandra waited for the next questions. Teal might be the perfect way to get to Renee. But Teal disappointed her expectation. Teal asked only one.

"When did you see this?"

"December," Sandra said and decided to keep talking.

"About your friend's death? I don't know if it will help, but Renee's car passed me that morning in Shell Bay."

Sandra tried to look upset.

"Did you see Nancy on the road?" Teal had Sandra's wrist.

Sandra shook her head and stepped back. This wasn't going quite as she'd hoped.

? Twenty-One

Wednesday.

"She lied," Renee said from behind the barrier of desk and chair.

Teal refused to be gracious, to agree and go.

"I don't think so. She quoted 'you filth atone or die' verbatim to me," Teal challenged.

Renee shrugged a wrinkle across the front of her charcoal suit.

"I'll tell you what I think," Teal said.

Renee remained immobile for a beat before she shrugged again. No expression marked her face.

"There is freedom of speech," she said.

"I think you harassed Nancy and sent 'you filth' to yourself. Her talk of leaving Michael for you had you scared. Did the idea come with the May *laMode?* The article talked up the importance of Nancy's husband and perfect, suburban life. You wanted her to continue to live the big lie. You'd been living with your own for years." Teal stumbled over the words.

Nancy had lied to her, too. All the times Teal assumed Nancy's lover was a man and Nancy never said no. Never trusted Teal with the truth.

"Are you quite done?"

"Not quite, no," Teal said. "You marked the article in fluorescent smears and sent it to Nancy, but it didn't deter her, did it? She might have been frightened, but she wasn't malleable. She forced you to threaten yourself. And Carole? Did you think to enlist her into pressuring her sister, too? How can you live with yourself?"

Renee sat as still as a snake. She brought her eyes to Teal.

"Now I have something to say."

Teal's passion dissipated like helium fleeing a punctured balloon. Renee sounded confident. Teal didn't want to lose this object for her rage.

"Perhaps Sandra did see that ridiculous message here. I'd brought it from home. I wanted to identify the author who, by the way, was not me."

Renee stared into space for a moment.

Teal's discomfort increased as she recognized unwelcome candor. She needed indignation to mask the horror of her loss. She needed to despise Renee.

"What were you doing in Shell Bay the morning Nancy died?" Teal asked.

Renee's tremble evidenced an uncharacteristic struggle for composure.

"I don't owe you this, I owe Nancy," she hissed.

Renee fixed her eyes on her desk a long time before she spoke.

"There are two pathetic truths about 'you filth atone or die,' " she said. "The first is that my cleaning man sent it. His homosexuality tore him apart. He found the Italian letters and fixated his personal denial into an attack on me. You wouldn't understand."

Renee raised her eyes to Teal without apology and continued.

"He read them during the time he attended Mass every morning and gay-bashed outside the bars every night. No one exactly chooses homosexuality."

Teal broke in. "Your second point?"

As suddenly, she realized she didn't want to hear another word. Nancy might never forgive the animosity Teal had turned on Renee. Jealousy, Teal admitted. The convoluted jealousy of a friend for a lover.

"Please—you needn't say more," she said. But it was too late.

"I was afraid of exposure. Do you think I wanted to be the butt of locker-room jokes? Opposing counsel with discreet grins and the cops smirking openly when I enter a court? But I loved her. I yearned for her to come to me. More than that, I was impatient. When she received the *laMode,* I didn't consider my reputation or her fear. I was happy it raised the pressure another degree, and I decided to pretend 'you filth' had just arrived to scare me. *I* filled her last weeks with anxiety."

"You never told her your cleaning man stood behind the threats to her and you and Carole?" Teal asked, incredulous.

Renee shook her head in denial. "But he didn't. Not to Nancy or her sister. He settled with himself over the winter. I asked, of course, but he didn't know Nancy. I believe him."

"What about the journal, Renee? I saw it yesterday. She gave me one, too, years ago."

Renee sighed. "Her birthday present for me this spring. Believe me, he'd long since resolved his problem. He didn't threaten Nancy. The sketches and poems only reveal her identity to those familiar with her work in art and verse. He wasn't."

"I want to believe you," Teal said. "What should I believe about Monday morning? You in Shell Bay?"

"Believe that Nancy told me not to come, but I needed to see her. I wanted to catch her on her run. I wanted to be there as emotional support. No."

Renee drummed her fingers on her desk in a frantic tattoo.

"No?" Teal prompted.

"The truth is, I came down for me. Selfishly." Renee's voice cracked. "I guess I realized that when I lost my nerve. You may not understand, but I never recognized Nancy. I was blind with rage at myself when I drove by the accident."

Teal looked at Renee. It was their first unencumbered exchange.

Renee stared back. "Do you know how much I resented you, Nancy's best friend? The public acceptance of your relationship? Do you know how horrible it is to hide? I loved Nancy."

"Please." Teal gestured, then dropped her hand. "When I saw Nancy's picture on the Cape, her drawing of herself in your arms . . . maybe I needed to blame you."

"What do you imagine I thought about you?" Renee asked. "I wanted to humiliate you on Fruiers, demonstrate my superiority to Nancy."

"You almost succeeded, at least in queering my shot at the partnership this year." Teal laughed and as suddenly stopped.

"No pun intended, I'm sure," Renee said.

"None." Teal warmed in confusion.

Renee leaned across the desk. "We both loved Nancy, Teal. Wouldn't it make more sense to become friends?"

Seconds after Renee stepped out of her office, the telephone rang.

Teal hesitated. Another ring and a secretary should take it, but it pealed again, twice. Oh, why not? Teal decided. She could take the message for Renee.

Teal raised the receiver. "Renee Maxwell's line."

"Miss Maxwell, this is Sister Celia of St. Mary's returning your call about Sandra Jordan. I'll be happy to answer your questions."

Teal pulled the cord taut as she reached to close the door. She didn't rationalize her action as motivated by an interest in helping Renee. No, she hoped the lawyer stayed in the bathroom a good long time.

"Stimpson, Grey & Minot is so pleased with Sandra's accomplishments," Teal improvised. "The firm is developing a program to reach out to target students of color in high school to stimulate an interest in a law career. An in-depth understanding of the formative years of top performers like Sandra could help the program. Your comments about her background will be an enormous contribution."

Teal kept an eye on the door and began to pace with the telephone.

"Sandra makes us so proud at St. Mary's. When I think of the child's terrible history, well, God's ways are ever a mystery to man. Our little Sandra a lawyer! I'd never have believed it possible after she saw the man who had killed her mother walk out of the courtroom, free. I never understood, but everyone said it was as legal as you please. Her poor daddy hung himself the next day, God tend his soul. Look at our Sandra now. A lawyer!"

City heat, heavy with humidity and the grit of airborne dirt, surged around Teal. Her lungs tingled with pollution claustrophobia. The torpid air pressed closer, squeezing to the surface her true anxiety. Returning to Clayborne Whittier to start Kathy researching the Chicago court records could wait.

Teal crossed Congress and Franklin on the diagonal, as drivers honked and cursed. A free bench in the park gave her a place to rest. She sank to the seat as the pigeons waddled over to inspect her for bounty. They sauntered away after a minute, heads bobbing as though gravely offended. A scavenging gull cawed.

Teal gripped the edge of the bench and took a centering breath. The opening routine of meditation eased her fear. She counted up to four and back down until the inhalation and exhalation drove out the panic. Teal lifted her repressed thoughts to consciousness.

Nancy had intended to betray her.

Teal knew she wouldn't have cared that her best friend might be a lesbian, yet for the entire last year, Nancy never said. Never confided a thought or word, never turned to Teal until, without being candid and without being fair, Nancy brought Teal into the tangle of the affair. Nancy's death robbed them of the time for reparation.

Grief and anger rose in equal measure. The tension burst as tears.

Teal stood half an hour later. There was betrayal and betrayal. Surely Nancy deserved privacy—but it hurt.

At the FNEB building on Federal Street, Teal pushed into the revolving door. Her face, reflected in the glass, looked a fright of makeup streaks and puffed eyes. She twirled through the circle and stepped back outside.

Street noise forced her to shout into the public phone.

"Has anything vital come up, Kathy? I won't be back for about an hour."

"Nope, not vital. Felicia Barrette, that's it."

"I'll call her back when I return, Kath, and maybe you could start on a small project."

Teal summarized what she knew of Sandra Jordan's mother's murder.

"Get the details. It's not a top priority, but—"

"But don't let it fall off my list. Okay, boss."

Sitting on the high chair, before a lighted and magnified mirror, in the middle of the busiest floor of the department store, Teal felt a genuine fool.

The Clinique lady swabbed Teal's face with a "gentle, oil-free, daily-cleaning emollient" followed by pats of "clarifying lotion to stimulate the skin." The woman wore a wrap of surgical white and smelled of talc. She started to dot on an "oil-free, sun-protective, alabaster-hued foundation" and bossed Teal into closing her eyes.

Those blind seconds brought to mind the day Nancy had strolled into Chicago's finest department store. "I want the works," she instructed the cosmetic company's representative. "I need to look gorgeous tonight." She winked at Teal, an acknowledgement of the lie. That night they had planned nothing more than a movie.

"No, no, dear. Please! You'll bunch your foundation into very unattractive smile lines."

Teal opened her eyes, but the joyous feeling lingered. Nancy would always be her best friend. Was Nancy's reluctance to share so intimate a truth betrayal? Teal didn't want to think so today.

A second Clinique consultant stopped to watch the transformation. The woman's hair glowed redder than Felicia's and straighter, Teal observed. Teal wriggled in the chair. The red-haired woman seemed as bored. She walked away.

For a second, imagination and the receding flame of hair converged. Betrayal and Felicia, Teal thought. The moment of musing dissipated to the tedium of smile lines and blush.

Half an hour and many purchase dollars later, Teal entered Clayborne Whittier with her new face. Kathy's wolfwhistle rang long and sharp.

"Who's getting lucky tonight?"

Teal graced her with a smile. The truth would be a late dinner and alone.

"Here's Felicia's number. No other calls. I tried *The Chicago Tribune*'s morgue. The guy there did a quick check, nothing under Jordan. He'll take a second look, but it may be a week or so."

"If that's the best we can do?"

Kathy shrugged.

"Okay," Teal agreed. "I can wait."

She looked at Felicia's return number.

"Felicia isn't in New York?" she asked.

"Nope, Boston," Kathy said. "Business before the funeral, not that I asked. The woman, as ever, had an urge to tell. What don't people know about her?"

Teal grinned. "Felicia's not that bad. For example, I don't know the name of the man she's been seeing, although her cat's name is—"

"Portia!" Kathy rolled her eyes.

Teal read the message again. What about Felicia and betrayal? Teal decided it might be smart to step out this evening after all.

? TWENTY-TWO

Wednesday.

Albert heard the words and kept nodding his head as though he understood. As though he could.

". . . the first series of tests. I am sorry. There is the possibility we will qualify for the experimental drug study my associates and I are conducting. The admission protocol prevents me from promising anything," the doctor said.

We. Where'd the doctor get off saying we? Born alone, die alone, left alone. No fucking we. Albert knew the doctor saw him as a little nobody, impotent and scared in the face of disease. But Albert sat, obstinate in his immunity to the man's impatient look.

The doctor stirred as though to agitate action. Ignored, he pulled out his pen with an officious snap and endorsed a set of forms in an impatient flurry. Finally, he pushed back from his desk, his purpose clear. Albert remained immobile.

"Mr. Fontane, I know this is all very shocking, very sudden news for you. We'll start chemo tomorrow and hope to join the study by the end of the week, if that meets your approval."

Albert understood that it wasn't a question, not really.

Tina was just another lab animal available for study. Albert watched the man rise with a scrubbed and buffed hand extended. Albert showed a thin line of dirt under two of his nails and a thick line under one. What the doctor really wanted beneath the false sincerity, Albert knew, was to get Albert out of the room. The doctor grasped Albert's hand. Albert resisted the pull. He might be an uneducated man, he was not a fool.

"I'll see her now."

"I am sorry, Mr. Fontane, that is impossible at this point. Our ICU, as you can appreciate, strictly limits visiting hours in the interest of patient care."

"ICU?" Albert asked.

"I'm sorry. The intensive care unit."

In one morning, Albert realized, he'd become an old man. Tremors disrupted the motion of his arms and bobbed a nervous nod from his head. He couldn't make sense of the facts, couldn't accept being here. Why hadn't Tina given him a warning, a chance to fight back? Last night, she complained about her migraine again and rose from her chair, a simple, ordinary action.

"I want to go to bed," she had said and fallen to smack the floor.

She didn't answer to his touch or her name.

The doctor at the local hospital hemmed and hawed and frowned until Albert wanted to twist off his head. Maybe the intention shone in Albert's eyes. The doctor had backed away and waved.

"We need to transfer your wife to Boston after she's stabilized," he said before he fled.

The first hospital in Boston ran tests and scans and asked Albert the same questions again and again on multipart and carbonless forms. Doctors hurried in and out of the emergency room. Albert was passive until he couldn't stand it anymore. He grabbed the next white jacket to emerge from an unmarked door.

The woman tapped a pen to her clipboard.

"She'll require specialized care, but you must know that," she said.

The look she directed at Albert radiated scorn.

He shook his head. "No, I don't understand."

"This cancer is extensively spread. Who has she been seeing for it?"

Albert felt his stomach turn, and fear flattened the muscles in his throat. "Cancer? She doesn't have cancer!"

He had slumped with remembering Tina's many months of "headaches," the weight she'd bragged about losing. Yes, she'd visited the family doctor once or twice that Albert knew. But it was nothing, just female things after mid-life. It wasn't cancer.

The doctor touched his arm, her face softer. "Well, whoever it was, your wife requires specialized care. I've initiated a transfer to the best place for her in town. You can wait there."

The doctor wrote out the hospital's name and slipped back into the stream of people flowing past, forever exiting Albert's life.

At the special cancer hospital, famous enough for Albert to have recognized the name, he was greeted with more forms, more doctors dodging his eye, more hours passing until it became now, this morning and this conversation with this doctor. The man's words as good as admitted Tina would be dead soon. Albert's acquiescence transformed. He wasn't going to let anyone, doctor or not, tell him he could not see his wife.

"I'm gonna see her, Doc," Albert said.

The doctor leaned around Albert to open the office door. He pointed Albert out.

"Well, yes, of course you are. Let's see. ICU visiting hours can be arranged with a nurse at the station. This evening or tomorrow, at the latest, will be a good time."

The doctor pursed his lips in self-assent.

"No. No, you don't understand me, Doc. You tell me how long my Tina has and forget the experimental crap. Know what I mean?"

The doctor stared at Albert. "The nurse-social worker will be counseling you after my colleagues and I further evaluate your wife."

"You're not getting it, Doc. I don't want to hear from no special social worker what you already know. You're the doc, right? You tell me. What's left for my Tina?"

"Well," the doctor stepped away from Albert. "Premature diagnosis is a help to no one. The data is incomplete, but our time would be longer with the experimental drugs than without them, I must tell you."

"Would you take the drugs if 'our' time was your time, Doc, not hers? Would they let you live a normal life? Dim the pain?" Albert asked.

The doctor's extreme degree of discomfort drove his eyes to stare through Albert, then shift to the floor.

He spoke fast. "Well, of course, it isn't me."

Albert appreciated the deep silence between them. It restored Tina's dignity. "How long, Doc?"

"Maybe three weeks." The doctor sighed.

"Then I see my wife. I want to sit beside her. I want to hold her hand and tell her she's always been everything to me. Know what I mean, Doc? *We*'re going to break the rules."

"Fifteen minutes, Mr. Fontane. After that, you must follow my instructions and leave."

He held the part of her hand that wasn't threaded with an IV. He couldn't cry, it wouldn't be right, and he couldn't lie, not to Tina, not anymore. Love made his guts feel turned inside out. He leaned his face to her ear.

"I always thought you was crazy to marry me, Tina Norton. You coulda had anybody. How'd I get so lucky? You made me the happiest guy around. Proud. I even got used to all your sassy back talk 'cause, I guess, I knew you was better than me.

"Tina, I love you, baby. I love you even though you lied about this disease. I got so scared at times, thinking you might leave me. But you never did, and I never expected anything like this. You must have worried for me, but I still wish you'da told me the truth." Albert's shoulders jerked with sobs. "It's my fault, Tina. I'm not gonna burden you with my sins, but God, you're being punished because of me. The terrible things I done."

His heaving breath fluttered a stray hair by her temple, but her eyes didn't open and her head didn't move. The room pulsed with the hiss of machinery woven into and around his Tina. Guilt filled him with terror.

"No, look, forget what I said. Have I told you how beautiful you are? Sam's never let up on he thinks you're too good for me. That's how special you are, even to my crazy brother. So, honey, you rest up now, you hear me? I'm not leaving you, I'm gonna hold you right here in my heart while you let that beautiful body sleep. I'm not gonna lie, Tina. The Doc says you're in crisis, it's more than just R & R you need. But I'll be with you, understand?

"Now, I can't be getting the nurses in a snit this first day. Time's about up. Remember, honey, I've put you here against my heart."

Albert tapped his chest with his free hand and held to her a minute longer, then leaned to kiss her slack eyelids. He didn't tell her what he planned, or of his hopes for the bargain he had proposed to God in the instant the Doc said three weeks and sighed.

As before, the Shell Bay cops treated him with nice respect. They recognized him at the desk and brought him in to see the chief right away. As before, the policewoman took the notes. Unlike before, the chief did the talking while the young sergeant lounged in the door.

"Well, well. Mr. Fontane. Good to see you. And to what do we owe this visit, sir? No damage to your automobile from our tow, I hope."

Albert saw the chief grin at his own joke, so Albert tried to smile in return.

"No. Nothin' like that." He couldn't say what he'd come to say wearing a damned smile.

"Is something wrong?" the chief asked.

"The accident," Albert said. "I killed her. All that sand, slipping like crazy, sure it was a factor, but I killed the lady. She was supposed to live. You know what I mean?"

The sergeant straightened and pushed the door shut. The policewoman wrote faster. The chief made soothing gestures with his hands.

"Of course you wanted her to live. Anyone with a conscience would be upset if their actions, however accidental, cause a person to die. Your feelings are what distinguish man from beast." The chief looked satisfied with his wisdom.

Albert didn't care about the chief. Tina was about to die. Jesus, Tina was about to die for his sins. Tina, the love of his life, the only love. Whadda he and Sam been thinking all these years?

"Mr. Fontane, sir, are you all right?"

What could he say? He couldn't rat on Sam. He could only guess who contracted the hit, he had no evidence. Their system didn't work sloppy. But he had to make amends, make God see he was serious. Punish him, Albert, okay, but not his Tina. Albert took a deep breath.

"I want to confess. I murdered that poor girl. I'm the one deserves to die."

Albert didn't see the glances exchanged over his bent head.

"Have you had a shock, sir? Is everything all right?" the chief asked.

"How the hell can it be?" Albert's control broke. "You tell me how the hell can it be with that damned Doc saying Tina's as good as dead. It's God's punishment for what I done. I killed that woman and she wasn't the first. Look at me, I'm confessing, goddamn it. Charge me."

The glances became more obvious. The sergeant shuffled foot-to-foot and watched the chief. The chief took his time. He steepled his fingers and furrowed his brow while he soberly regarded Albert.

"No automotive priors, no record at all. We checked. An eyewitness to the accident, her husband, saw you try to steer out of the way. Tina is your wife, is that right? I am sorry. Now, you go home and get some rest. The sergeant will see you to your car."

"Please, let me, Chief." The policewoman spoke up.

The sergeant stepped away from Albert and shrugged.

"Fine. Mr. Fontane, sir, it's damned bad luck." The chief stood.

Albert recognized failure. "I lost it, didn't I? Tina, see—I'm sorry."

"No apology called for." The chief waved Albert out.

The policewoman stopped for a quick rummage in her desk drawer before they continued to the sidewalk. The heat prickled at Albert's skin. Failure oppressed him.

"Is this your car?"

The policewoman opened his door.

"Look, it's not my business, but a friend of mine hit a guy. It about tore my friend apart. The guy's fianceé let my friend apologize. It helped. Anyway, in there," she inclined her head to the station, "I found this. She was Ms. Vandenburg-Britton's friend."

Albert automatically took the rectangle of paper. He sat heavily in the car and fingered the card. The policewoman was entering the station when he read "E. TEAL

STEWART, CLAYBORNE WHITTIER." He flicked the card's stiff edge. Yes! God had a plan.

Felicia watched Carole behind her desk. Carole looked cool and fresh in pale cream linen. Felicia sighed just as the hotel clerk returned to the telephone line.

"Any messages for me? Barrette, room twelve-oh-four?"

"Please hold."

Canned music flooded Felicia's ear. She wondered what it was to be Carole, to be so sure and poised, not even undone by death. Old envy bubbled up. The clerk spoke.

"Two messages. Shall I read them to you?"

"Please," Felicia said.

"The first came in at three from a John. 'Not to worry, dear, everything is under control and the date set. Will celebrate when you return.' He did not leave a number."

"No," Felicia murmured. Dear, dear John.

"Your second, at three-fifteen, a Teal Stewart. 'Any chance you are free for dinner tonight? I'll be in my office late, call when you can.' Would you need that number?" the clerk inquired.

"Yes, thanks."

Felicia wrote as he spoke, then began to dial when she thought the better of it. No reason to let Carole know she planned to dine with Teal. Felicia tensed. She had one more thing to say to Carole before the afternoon's business was ended.

"Carole, I have to tell you how sorry I am about my argument with Nancy. I should have called her about selling *SELF.* I had my reasons, but, well, I still behaved poorly. The minute I heard, I canceled with Sotheby's. It's too late, I know, but—"

Carole's voice cut Felicia to the quick.

"You made the last days of my sister's life a miserable

hell. Don't ask me for forgiveness. You'll have to perform that miracle for yourself."

Panic gripped Felicia as the seconds accumulated. Humiliation flamed Felicia's face as her capillaries burst wide. Everything, instead of working out, seemed a greater mess.

Carole knew, but how much? Felicia tried to control the panic engorging her chest. Carole couldn't know everything, could she?

More than ever before, Felicia wanted to find a sanctuary from the repercussions of her sins. She wanted to confess.

? TWENTY-THREE

Wednesday.

Teal waited in the hotel lobby for Felicia. She didn't mind Felicia's tardiness. The delay gave her an opportunity to consider Carole's call.

Had Teal made any progress? Had she considered Felicia might be the source of the threats? For all Carole knew, Felicia was responsible for Nancy's death, except that Carole believed what the police always claimed. Look to the spouse. And Teal was looking, wasn't she? But Felicia's duplicity infuriated Carole. Why, the woman had spent the afternoon in Carole's office all apologies about *SELF* when, Carole discovered afterward, the sale date had been set. Carole assured Teal that Teal wasn't the only sleuth.

Carole proved the claim when she suggested Teal use dinner with Felicia to ferret out the truth. How did Carole know about dinner? Teal wondered.

The good thing about the conversation, Teal realized, was Carole didn't let her wedge in more than a word. Teal did not see an opportunity to address the identity of Nancy's lover. The circumstance made it easier to respect Renee's request and Teal's own inclination to let disclosure wait. Carole made the subject easy to avoid.

Teal jumped when Felicia touched her arm.

"Did I scare you?"

Felicia leaned to Teal in a greeting hug. They kissed the air beside each cheek.

"Deeply oblivious, as usual." Teal laughed, chagrined. "Thanks for joining me on short notice. The restaurant's not much of a walk."

"Let me drop this at the desk." Felicia waved an envelope. "Our final decisions on the retrospective. Carole and I made them this afternoon. I want John to start on the arrangements to collect the paintings."

The desk clerk listened to Felicia's instructions for overnight mail as if he didn't know how to send express. He grinned when she finished.

"Would you be wanting your messages a third time then, Ms. Barrette?" he asked.

Confusion slacked Felicia's face before it cleared to recognition.

"I spoke with you—that's right. You're Irish," she said.

"I am. Part of the international training. The company will open a hotel in Dublin next spring. You be sure to visit us."

"I hope I do," Felicia said and turned from the desk before she swung back to face him. "Why did you ask if I wanted my messages a third time?"

"A bit of a tease, miss, as you called that second time so close after the first, explaining about mistaking a number. It got me to worry about my accent until you graciously blamed your sloppy writing and not a misspoken word of mine. You have a pleasant evening, now."

Teal observed Felicia hold her concern in check until they reached the street. Then her baffled expression returned.

"I never called him a second time," Felicia said.

Carole, Teal realized in a flash, too clever by half. That fact best remained withheld from Felicia.

"Maybe he used a bit of blarney to keep talking to a red-haired colleen."

"Now who's talking blarney?" Felicia laughed. "I look a harridan these days."

Teal shook her head politely, but didn't speak up to disagree. Felicia looked awful, her freckles dull against a face the color of old window putty. Her body, leaning to lush, seemed thinner but less lovely. Teal understood Felicia's skepticism.

Past the Cathedral Church of St. Paul's and a pizzeria, they turned from Tremont onto West Street. A row of trash-filled plastic bags edged the narrow sidewalk. As a matter of convenience, Teal stepped ahead. Humid air held the exhaust and stale odors of city living. The luminous pearly-gray of a summer sky showed through a brown veil of smog. She could about chew the air.

The hour was too early for a sunset and, anyway, West Street ran south to north between buildings of brick and granite, which, if short by modern standards, rose tall enough to block the natural horizon. The prior restaurant in the converted house had been fitted with arty glass lights and Mackintosh-inspired chairs and served "new American cuisine." Now it was the city's most popular grill. Teal still liked the food and atmosphere, so different from the world of Clayborne Whittier, so suitable to a visitor from New York.

Felicia rolled the edge of her napkin between her fingers and unrolled it flat against her leg again. She repeated the silent motion over and over, her bright nails punctuating the field of white damask. She fiddled with her roll and transferred butter to her plate. She tilted her glass of wine against her lower lip, inhaling the vapors.

She kept the conversation humming, one banal comment skirting and diverting from another.

This was not why she'd agreed to come.

She studied Teal, a woman she knew as Nancy's friend. Felicia remembered their first meeting. Teal had walked into the gallery with Nancy, and Felicia saw the bond between the reticent, statuesque artist and her voluble, incisive college roommate. Felicia remembered her twitch of envy. Despite what Nancy owed to Felicia, their relationship never evolved to anything as close.

Felicia went back to worrying her napkin. Nancy was not here, would never be again, leaving her only recourse, her only hope with Teal. Felicia did not want to miscalculate. She did not want to bring derision and disdain upon herself. She did not want to answer questions. She wanted the absolution for confession—forgiveness and a new start.

Felicia had considered confession with care. What was the truth but putting blame where blame was due? She pinched the napkin harder and broke into the conversation's flow. Felicia did not think to care that her action informed Teal she really hadn't been listening.

"This whole mess with Nancy—you heard about our fight on the Cape? I tried to apologize to Carole today. I loved Nancy, too, only Carole isn't interested in what I have to say. She'll never forgive me for discovering Nancy or that Nancy stayed with Barrette over the years."

"That's not true, Felicia," Teal said. "Carole understands your importance in Nan's career. You've just been a bit erratic lately, that's all, and Carole is concerned."

Felicia pulled back. "I never forgot what Nancy meant to the gallery, whatever Carole says. Never, no matter how stupid I've been these last months."

All the starch in the napkin gave way at once. She held a rag and stared at Teal, who had stopped eating and sat across the table, waiting. Felicia pulled at a thread hanging from the corner. Her eyes fixed on the strand of cotton her fingers yanked taut. The length of cloth puckered.

"Basically, I guess I'm angry at myself."

The thread broke in a snap, rocketing her hand to slam the table's deep edge. In that instant the waiter arrived to present two plates of entrées assembled like art. He topped their wine. He inquired if there might be anything else the ladies needed or desired. The break in her concentration made her think twice.

The interruption relieved Teal. Felicia sought a forgiveness best received from Nancy. But Nancy was dead, and her sister angry. Teal knew she remained Felicia's hope. And what did Teal want?

What Carole suggested, the truth.

"What did you do, Felicia?" Teal asked.

Felicia turned the question in her head. There was confession, and there was confession. What did she want to tell Nancy's friend?

"I've been having problems, money things affecting the gallery. Anyway, I went by her studio in Lincoln a few months ago for her advice. I wasn't thinking about selling *SELF* then."

Surely that, of all she planned to say, was true.

"When she wasn't there, I decided to wait. I admit I shouldn't have gone upstairs. Nancy hated any violation of her work space, but I was curious and, as her representative, thought I had a right to be. She had hinted about an evolution in her art."

Felicia remembered the day too well.

"And did you see a change?" Teal prompted.

"It reminded me of Paris—canvases everywhere. I became optimistic, maybe everything could start over. But

184

that pretense didn't last long, not when I looked at the art. I couldn't sell them. They weren't by the Nancy I knew, but all abstract and raw. But that's not what upset me. Worse than the art, SHE'D NEVER SAID A THING TO ME!"

Felicia fought to control her voice.

"I didn't want to see her then. I didn't want to talk about anything."

Felicia pressed her index finger against the crumbs of bread littering the tablecloth. She dropped them on her plate. There were some things she needed to figure out how to say. Teal evidenced no judgment or impatience.

"Just when I turned to go, I heard the downstairs door. I panicked and jumped into the closet as the telephone started to ring. No one answered, and the machine kicked in. Some man with a message about her book being ready. As he talked, she still didn't pick up. That's when I guessed the person on the stairs wasn't Nancy."

"Could be she didn't want to talk," Teal said.

Felicia hesitated at the sharp tone of voice. Maybe she wasn't ready for the price of absolution. She rolled her napkin into a sausage again.

"Who came in?" Teal asked.

Felicia considered her answer. "I'm pretty sure it was Michael."

Teal focused wide eyes on Felicia, and Felicia hesitated.

"This was when?" Teal asked.

Why do you care, Felicia wanted to scream, but she didn't. She was afraid of breaking down completely. She decided it wasn't the best time to confess to the affair or other unspoken things.

"Let me think."

Felicia stared at the stem of her wineglass. She tried to press back the paralyzing guilt.

"May. Maybe mid-May."

The silence held. Teal couldn't think of anything to murmur. She watched Felicia's nervous fingers fiddle her napkin.

"You haven't told me everything, have you?"

Felicia's face reddened to clash with her hair.

"Almost," she croaked.

The silence returned.

"Well?" Teal said.

"Don't be upset, please, but I'm going to the Ranch next week. I made the reservation yesterday before I remembered you always take this week in July with Nancy. Are you still going this year?"

Teal hadn't given the Ranch any thought since Nancy died. The question surprised her into accepting Felicia's extraordinary behavior.

"Yes," she answered, suddenly determined. "Yes, I am."

"Please, don't feel you have to spend time with me, but I'm so out of shape." Felicia evaded Teal's eyes. "I was afraid you'd think I'd tried to hone in on what you had with Nancy. Silly of me."

Teal didn't say, I can understand you might. She was too bemused. What sin, exactly, was Felicia confessing? The stricken face made Teal smile.

"I'm glad you'll be there. Really."

The waiter pointed to each dessert presented on the tray and recited a baroque description. Teal paid no attention.

Felicia had seen Michael in Nancy's studio. And there was something else in what Felicia said, but Teal couldn't make the thought come together.

"Are you feeling guilty about selling *SELF?*" Teal asked, wondering if that's what Felicia meant to confess.

"I'm not going through with it," Felicia said, her voice dismissive.

"But I heard that the sale date had been set."

"You did?" Felicia looked astounded. "What I'm selling is half of Barrette Gallery. To John. It just made more sense."

"That's great Felicia," Teal said, happy with one answer for Carole.

Waiting for the check, Teal returned her thoughts to Felicia's mention of the telephone message. What book of Nancy's was ready to be picked up back in May? Renee's birthday present?

Nancy gave the first journal of illustrated verse to Carole, years before either sister accepted Nan's poetry as mediocre and her paintings as inspired. Teal couldn't remember if she ever knew to whom the second was given. She had received the third.

Michael's courtship inspired number four, and Libby merited the fifth on the occasion of her birth.

The journals, filled with line drawings and uninhibited verse, celebrated the subject relationship and spoke intimately, even eloquently, to the recipient. Teal cherished hers. Nancy had each custom-bound. These were the familiar details. Teal began to smile when she realized something else.

Felicia's story told Teal about journal number six, and it troubled Teal. Nancy's answering machine gave Michael knowledge of the journal filled with Nancy's adultery.

? TWENTY-FOUR

Thursday.

Nancy's lawyer read the will in a calm and neutral voice. Everyone's position was quite clear, and clearly Michael lost. Nancy had passed to him the perquisites of a spouse in Massachusetts and nothing more. Her use of trusts reduced that inheritance to almost nothing.

Carole appreciated the United States Postal Service for the first time in years. Will and trust documents, signed by Nancy and witnessed on the Cape, had arrived in Boston a few days after Nancy's death.

Carole refused Michael's offer of a ride to her office after the reading. She didn't care if she drowned in the rain which gusted against her legs. She bent her head to deflect the wind and indulged in a single-minded focus on the morning. Michael's face had transformed from a study in perfect grief to surprised rage when he realized what Nancy had won.

Carole turned into her building, the squish of water on the foyer's marble floor echoing along the ancient marble wainscoting. A vintage elevator whined on hidden pulleys and gears at her call before it shuddered to a stop. She pulled the heavy door and squeezed the accordion grate. The shadowed interior did not brighten when she pressed number four.

Water from her raincoat dripped to join other rivulets rolling across the floor. She didn't notice, but continued to dwell on the morning.

The car began its tremble to a stop, and she stepped forward. Her hand no more than touched the door when another jerked it open. The fingers reaching in from the corridor glistened with dark hairs. Carole froze. The hall's wan light outlined the looming figure of a man. He blocked her exit for one long second before he stepped aside.

"You should have accepted my offer, Carole. You're soaking." Michael chuckled.

Carole stumbled, her coordination impaired by residual fright. She nodded scant acknowledgement and set her teeth. Her brother-in-law fell in beside her.

"If I'd realized you wanted to speak to me . . ." Carole gestured with forced disinterest.

"Oh, but of course I do. We have so many common business interests. You didn't understand that when I offered you the ride? No?" He laughed. "I guess you thought I'd be that easy to get rid of."

Carole wanted to slap his insolent face. Instead she busied herself locating her office key. She pushed a hip against the door and turned to snap her umbrella open, sending a shower across his front. Water bled an oval pucker in his tie. She flipped the light switch. The sudden illumination isolated the room from the darkness of the stormy day. She stepped inside and did not offer him a seat.

He ignored the lack of hospitality and lowered to the couch. He took time in leaning back and spreading out. He ran a hand down his tie, hesitating where dry silk feathered to wet. Carole enjoyed its pattern of yellow and gray against his pale blue shirt despite herself. Natty as always. It set her teeth on edge again.

"You must know when she changed her will," he said.

Carole continued to stand, her face held impassive.

"I expect you advised her to, and, conveniently, right before her death." He actually grinned. "You do well as Libby's fiscal guardian."

Carole fought an urge to smack the arrogance from his face.

"She didn't need a suggestion from me. Too bad for you she managed to sign and mail the originals before her accident." The word twisted through tight lips. "There's not much in the estate for you."

Michael leaned forward.

"But you're wrong, Carole. There's Libby. She's my child even if you control the money. We'll enjoy working together, closely together, for the benefit of my daughter and your niece."

His grin spread until she saw his big, white teeth. She wanted to throttle him.

Teal spent the morning sorting through her backlog of work.

By noon, rain still pinged and rattled her window, the building still creaked and swayed its forty-nine floors. She realized there was nothing to wait for, no chance the storm might pass. She kicked aside her flimsy leather shoes and pulled on her boots. She hesitated over her oversized umbrella. It could be a lethal weapon on a city sidewalk. She checked the address in her hand. Better than seven city blocks. She took the umbrella.

Midday could have been midnight as thunderheads eclipsed the sun. Drivers used their car headlights, and the Boston monochrome of red brick and granite and glass transformed to slick gray. Puddles grew over failed storm drains. Teal cursed that any errand sent her out this noon.

Strands of hair at the nape of her neck twisted and curled in the one hundred percent humidity. At least when she had looked out her window that morning across the storm-stirred Charles, she chose to wear her rubber boat boots. She didn't care that they were a bright, unprofessional yellow, a screaming yellow. They were waterproof, guaranteed as one hundred percent as the humidity.

She thought about Don Clarke. He commuted from a monster house in the suburbs. His journey started in his climate-controlled car which he entered from a kitchen attached to the garage. He exited the turnpike to park in the FNEB's underground lot. His eating club, Ivy, was on the building's top floor.

Don Clarke never needed to venture outside. He never navigated the bodies of prone alcoholics, the destitute or homeless. He never battled the harbor's stiff breeze. Teal suspected he couldn't walk four blocks from the office without getting lost. Yet Don held a seat on the Vault, the group of powerful executives committed to Boston's future.

Somewhere in this, Teal concluded, lay a great irony.

Don Clarke illustrated another of the differences between *her* and *them*. Not one partner lived in the city. Not one was single. Clayborne Whittier's sole female partner worked in a special consulting group and was an individual with whom Teal could not claim rapport. The profile of the typical Clayborne Whittier partner—male, married, and suburban—raised the question again. What did she want?

She wanted to discuss her ambivalence with Nancy. Her oldest, best, and most dead friend. Teal misstepped to kick a puddle up her leg. She hated the question.

What did she want? How did anyone know? Had Nancy?

Clutching the book wrapped in double plastic bags, she angled across the cobblestone plaza between Faneuil Hall and Quincy Market. No mimes or magicians performed to spellbound crowds today. The square opened empty before her.

She hurried through to Blackstone Street with its franchise McDonald's that had caused so much controversy. Rumors and intrigue accompanied the location of the fast-food outpost in a historic district. A few cheese and meat purveyors remained around the corner to mark the origins of the block.

A right turn took her across a bronze trail of rotting vegetables, faux paper wrappers, and packing crates flattened like garbage in the asphalt. The humorous sculpture, strewn across the street, paid tribute to the locale's history as an open-air haymarket. The jam of carts heavy with inexpensive produce and fish now operated on a restricted Friday and Saturday schedule.

Teal stepped on "corn" and a "crate," then sped down concrete steps and through a short tunnel reeking of urine. On the path through the municipal lot under the expressway, she opened her notes. The bookbinder's address was further into Boston's North End.

A better day, and she would have paused in the salumeria on Richmond Street for Parmesan and prosciutto, Calabresi olives and imported oil, but she didn't want the burden of another bag to shelter from the rain. Her purpose for this journey was burden enough today. Italy's delicacies could wait.

Two blocks and two turns brought her to the storefront she wanted. A voice called, *"Momento, momento,"* at the bell announcing her entrance. Nothing in the small shop advertised its purpose. Teal slumped with depression as her expectations faded.

A handsome and distinguished old man emerged from the back to regard her from his side of the wooden counter. In Boston's most Italian district, famous for a population of Sicilians and other émigrés from southern Italy, he stood out a born Venetian. Teal smiled, flooded with happy memories of the melancholy city.

"*Venezia?*" she asked.

"*Bene, bene, signorina.* I am Venetian."

His voice held an equal measure of music and courtesy and was devoid of curiosity. But his bright and pale blue eyes watched her like an alert bird. He spread his elegant, long fingers.

"How may I be of help?"

Teal removed the journal from its protective wrapping. She lay it on the counter as the craftsman removed his gaze from her face to the book. He stroked the top edge with a flat palm.

"Yes, this is my work. That is what you want to know?"

Pride illuminated his face.

"A friend gave it to me years ago. Nancy Vandenburg," Teal said and watched.

He inclined his head, showing more of the thick white hair that waved back from his face.

"The famous artist, the lady who just died," he said as a statement of fact.

He lifted the book, his hands gentle against the covers.

"This is my first for her. I do others. That's what you want to ask."

His comment was not a question.

"I love Americans after the second war. Not the Brits, no." He gave an Italian snort. "The Americans so friendly at the end. Shoulder-to-shoulder. When I can, I come here to your America, but it is not like I think. These southerners."

He dismissed the other residents of his neighborhood

with another snort and an articulate hand. Teal recalled her time in Italy, that country assembled in the nineteenth century from powerful and insular city-states. Old animosities and fraternities lingered.

"Your friend, she was very good to me. Shoulder-to-shoulder. She brought me my first museum commission, the first scholar from a university press. I am very sad she dies."

The melancholy of Venice hung in the deep set of his eyes. Teal had visited the water city many years ago in September, the young men shy but attentive, the sky gray and misty, herself ecstatic with the trip.

Teal returned to her mission and began to ask with tact about the book he might have bound for her friend in May. Anything about it he might remember. He raised both hands to protest.

"I no read but *Italiano.*" He tapped the book. "I bind with the finest materials, paper from *Firenze,* hides cured in Germany, twenty-three karat for tool. But I no read."

His expression communicated the depth of her offense.

"No. Of course. That's not what I meant. I only need to know if she or her husband picked up that book?" Teal asked.

They both knew what she'd meant.

"Sometimes she collect, sometimes I send. Nobody else."

Dignity remained offended. Teal tried a helpless smile.

"Nancy Vandenburg was my best friend. I cared about her, care still. You see, I think someone was trying to scare her at the end before her death, and it makes me mad. Knowing this about her last book might tell me who."

Northern or southern, Italians unified on issues of loyalty to friends and family. The man's expression softened as he nodded his agreement.

"I look," he said and disappeared into the back room.

He returned with a flat desk calendar, "DIMASI'S PLUMBING AND FIXTURES" printed across the top. Still behind the counter, he paged through the months to May. May 1, 2, 3 . . . 15, 16—he tapped a knuckle at the date.

"I call her, leave a message it is ready." He pursed his lips at May 17 and 18. *"Sì, sì.* First she call back to say send, then before we can, she collect. My wife makes the note."

He handed the calendar over to Teal.

Teal shook her head. "I'm sorry."

The craftsman chuckled. "You no read *Italiano? Sì?"*

"Sì." Teal smiled.

"I read it to you. 'Lady come for book. Very pleased.' " He beamed.

"So she picked it up this time." Teal tried to hide her disappointment.

She suddenly hated all the rain she'd walked through, all the hope accrued with each footstep. The rain continued to pound the street outside the store. Depression settled to the base of her throat. She hated the whole lousy morning.

"You couldn't know what time of day she stopped by, could you?" Teal asked.

The question was a stall. A percussion of drops chattered against the window and the door.

He placed a finger to the side of his nose. He lifted it and shrugged before he nodded.

"My wife is visiting her sister, I ask her next week and *telefonata."*

"Don't bother," Teal said.

She only meant to delay her exit into the grim day. An answer wasn't important enough to be complicated by her being away next week.

"No, I telephone." The man spoke with force.

"Of course," Teal revised.

She'd enlisted his help and must accept it with grace. She dug a business card from her purse.

"I won't be available, but please, my secretary will expect to hear from you."

Teal wrote Kathy's name above the printed "E. TEAL STEWART" and circled the office number.

Outside, a persistent wind and darker sky brought the rain up under her umbrella. Her disappointment matched the soaking. She had to admit to herself she couldn't prove Michael's guilt in one easy trip.

And she hadn't.

On Hanover Street, she stepped into the Cafe Pompeii. Men in sharply tailored suits sat at the front tables smoking unfiltered cigarettes and arguing in loudly expressed Italian. The shadows of the back revealed a pair of adolescent lovers. Teal chose a midpoint and ordered cappuccino with a *sfogliatella,* trying to pretend a continental air. In Italy, of course, only tourists took cappuccino at this time of day. She shrugged. Boston was not Italy.

The pastry shattered into sweet flakes and the milk-foamed espresso slid hot and strong over her tongue. She almost never drank coffee anymore. The java jolt raised her pulse and stimulated frenzied thoughts. She made herself turn from Nancy to next week's vacation.

She succumbed to her yearning to be in Baja, to climb the mountain at sunrise, to smell the hot, dry Mexican air, to join the conversation of women at the end of the day. Memory stirred in new apprehension. How would the Ranch feel without Nancy?

How could Nancy be dead?

Michael.

Teal lingered over his name. Felicia's story of her trip to the studio pointed to Michael's knowing about the journal that celebrated his wife's infidelity. Teal could imagine his anger.

Her surety deflated as quickly as it had come. The

bookbinder had said Nancy fetched the journal. Teal pressed her temples with her thumbs to think again. Maybe Michael saw the book another way, maybe in the Lincoln studio. Felicia had caught him there once.

Now Felicia's confession made Teal queasy. So Felicia had wanted to talk to Nancy enough to violate the privacy of Nancy's studio. The action may have been unfortunate but not heinous. Not enough to merit a confession. What unspoken guilt made Felicia claim a need to tell all to Teal?

Teal shrugged as she stood. Felicia's story provided a strike one for Dan: Michael had overheard the bookbinder's call.

Did Michael learn more? Teal nodded. Yes. In the euphoria of a caffeine high, she imagined finding strikes two and three.

Absolutely.

Albert shifted, uncomfortable on his feet. When he asked for Mrs. Stewart, the receptionist gave him one of those looks. When he stood closer to the high barrier surrounding the opulent desk, she pointed him to the reception area. But he didn't like sitting, sunk trapped and foolish in a big square thing that passed for a chair.

"Excuse me. Are you looking for Ms. Stewart?"

The girl was as pretty as any he'd seen. Face like a heart framed by a cloud of dark hair and given grace by such kind eyes.

"That's me," Albert said.

He tried to lever himself up by pushing against the seat. His hand sank.

"I'm afraid she's not in. I'm her secretary. Can I help?"

Albert liked her even better now as he stood. Like his Tina, she made him feel tall. He wished it was as simple as accepting her offer.

"No. I need this Teal Stewart." He waved the business card.

The girl hesitated and he wondered if she planned to ask him, politely, to come back again. But he couldn't. He couldn't come back ever again. This was Tina's only chance. He'd been awake the night, making calls to Sam and battling the demons of terror. He bargained away everything in his deal with God. He couldn't leave.

Perhaps the girl saw his resolve.

"Why don't you come with me? I expect her back any time now."

He wanted to kiss her bright engagement ring and tell her fiancé he was one lucky guy. He wanted to sing.

Tina, honey, he kept thinking as he walked the fancy corridor, *Tina, honey, trust me. I can make things fine. You know what I mean? I can make it so you won't die.*

That's the deal, right, God?

? TWENTY-FIVE

Thursday.

Impulse made Teal stop at the massive skyscraper housing SGM. She scanned the lobby directory and set out to visit Renee. The elevator shot her through forty-seven floors in the minute during which she wondered what words to use. A minute proved insufficient.

"Please. I realize my request is a terrible imposition on your privacy," Teal concluded at the end of her speech.

"Do you?"

Teal heard a tired cynicism at the edge of Renee's droll comment, but Renee did not turn away. Teal restated her point.

"If I could read the journal, I might see what triggered the threat. It could lead me to the creep."

Renee, composed and controlled, little resembled the drunk and devastated woman of two days ago. Every hair lay groomed on her head, her pin-striped suit denoted restraint. Her eyes remained calm and opaque and her lips still.

Impatience hurried Teal, but the silent seconds accumulated. She tried to contemplate the distant view and wondered, for a moment, if her request disturbed Renee. Teal wouldn't want her affairs exposed, the innards of intimacy laid bare. Teal prepared to give up when Renee inclined her head.

"I want you to understand my agreement has nothing to do with those disgusting mail threats. They aren't important. I want you to learn how she loved me, whatever the world may believe. Yes, I'll get the journal for you." Renee gestured for Teal to wait.

Teal considered the unspoken challenge laid down by Renee. *Accept me. Recognize me.* This was not the attitude of someone afraid of public exposure.

Renee returned with a briefcase. She opened it, then hesitated.

"I'll expect this back tomorrow."

"I understand," Teal said.

"Do you?" Renee asked, but withdrew her hand and extended the journal to Teal.

Senior managers at Clayborne Whittier enjoyed a certain freedom. As long as Teal satisfied client demands, directed her staff, and pleased the partners, she could use the occasional daylight hour for herself. She called Kathy from the lobby.

"I don't think I'm going to make it back today," she said.

"What should I do with the man waiting in your office?" Kathy asked.

"What man?"

Teal as much as heard Kathy raise her hands in a gesture of doubt over the line.

"He's old and small and refuses to tell me his name. But he must really want to see you since he's been sitting in there for over an hour."

Nan's journal burned in Teal's hand. Teal couldn't return to Clayborne Whittier right now, not even to help Kathy get rid of the guy.

"You can tell him to try me after the funeral tomorrow. Otherwise, he can see me when I return from vacation."

"Okay, boss," Kathy said.

Teal smiled at Kathy's disapproval and placed the handset in its cradle. The plastic bag she had carried to the North End teetered on the shallow counter and threatened to slide to the floor. Now it held two books. Teal almost did not save the bag from its fall.

She wasn't sure she wanted to read Nancy's private words to Renee.

The sky's murderous gray cleared to worn blue as Teal walked up Devonshire Street. In this section of the financial district, to see the sky at all required contortions of the neck. Few people did other than push ahead. Lone individuals were forced to dodge sidewalk-clogging groups, and everyone played chicken with the cars at a green light.

Teal turned at Milk, the street's buildings older and lower, and skirted the colorful flower stall beside the Old South Meeting House. She circumnavigated a couple who were eating take-out as they ambled down the street. Finally, the edge of Boston Common opened a broader horizon. Teal quickened her stride.

The aged, the unemployed, and the lonely made the park their home. Bold squirrels and scavenging pigeons snatched stale and sodden popcorn off the ground. A messenger on roller blades sprayed through puddles as he whirred by, spinning city mud across anyone in his path. The yellow rubber boots spared Teal a splattering.

She paused to watch a child urge his kite into the sky. The bright pink fabric teased and stretched and bounced, but would not catch the air. Teal chose to ignore that a certain reluctance, not pleasure, dragged her step. Renee's journal, clutched to her side, began to feel like unwanted freight.

Should she read the journal uninvited by Nancy? Worse, would it rob her of the Nancy she was comfortable knowing? The irony of life, Teal realized, is in getting what I sought.

A little girl ran across Teal's path. Blonde curls bounced around a serious face as she ran to challenge the boy for control of his kite. Teal grinned and thought of Libby.

Libby. At once Teal longed to hug her goddaughter, to bring back an image of Nancy innocent of adult passions and desires. A visit to Libby could be a legitimate excuse to defer inspection of the book. Teal turned from the path home to the entrance to the garage sunk under Boston Common.

The garage smelled heavy with exhaust. Some vehicles owned by residents of Beacon Hill were crusted with grime from lack of daily use. Teal spared her car that abuse with a canvas tarp. She found her car parked, as usual, close to the security of the exit.

Even under a shroud of bilious green, the 1959 Mercedes 190SL sports coupe pleased Teal. She rolled back the canvas to reveal a charcoal gray hardtop which gleamed in tribute to her hours of hand buffing. The cream body gave Teal a shiver of pleasure as she eyed the car's curves and soft edges. She stowed the cover in the trunk, then opened the driver's door. The interior scent of saddle soap on fine red leather filled her nose.

Teal dropped into the seat, swiveled her legs under the low steering wheel, and closed the door with a satisfying thump. She turned the key and pressed the starter button before she shifted into reverse. The dowager car backed into the lane. She clutched to engage first, and the trip to Lincoln was underway.

Throughout the drive, her mind never left the road or her senses the feel of the automobile. She let herself forget Nancy and the journal and her own concerns. She succumbed, as she always did, to the joy of driving. Time spent with the 190SL never disappointed.

Libby greeted her with shrieks of delight and the young nanny with gratitude for an hour's relief. Together adult and child sat on the porch swing and tended to Victoria's endless needs. Bottle, burping, changing, dressing, teaching, and hugging until the doll became as alive to Teal as to Libby. Teal finally rose to go.

"Victoria has a secret for you," Libby said as she grabbed Teal's leg.

"And what is that?" Teal asked. She regarded the girl and doll with a serious face.

"She wants to whisper," Libby said as she lifted her doll.

Teal knelt and inclined her head to the little plastic mouth.

"The night before Mummy went to heaven on the Cape—"

Libby stopped to evaluate Teal's attention. Satisfied, she resumed. "The witches and warlock hid under the bed with the stupid old alligator. Victoria says she was afraid, but I wasn't."

Teal remembered Nancy telling her about this new phase, the phase of imagined beings. They provoked a curious terror and delight. They were also, Nancy said, a handy insight into Libby's fears and fantasies. Teal recognized she lacked the skill or familiarity of a mother, but the little girl expected her to try.

"I imagine you were very brave," Teal said and held Libby and Victoria in a gentle embrace.

"I was. I was even when they screamed at each other. Yelling isn't right."

The child's self-righteous assertion contrasted with the expression on her face. There she fought the urge to cry. Libby held on to Teal in a tight hug.

"What did I do to make my mummy leave?" she whispered.

Then the tears came, as dense and furious as the morning's rain.

Teal's surety grew on the drive home. Libby had heard telephone calls and arguments among the four. Nancy. Michael. Carole. Felicia. And, after Felicia left, the three.

Libby's childish voice had repeated Michael's words to Nancy, "don't you dare walk out on me."

Then innocent Libby had mimicked Carole's intervening, "leave her alone."

At least that was Teal's interpretation of the tangled words Libby mouthed in a pitch of fear and emotion. How awful for a child. No wonder Libby asked Teal about the bad warlock. Nancy's daughter believed he had spirited her mother away.

Libby had strung "lover, a fair, no shame, done tomorrow" from her memory of voices mixed, confused, and raised.

Teal had rocked Nancy's daughter until the child grew peaceful, then Teal laid her cheek against the silky hair. When the nanny entered the porch, Teal passed the dozing girl into her arms. Teal kissed the sleeping cheek one last time before she left.

In the miles between Lincoln and Boston, Libby's jumbled words repeated in Teal's mind.

"I could kill you," the warlock had said.

Did he add "before I'll let you leave me?" Did Libby repeat Michael's words, or was that what Teal wanted to believe?

A car roared across the painted lane line to dart in front of the 190SL. In the downshift, she ground the gears.

"Shit," she said, desperate to be home, and tried to remember a world as innocent of true evil as Libby's.

Home would mean a glass of wine, a loaf of whole wheat bread, and reading Nancy's journal. Resignation shook Teal's head. There was no escaping duty. No escaping her promise to Nancy or the challenge of helping Nancy's child.

The sporting activity beside the Charles presented its usual after-work pitch.

Bicycles and joggers, diminutive children and darting dogs crisscrossed the paths visible from Teal's kitchen. A lowering sun reflected silver streaks across the water and brought orange-tinted pink to band the western horizon. The triple-glazed windows and Hunt's clever installations deadened to near silence the whine of traffic on Storrow Drive. Tonight Teal, who had insisted on this construction, felt not gratitude but abiding isolation.

She chose to describe her life as solitary, but this evening she could not avoid lonely.

A single glass of wine stood on the counter. A single book waited by the living room's most comfortable chair. Tomorrow she must attend the funeral of its author and her most intimate friend. She fought the panic of desertion, the anger of despair.

Teal sipped the Calera Pinot Noir and spread goat cheese on a piece of whole wheat bread. She pretended that she chose to eat alone at the kitchen window. She gazed at the Charles, contemplating what?

Her failure to be there for Nancy? Her dissatisfactions with her career? Even the Ranch promised little solace this year. The hacienda for two would make her feel more alone. Nancy's death had stripped a protective illusion of community from Teal's life.

The sun rested on the river's distant bend as Teal raised her glass. There were many ways to be dead.

The buzz of her doorbell broke into her morose thoughts.

"Who is it?" Teal asked at the intercom.

"Private business with Teal Stewart," came the reply.

"And you are?" Teal asked.

"Albert Fontane," the voice said.

Albert Fontane. The man who had killed Nancy.

"I'll be down."

Teal didn't explain she couldn't buzz him in, a practice unsafe in the city. She descended three flights to the street door and flipped the dead bolt.

The minute Teal saw Albert on the stoop, she recognized him for Kathy's secretive little man. His brow glistened with perspiration. He rocked from his heel to his toe and back again.

"Miss Stewart, I have to talk to you. Know what I mean?" he begged.

Teal only cracked the door ajar. She didn't know what he meant. She didn't know what he wanted her to do.

"Look, your pretty secretary didn't give me your address. I snooped. Don't take me wrong, I wouldn'ta done it but for Tina."

He raised his shoulders and let them fall.

"Please. The police at Shell Bay laughed at my confession, but I told the truth. I killed your friend," he said.

The hairs tingled on Teal's arms. Albert Fontane hadn't meant accident when he said killed. She jerked the door wide.

"No. You come out. I don't have time. Hospital rules. How can they be so crazy when my wife needs me? They say she'll die. Not Tina!" Albert grabbed Teal's arm. "The sand messed me up. The car skidded and I hit her bad. The contract'd been specific. An accident, see. But the sand screwed me up."

Teal could smell fear in his sweat. She began to sweat, too.

"What do you mean, contract? Someone paid you?"

Teal couldn't feel the step beneath her feet. "Who, Albert? Who?"

She shook him, hard.

Albert's eyes darted around. He wouldn't look at her, but began to mumble.

"First the deal's on, then off, then last minute, the kind I hate, it's go. Last minute means problems every time. God, I'm sorry. Tina, she's everything to me. Somebody has to believe me."

"Why? Why, Albert?" Teal yelled in his ear.

Michael might be capable of playing silly paper games, but set Nancy up for murder? Teal didn't want Albert to make sense, but in her core she believed his words.

"Why?" Albert stuck out a lip. "I never ask, know what I mean? Now there's Tina's sickness and all, so I wrung his guts to tell me. All he says is make the lady forget the affair. Crazy, isn't it! I'm supposed to knock sense into her with a car? Jesus!"

Anxiety pierced Teal while Albert Fontane confused her.

"Who is *he*? Who wanted to end the affair?" she hissed.

Albert stared at Teal. She tried a different question.

"Why come to me?"

Albert nodded. "You get somebody punished. Make the cops find the crazy who hired me. I gotta get justice for Tina."

Teal had to be sure of what her gut believed.

"Mr. Fontane, the Cape investigation concluded Nancy's death was the result of an accident. You said accident just now. Your wife's illness must be a terrible stress, but this new fiction won't help."

"Fiction? This isn't fiction, lady." Albert backed away from her down the steps. "You don't get the cops, I'll go after the contract myself. I thought you'd want to help because of your friend."

He spit the words out between a snarl and a moan.

Teal collected her wits as he unlocked the door of his double-parked car.

"Is 'he' Michael Britton?" she shouted as he climbed in.

"You tell the police," the agitated old man screamed.

Teal watched him drive away.

Strike two, she realized, must be the threat Libby heard Michael yell at Nancy. But strike three? Teal considered Albert Fontane's words. Horrible images crowded her mind. Contracts and accidents and Michael. Could it be?

Could she prove it?

? TWENTY-SIX

Friday.

Yes, it could, Teal realized at three in the morning, the journal resting on her lap.

If Michael *had* read the intimacies it exalted, *had* known himself cuckolded—Teal could only imagine the extent of his humiliation. She sat straighter against her pile of goose-down pillows.

One recounting of Michael Britton's history could sound like the American success story. An intelligent, charming young man born into adversity who worked hard to make good. But Teal considered Carole's unsentimental assessment—Michael Britton would revert to his origins as a petty hood without Nancy.

If her loss was imminent, what might Michael have done?

Teal knew he read the occasional mercenary rag. He was capable of hiring an Albert Fontane or worse. If Nancy's affair made him angry, imagine his fury if he had read Nancy's will, the proof she was preparing to leave. The chronology fit Fontane's description of a contract switched on and off and on again.

Maybe the onset of the long family weekend gave Michael the hope of settling issues more amicably. Michael didn't want his wife dead. He wanted what was hers to continue to be his. Did Nancy's assertion the marriage was over force the final contact with Albert?

Teal tried logic.

Logically, the scheme was ludicrous, but human emotion didn't operate like an equation. Teal considered the emotion in Nancy's journal. For all the many things it told Teal about the depth and pleasure of Nancy's love, it revealed nothing to identify the lover or the lover's gender. An intuitive eye might have guessed, maybe right and maybe wrong. Nancy, even baring her joy, had remained vigilant in shielding her privacy. One was left to wonder, not to know.

Wonder enough to allude to perversion in streaks of orange?

Nancy's love, in any manifestation, was not perverse to Teal, could never be. Her best friend's words, strung in artless poetry, in doodles and drawings, proclaimed Nancy loved as a fully realized woman is able to love. The record of her evident joy returned a memory of Nancy whole. Teal could imagine Michael's reaction to reading the journal.

Teal laid her cheek against the cover and traced the tooling of the bookbinder's art. She had resisted Carole's wish to meet the lover, mindful of Nancy's privacy. The reluctance had faded with this reading. Renee deserved the comforts of Nancy's sister and community.

Teal thought about the service tomorrow, its implicit demand on the living to loosen Nancy to eternal peace. Teal wasn't ready to let go. Not when her failure to help Nancy left so terrible a guilt.

The green digits of the bedside clock read too late to disturb Dan Malley, but the reservations desk in Baja, California, remained open twenty-four hours. Teal reached for the telephone. When the conversation ended, she cradled the book.

"I'll make things as better as I can, Nan," she vowed.

Felicia tossed and turned, restless and uneasy with dreams.

A distorted Nancy chased her down an elongated corridor clutching *SELF* while John smirked and sang "you report to me, no choice, no choice." The sports car rose from her trash reassembled to start with a bigger-than-life roar. It pursued her through a hospital's day surgery, IVs tumbling and nurses screaming. Felicia jolted awoke at three A.M. to the croak of her own voice trying to say "no."

The bed was a night nest of sweat and tangled covers, the pillows flung to the floor. The hotel ventilation system ground out stale air. The sticky glaze of a nightmare's fever burned her brow, gummed her eyes, but she shivered. Tomorrow she must stand beside Nancy's ashes lowered to the ground, must weep and murmur comfort to the other bereaved. The thought set Felicia shaking.

Dinner rose in her throat and stung the back of her nose. She gagged it back down. Amends, she must make amends. She took no comfort from her cowardly altered confession to Teal. Somewhere in Carole must reside the capacity for mercy. Somewhere it must reside in herself.

Felicia did what she had never done as an adult. She slipped from the bed to her knees.

"Our Father," she started as she knelt.

Carole slept with her hand on Libby's head, and the little girl snuggled against the comfort of her aunt.

The old farmhouse in Lincoln gave an occasional creak and moan, the dog busied himself with a hunter's dream and the grandfather clock chimed three.

Carole bobbed and surfaced in the depths and to the

edge of sleep. She hugged Libby closer and murmured, "Nancy, Nancy."

They drifted together in Carole's head, back to the house on Lake Michigan's shore, back even to the time before, Nancy in utero, when Carole had said, "Mummy, Mummy, we don't need another little girl. You make me a kitten!" And Carole dreamed a sleeper's silent laugh at that family lore.

She wrapped herself more against memory, her sister embodied in her sister's child. Neither woke until dawn.

At three A.M., Michael crashed his fist through the studio's wall and kicked his foot at the baseboard molding.

Nothing at all had turned out the way he meant. The years of upward mobility had come down to this, him being shown the figurative door. He boxed an uppercut with his right and plaster fell. The old moves came back, the moves that had made Mickey Brosky the toughest kid on the toughest block, the moves that had made him a contender for the Golden Gloves. All a long, long time ago and in another lifetime. Only that wasn't really so.

It was in his lifetime, his lifetime of using every shitty little advantage, seizing every sop available to the demographer's invention, the working poor.

Things began to change when he was admitted on academic probation to the state university. He entered as Michael Britton and hung up the gloves. He never turned back, never went home again, not even when the old man died, finally, of emphysema. Served the bastard right.

He shed his past with ease. Public relations moved him from shop to shop, always moving up, until he formed his own company. Meeting Nancy on that plane was like found money. A classy, famous, gorgeous blonde who'd never been laid. Imagine that, Mickey B. marrying the equivalent of the American flag. It had been some life.

He hooked a left against the hapless wall and listened

to something else fall. Why'd she have to mess it up and die? He pounded the door.

Michael Britton collected himself. He stroked an imaginary tie to push away the memory of undershirts at the table, the echo of the old man's disgusting hack. He flicked the dust from his hands. Tomorrow his wife would be laid to a final rest. He thought about Carole sleeping with Libby in the house.

He thought he might just get away with it.

Renee slept the sleep of the drugged.

She did not hear the three A.M. round of the building's security guard. He passed through the quiet floors and in the health club settled down to watch television.

Not a dream busied Renee's head, not a movement disturbed her body. She had deliberately saved, and as deliberately taken, her last two sleeping pills. They allowed her to find relief through the hours of the night before Nancy's funeral. *The Globe*'s obituary had reported the service was closed to all but close friends and family.

Before she slept, Renee considered the notice and laid out her decision on a bedroom chair—a suit in sober blue and an ivory shirt. Pearl earrings waited on her bureau. She fantasized an introduction which identified her as she was, Nancy's lover. But Renee recoiled in horror at the threat of exposure. She accepted the camouflage of her public persona. She would attend the funeral as the minor collector she was, giving to Michael the claim of spouse.

Before the tiny pills had taken their merciful effect, she shook with a terrible understanding. It had never been meant to turn out this way. Never.

Suddenly it didn't feel good at all to be Renee in bed at forty-one, alone and living a lie. Nancy had promised to be the turning point. Renee clutched her head and curled in anguish before slowly, inexorably, the pills dulled guilt and pain to oblivion.

Three A.M. woke Sandra Jordan with an urge to raid the refrigerator.

The freezer yielded a frostbitten quarter of a Sara Lee double-chocolate fudge cake. Sandra hit the microwave defrost button. Seconds later, she removed the slice, an uneven hunk of steam and ice. The frosting slid off one side, slick and melted, where on the other it clung in icy shards. Sandra did not notice. She heaved the cake into the trash, her breath in short, shallow gasps.

The gooey lump could not fill the empty place, the anger chewing her inside. There had to be a better way.

Sandra could name the obsession of her present, the obsession of her past. She could name the woman who, fifteen years ago, had ruined her life.

Renee Maxwell.

What she couldn't name was a way to make the obsession go away. Eating certainly didn't do it. Sandra wanted to laugh but found herself crying, sobbing largely, her head banging defeat against the table. The joys of vengeance had turned out a bitter brew.

❓ TWENTY-SEVEN

Friday.

"Amazing grace how sweet it is to save a wretch like me who first was lost but now am found, was blind but now can see."

The choir of Roxbury's Baptist Church rose in an abundance of gospel energy. They sang at Nancy's specific request. "No pallid eulogy for me, but please, a triumphal celebration of dust's return to dust and the spirit loose and free. Sing and clap me home," her will read.

If there was no thunderous meeting of hands, there were backs that swayed, heads that bobbed, and voices that soared in the Lord's praise. The staid New England church overflowed despite the obituary's instruction. People crowded the outside steps as they spilled from the building. A gentle breeze brought the smell of new mowed Lincoln lawns to fill the nave.

The service ended with a benediction for everlasting peace. Michael, Carole, and Libby accepted condolences at the door while the minister hovered around the trio. He ordered the pace at which the line of mourners passed the family. His ministrations left them free to hug and cry and greet.

Carole tried to believe the service's offer of peace.

Healing might come slowly, but it must come. She nodded rote acceptance to words of sympathy and sent each shaking hand or pair of lips grazing her cheek to Michael all but sight unseen. She steadied Libby, cupping the child's fair head against her body. Many reached down to stroke the little girl with a light pat and word meant to buttress the child's bravery.

Michael marred the picture and Carole shrank from his presence at her side. He repelled her like a magnet placed wrong-way-round. Today Carole judged him guilty of the worst sin, the sin of inadequacy. His failings sent her sister into a lover's arms and brought to their lives fighting and disharmony. Carole blamed Michael for Nancy's death.

Worse, she blamed herself.

She had stood in the bedroom window, mute, to wave at Nancy as her sister ran to meet her death. Carole remembered pleading with Nancy the night before to confide her plans, to move with caution. Now Carole wondered. Could any words have changed the outcome? She would never know why Michael had insisted on running with Nancy.

Carole wanted to scream, but found herself struggling to nod at the phrases of comfort whispered in her ear.

Finally, the last solicitous hand freed hers, the last kiss dried on her cheek. She stopped murmuring automatic gratitude for each attendee. Libby gave a last bob and curtsy, and Carole felt a pang of pride. Libby deserved an aunt who tried to make up for the child's incomprehensible loss.

Teal joined Renee at the edge of the crowd.

"You came—I'm glad," Teal said.

Renee tipped her head to Carole and Libby in the distance.

"She's such a beautiful child. I'd only seen pictures. I

met Carole before, an opening." Renee shrugged away an unspoken pain. "I never saw Nan with her family. I never really thought of them together."

Teal looked across the lawn before she turned back to Renee.

"Carole wants to meet you."

Renee's face showed confusion as Teal realized the error.

"I meant she wants to extend Nancy's lover the comfort of family. She has no idea you—"

"Are a woman," Renee said.

"No," Teal agreed.

Renee shook her head. "I'm not ready. Not yet."

The reaction surprised Teal, but then she'd never been in Renee's position. Teal hesitated. She hadn't considered Renee might reject the plan. Teal decided to change her strategy and omit further mention of Carole.

"You can't have much work next week with Fruiers settled early," Teal said. She realized she sounded silly.

"Criminal lawyers never want for work," Renee replied.

The offense in Renee's voice expressed a disbelief Teal could speak of work at a funeral.

"That's not what I meant. You see, every year Nancy and I spent time at a place called The Ranch. We were booked for next week. Starting tomorrow, actually."

Renee continued to stare with disbelief.

"I'm asking you to come with me. Please," Teal said.

Waiting, she discovered her offer wasn't simply a favor to Renee. Perhaps Renee understood.

"Tomorrow?" Renee asked.

Teal inclined her head.

"I'm a way of not losing Nan, aren't I? You're lonely, too." Renee's lips almost smiled. "What time's our flight?"

Teal watched Renee walk to her car. The private inter-
ment included only family and special invitees. Teal
would ask Carole then. She turned to join the family.

Carole patted Teal's hand. "The music was lovely,
don't you agree? It brought her into the church."

Teal looked harder at Carole, beside whom she'd sat
through the songs and spoken remembrances of Nancy.
Carole's demeanor, elegant and groomed, almost
masked her exhaustion and denial. Teal hoped Carole
would agree as she shepherded Carole and Libby to the
waiting limousine. Michael slid in from the other side.

"I'll meet you all at the cemetery," Teal said and bent
to kiss each offered brow.

Michael caught her eye, smug in his role as husband.
He allowed her a somber nod. She wanted to shake the
insolence from his face, but knew she must not make a
scene. Not today.

Teal kept the dowager to a creep behind the black
hearse. Temporal majesty, Teal thought. That life was
fleeting for everyone did not help her accept Nancy's
death. Carole couldn't accept it either, Teal realized, and
understood Carole's passivity.

Mount Auburn cemetery was cool and green beneath a
powdered blue sky. A late dogwood shadowed Nancy's
plot and dropped white petals on the pond. Monuments
and headstones bordered curved paths which rose with
the gentle roll of grassy hills.

Nancy's mourners bunched together to stare at the
foot square of earth into which her ashes had been lowered earlier in the day. A single calla lily lay across the
dark soil.

The plot had come to Carole and Nancy through their
mother. The sickly bluestocking was interred in Michigan beside her robust Dutch husband. Carole, wanting
her sister close, chose to bury Nancy beside more distant
relatives.

Teal turned Carole aside before the group broke.

"Carole, come with me to the Ranch this week. Please. Nancy would approve," Teal said to prime agreement.

"I booked a day ago," Carole replied.

The statement set Teal back. She'd been prepared to persuade Carole, make the case Libby could survive a short separation and Carole needed respite. For a moment, Teal found herself resenting Carole's independence. The relationship with Carole would never be like the one with Nancy, but she had the right result, a chance to introduce sister and lover.

Carole's face contorted as she pointed to Michael. He held Libby high in the air. His daughter squirmed with delight and terror.

"He thinks he can seduce me, the fool, because of her. As though I'll let him get away with using my niece. 'We'll work together, won't we, Carole? For Libby,'" Carole mimicked. Fury distorted her voice. "Why did Nancy let him go with her? Why did she do this to me?"

Teal could see Carole's grief progress to anger from denial. Carole might blame Michael but she raged at Nancy. Teal recognized her own inability to accept Nancy's death. Why hadn't Nancy said anything that afternoon at Clayborne Whittier? Why hadn't she told the whole truth?

But Nancy hadn't nor had Teal kept her word. Help me, Nancy implored and Teal promised to. But Teal chose to push the obligation aside for a more convenient time.

Teal shuddered. The cemetery's raw earth told the story. Her help would come too late for Nancy.

It wasn't too late for the truth, Teal decided. If nothing else, she'd press Dan Malley to place Michael under police scrutiny while she introduced Renee to Carole at the Ranch.

Carole stroked the family obelisk as she spoke. "I can't make it to Baja until Monday."

"That's okay," Teal said.

Carole shrugged as though nothing could ever be okay. She left Teal to take Libby from Michael's arms. He sidled over to Teal's side.

"Lobbying hard against me? Don't believe everything you hear." He snorted his derision.

Teal shrugged. "In fact, we hardly mentioned your name. We talked about Carole's coming to the Ranch next week."

"Ah yes, the place of the annual pilgrimage with my wife. This year you go to mourn, no doubt, and Carole with you? How sweet. Let me thank you. *Gracias, mi amiga por su preocupación y su generosidad que les has prestado a me familia,*" Michael said in Spanish.

Teal knew she looked blank.

"Do you understand?" he asked. "No? Well I thanked you, my friend, for your concern and generosity to my family. You mean all these years going to Baja and you don't speak Spanish?"

"No."

"More's the pity. A second language is so useful."

Michael squeezed her arm hard as he turned to join the minister.

Felicia watched the black limo pull out. Teal followed in her signature Mercedes. The rest of the group had departed earlier. No one remained to recognize Felicia.

Under the dogwood she rehearsed her private eulogy, but could say only, "Nancy, forgive me," over and over.

"I took your suggestion and interviewed your Mr. Fontane at the hospital this morning," Dan said.

"And?" Teal asked.

"And he denied about everything you told me. Oh, he

admits he said he'd been hired—because his wife's illness has him rattled. He couldn't apologize enough to me for causing trouble. Teal, he doesn't have a record. He doesn't have a motive I can see, so I'm not sure what to say."

Dan Malley leaned back in the chair and stared at Teal. He shifted forward and cracked one knuckle then another.

"But I don't b-b-believe him," Dan said.

"No?"

"No. What are you doing to me?"

Teal raised her palms. "Help."

"Right." Dan set his hands on his knees. "The man is a wreck about his wife. The doctor treating her at the Farber considers your Albert a first-class nut."

Dan enjoyed the shared silence, Teal's face, attentive and alert. These were rewarding moments as a detective, the moments when fact and imagination began to arouse his enthusiasm for finding a difficult truth.

"You think he's lying," Teal suggested.

Dan cocked his head to the side. "I think he's a weird guy. I think he may be lying or unable to sort fiction from reality, but I don't know why. I think it will be hard as hell to prove."

Teal tapped her fingers on her desk. Dan heard the impatience, but there was nothing he could do. She slapped down her palm.

"Michael is the key. Don't you see—Albert Fontane has given up on the police. Shell Bay laughed at him, and he's scared you could take away his freedom while he needs to be with his wife. I think he figured out another way to even the score. He's going to go after the contractor. After Michael," Teal said.

"Maybe."

Dan didn't share Teal's optimism, but he knew the statistics. A female homicide screamed look to the husband.

"I'll be away next week. San Diego to visit my brother. Kathy says you'll be south of me at some resort?"

"Not exactly a resort," Teal said.

Dan chuckled at Teal's protest of his characterization of her destination.

"Let's give Britton-Fontane a rest for now. Your Albert should be tied to the hospital for a while, and the doctor promised to keep the police informed of anything too unusual."

"Michael's going to be in San Diego, too," Teal said after a beat.

"He is?"

"Yes. Organizing the West Coast leg of Nancy's retrospective." Teal pressed a thumb hard against her teeth. "I guess he can't do much harm in California—"

"But you'd like to be sure." Dan sighed. "Okay. I have a few friends out there. At least I can learn where he checks in and when he flies out. Don't worry, Teal, we'll get him sooner or later if he set up his wife."

Don Clarke walked in as Dan Malley walked out.

"Won't keep you but a minute," Don said. "Talking to Detective Malley again?"

The partner-in-charge sounded uneasy. Of course, the last time Teal had been involved with the police, she'd almost gotten herself killed. She grinned. That wouldn't be Don's concern. No. More likely he was worried she might embarrass the firm. The great firm. Teal grinned.

Don refused her offer of a seat. He loomed over her chair and she felt pinned to the spot. The silence became uncomfortable. Finally, his eyes seemed to latch onto Nancy's painting.

"She was quite a talent," Don said as he swiveled back to face Teal. "You've suffered a terrible loss with the death of your friend."

He cleared his throat. Teal waited.

"I just wanted you to know, while you are on vacation, Boston will be pulling for you, and there's always next year," he concluded with a pat on her back.

Teal tensed for all she'd been concentrating on her meditation breathing. She didn't bother to be polite. She forgot office protocol.

"What does that mean?" she asked.

She wanted to stand and pull Don square to look her in the eye. She didn't, of course. She started her apology.

"I mean—"

"No offense taken," Don interrupted. "I understand it's an emotional time for you, Teal. I'm not saying there's a problem."

Great, Teal thought. Clayborne Whittier doublespeak.

"We'll discuss the result of the partnership vote when you return. If it's yes, you already know Boston thinks you'll make a fine addition. If the full partnership doesn't think you're quite ready yet, remember there is next year."

"Not for me," Teal murmured.

Don looked uncomfortable.

"I'm not going to belabor the partnership's questions about you, Teal, but commitment is a big, big factor in admission and, frankly, that attitude of yours troubles even me. With the distraction of your friend's death right on the eve of the vote . . . Well, it can't be helped I realize," he fumbled.

Teal stood.

"Of course. How inconvenient of Nancy," she said.

"Now there, there, Teal! You've a good chance this year and as good or better next. That's all I came to say. Relax and enjoy your vacation."

She forced herself to nod agreement.

Clayborne Whittier, she thought after he left, who needs it? But suddenly nothing felt like it could ever be the same again.

"I can't think about this now," she whispered to Nancy's passive, painted woman before she pulled a set of financial statements to the middle of her desk.

At the end of the day, Teal unearthed the Nancy file with its copies of the creepy threats. She read her messy notes and remembered the morning she had created her suspect list. She couldn't pretend anything else to herself, the real purpose had been to escape the tedium of the Fruiers suit. But Fruiers had been settled with ease. Not so the troubles plaguing Nancy.

Teal read down the list. Did anyone, really, stand out as a murderer?

At the end she circled with a red pen "WHO BENE-FITS *NOW*—THE STATUS QUO?" and "Michael," and drew a tidy line through from "Carole, Felicia, Sotheby's" to "the lover? maybe." She considered the speculation listed beside "WHY THREATEN?"— "force Nancy to end the affair, force Nancy to show her hand, force Nancy to run to the lover—or force her away?"

Poor Nancy had reaped the harvest of betrayal, Teal mused. It didn't make a difference to see love provided the motivation. She crumpled the page into a ball.

Her lob missed the wastebasket. She picked up her briefcase and changed into walking shoes, then spent a minute with Kathy going over last instructions for the week. Kathy did the work of pushing her out the door.

At home on Brimmer Street, Teal found herself humming as she packed. *Amazing grace how sweet it is . . .* she stopped. How sweet was it for Nancy? She said aloud what she had to believe.

"The police will take care of him, Nan, you'll see. I'm sorry I failed you. God, so sorry. I'll do anything to let you rest in peace."

No, Teal thought. *It's not just for Nancy, it is for me.*

? TWENTY-EIGHT

The Ranch—Saturday.

The aircraft taxied to the end of the runway and began the thrust which raised it from the ground. In seconds, Boston receded, then disappeared below. They were flying to Baja.

Renee pressed back her seat and tried to gain reassurance from the hum of the engines bringing the airborne vehicle level from the steep ascent. She sort of listened to Teal's tales of her visits to the Ranch with Nancy, but as her attention drifted, Teal's voice linked with the other background noises.

Bumping turbulence and the bells that signaled reactivation of the seat belt sign jolted Renee to attention. Panic sharpened the nerves beneath her skin. She hated flying. Teal's deluge of words became a lifeline and Renee held tightly.

"And don't be intimidated by the know-it-all attitude of the annual returnees. The Ranch actually changes constantly. I think there is a special tax incentive in Mexico for capital improvements and management uses it. They are always ripping up and rebuilding the place."

Teal gave the details of last year's construction as the

seat belt sign clicked off. Renee's mind began to wander. Then the plane slammed into an air pocket.

". . . dispute last year. We were outraged. It cut off the sunrise mountain walk up to Skull Rock," Teal said. "You have to understand, Ranch folklore says souls inhabit each of the mountain's monolithic stones, but Skull is the most revered. I admit I've left small rock offerings at the base. The Ranch's answer to prayer candles, I guess. Nancy was more daring. She balanced little stones on Skull's top. A few of us took the unsanctioned walk. I promise to show you."

The plane rattled with a new pocket. Renee gripped the armrests and gasped shallow, airless breaths. The terror never abated, no matter how many miles she flew. Sweat began to itch her scalp. Fear rippled through her stomach. Teal stopped talking long enough to touch Renee's arm.

"This will be over when we break through the clouds."

Teal resumed her side of the conversation and Renee understood the CPA meant to help. She worked to pull herself from the abyss with Teal's words and concentrated hard.

". . . when I was maybe five, so I've never been afraid of flying. But snakes—I don't care what they say—snakes really bother me. Which reminds me, never climb the mountain in the heat of the day. Rattlers sun on the rocks. At least that's what they say, and I take the caution as gospel. Anyway, midday is far too hot for that walk. I like very early in the morning."

The ride stabilized. Renee's eyes came back in focus.

"Thanks," she croaked.

"No problem."

The remaining hours passed without incident.

They debarked in San Diego into an airport surging with the arrivals and departures, greetings and leave-takings. Renee followed Teal's lead. The luggage carousel stood four-deep with people from the full plane. Teal and Renee walked by without a pause.

"The one joy of carry-on," Teal said.

"Umm." Renee did not mention that her arms ached.

They dropped their bags at a gathering spot marked "The Ranch" and waited as the attendant ticked their names on a list.

"The next bus is in an hour. Please return ten minutes before and welcome to The Ranch, ladies," he said.

"There's pretty good soft-serve ice cream around the corner," Teal said. "Nancy and I always indulged. The last sin before a week of abstinence. Maybe the ritual . . ."

Renee recognized the uneasy hesitation.

"Isn't right this year? No. Let's eat," she said.

Teal was half-turned to Renee when they walked into the shop, but Renee could see the line beside the counter. She raised her eyes to concentrate on the list of flavors chalked on a blackboard and for a moment didn't notice the woman leaving with a double-chocolate cone. When Renee did, she couldn't believe her eyes.

"Sandra! What are you doing here?"

Sandra turned at her name, pretending surprise. The prop of the cone helped her steady her hand as she waved to Renee. After, her stomach pulled in knots when she dropped the ice cream in the trash outside the store's door.

"I don't believe a word she said."

Renee stood on the hacienda's patio, looking across the valley to the shadow of a mountain.

Everything about the Ranch had been as Teal promised. The grounds covered with flowers in bloom and the extensive facilities beautiful in the hot, dry desert air of Baja's interior. The staff welcomed Teal like an old friend and Renee like a new one. They had heard about Nancy and expressed sympathy with a promise the Ranch would bring her soul to her friends.

Right now, as twilight dropped to dusky night, Renee didn't know what to believe.

"She's using her year-end bonus? She just read about this place and decided to come?"

Incredulity pierced Renee's voice. She shook the handout from the front desk listing the week's guests.

"She booked too late to be included? That's my story, Teal, only you asked me to come. Do you think she's following me?"

"She says she read about the Ranch in *laMode,*" Teal said. "Articles like that always tempt me."

She shrugged.

"Doesn't it bother you it was the May issue?"

Renee thought of Nancy's beautiful face floating at the bottom of a mutilated page. What *did* Sandra know?

Teal shrugged again. "The May cover story was on spas. Nancy and I actually got a laugh out of the write-up on the Ranch. It said something stupid about sweating side by side with the *haute-monde* if you can believe it."

Teal's joking tone didn't hide her sober eyes. Renee rolled a cold glass of mineral water across her forehead.

"I can't figure Sandra Jordan out," she said. "Last week I asked her to join my practice group, although I was a little worried about the decision. She can be so, well, over-the-top somehow. But she hasn't said yes, not yet."

"Could she be, well, attracted to you?" Teal asked.

Renee started and searched Teal's face.

"No. Not according to my radar."

Teal looked blank.

"Radar—the homosexual's ability to identify a fellow traveler. No radar pickup with Sandra, trust me."

Renee watched a spontaneous smile curve Teal's lips.

"Radar—how wonderful," Teal said. "Is that how you and Nancy . . ."

Renee realized Teal would not finish her thought as much as she might want to know, to understand. Both of them needed a memory of their place in Nancy's life as whole, without secrets and doubt and betrayal.

"About Sandra," Renee said, cutting off a further probe, "her reaction to my offer doesn't sit right after the sucking-up she's done with me. I expected a yes and was so surprised, I called her old high school, but I never heard back. Now I really wish I had. There's something strange about—"

Teal's expression stopped Renee.

"You did hear. The day I stopped by your office? When you stepped out of the room the phone rang and your secretary didn't pick up . . . I meant to tell you. I spoke with some nun who was Sandra's teacher back then. The upshot is . . . I asked my secretary to do a little follow-up research."

Renee couldn't decide between fury and relief. Teal hadn't meant to tell her, at least that day. And she had forgotten about the conversation until now? Maybe.

"What did the nun say?" Renee asked.

"Oh, just some stuff about why Sandra became a lawyer. I guess she sat through some horrible trial involving her family when she was young. Kathy's trying to get the records and she's checking on the name change. She found out that Sandra Jordan was born 'Sandra Moses.'"

Renee dropped her glass. Shattered pieces spun across the brick patio, but she didn't notice. The Moses trial. How was she to know Sandra Jordan was the little girl sitting in that courtroom day after day?

Renee's laugh sounded nervous to her own ears.

"She thinks I killed her father."

———

Sandra lifted the banana from the welcome basket of fruit. She replaced it and ran a finger along the orange until citrus oils perfumed the room. She listened for the dinner gong as laughing women passed her window. Silence followed and left her feeling vulnerable and alone.

She closed her eyes and all the images that had chased her through years of sleepless nights gathered in her mind.

Her father behind the register in the corner variety store, the chewing gum and candy arranged in orderly rows, the cigarettes behind. Her mother bent over her with a picture book as Sandra repeated the letters her mother outlined with a long, tapered finger. The former schoolteacher brought to this late, beloved baby great patience and a greater ambition.

The images regrouped and Sandra was eleven, trying to make sense of what the whispering neighbors said.

My God, no! Tortured and killed for only $500! Lordy, Lordy save us all! And her such a Christian woman.

That day, Sandra's father barred the store with plywood and hid from judging eyes in the darkened room. Sandra hated herself now for wondering with everyone else why it hadn't been him. Why her mother waited for death between the rows of Christmas ornaments and trim, as ordinary as it was for her to mind the store while her husband made the deposit. "Keeps us from harm," he'd proclaim to everyone on the block as he walked to the bank twice each day. "No percentage in robbing us."

The stranger hadn't known that fact. Her mother faced the ignorant robber alone.

Sandra gagged, but she couldn't stop.

The police caught him only two hours later. The day before the trial started in late spring, Sandra's father left his room to remove the plywood and wash down the store. The smell of Clorox burned the back of her nose while her father talked to her about his faith in the rule of law and the power of justice.

The murderer received a young court-appointed lawyer. Sandra remembered she had prayed for him to die. "He'll be put away for life, that's enough," her gentle father said.

Her father was wrong. The man who murdered her mother had walked free within the week.

The court-appointed lawyer invalidated the case on evidence of the arresting officer's procedural error. After the judge dismissed, Sandra's father dropped her off at his sister's. Sandra had been too young to see what must come.

He reattached the plywood to secure the store. He pulled shut the blinds. He made fast the rope.

Poor man, the neighbors said. *At least he went quickly.*

At thirteen, Sandra stood before a different judge and affirmed her desire to change her name. But Sandra Jordan never forgot she was Samuel Moses's daughter. She never forgot the name of the young court-appointed lawyer, either, the one who garnered all the headlines, the one who forever defined a textbook arrest.

Sandra never forgot Renee Louise Maxwell.

? TWENTY-NINE

The Ranch—Sunday.

Teal accepted the pleasure of knuckles running down her spine. She exhaled to release tension as the woman moved to rotate her elbow in Teal's hip socket. The room was small and hot and dim. Berta, Teal's favorite masseuse, began to knead a buttock. The pungent odor of sage growing on the mountain swirled into the room. Teal inhaled to fill her lungs.

Other winds brought a whiff of boiling beans and a hint of sewage up from the village. That very earthy aroma also pleased Teal. Early morning blew sharp, astringent air across the grounds. Mesquite smoke perfumed cool evenings. She mused about them all, the hot and dry and spicy scents borne through the Ranch by the wind.

Her mind floated free of any boundary as muscles and joints loosened under Berta's attentions.

Teal blinked her eyes open and closed. She recalled her walk from the hacienda to this first of the week's massages, the far landscape a collage-drying green against a brown-red earth. Irrigation brought succulent green and bright flowers to the immediate grounds.

Everything within her sight and scent assured her she was not in Boston anymore.

A melody of New Age music sprinkled from a speaker into the tiny room. Teal heard oil squirt from Berta's plastic bottle before greased hands slipped against her flesh. Distant traffic carried an engine's whine, gears groaning on the rise and the suck of tires tugged by hot asphalt. Closer was the noise of work, of bricks tapped into place and the high-pitch whine of power tools.

The corridor outside echoed with the staff's gentle footfalls, their whispered voices trilling Spanish. A stool scraped across an adjacent floor and, from down the hall, Teal heard the faint slap, slap of hot sheets spun around the bodies lying prone on hard cots for an herbal wrap.

The hiss of a far fountain and driving beat powering an aerobics hour remained inaudible to Teal. She only heard the crunch of her hair pushed against her scalp by Berta's fingers digging stress and anxiety from her temples. Teal gave over to pleasure, the warmth of Berta's hands kneading the pectoral muscles beneath the sides of each breast.

Teal thought of Nancy and all the years of weeks shared at the Ranch, weeks of exchanged intimacies and confidences. But in this instant, Teal could think only of all that had been left unsaid.

They never wondered aloud at what Berta touched in their psyches. Teal hated that she would never know what Nancy thought. What impulse had made Nancy receptive to Renee?

Teal jerked.

"Lo siento, señorita."

"No, Berta, it's not you," Teal said.

She had flinched at realizing Nancy's decision to shut her out still struck her as a betrayal. Who else might feel the same way?

All of them, Teal decided, one way or another. Felicia

by Nancy's embrace of a new and different style in her art, Renee in not getting her own way, Michael with the disposition of Nancy's estate and the specter of divorce. Did this give Michael the greater motive to kill?

A breeze tugged Teal's naked, oiled skin, riffling goose bumps up her side. Berta rubbed strong fingers over Teal's spine and Teal's mind let the worry go. She'd leave Michael to the police.

"All done, *amiga*. No hurry to get up," Berta whispered.

The woman closed the door behind her exit.

Voices rose as women filled the corridor. Teal lay limp and drowsy. Something dropped in the room next door.

"Darn," Teal heard.

The intervening wall muffled Sandra's voice.

Teal listened for something further, but heard nothing. She sighed and rolled to her knees, then slid her feet to the floor. Tying shut her terry robe, she decided she didn't want to occupy a second more of her week with the mystery. She had come to the Ranch to find peace. Period.

Michael stared down on San Diego harbor as his knuckles turned white with his grip on the back of the chair. All manner of ocean vessel moved along the water, most owned by the U.S. Navy. Any other day, Michael would have watched the floating traffic with interest. Today he didn't register either the drama of sail or diversity of boats under engine power.

He faced the window blind with anger. He had been watched as he debarked, shadowed at his check-in. Mickey Brosky knew how to sense these things.

Well, someone was going to get what they deserved.

Michael dropped into the chair and pulled out his itinerary. Monday every hour belonged to the museum. Not so all of Tuesday, Wednesday, and Thursday. Here the schedule of meetings and negotiations allowed flexibility.

He raised the telephone.

"Front desk? I need to change my plans. Can you get me a car for the week?"

He nodded at the positive response.

"Fine. And can you give me directions now to a place just over the Baja line called The Ranch?"

He nodded again and hung up. Then he slipped the annotated paper into his wallet and rose from the chair.

Blood beat in his ears just like before a big fight, and he ducked and threw a right. Too heavy, too slow, and too old. The realization stopped him cold. He stared at the window again, sightless.

What had Teal always said when she and Nancy took off for their week? Something about how the Ranch and its mountain could bring inner peace. He smiled. This year he might just get to see if he agreed.

He saw the harbor come alive with aircraft carriers and yachts and kayaks. Mickey Brosky let Michael Britton relax.

? THIRTY

The Ranch—Monday.

Monday, Carole arrived in time for the morning stretch. She waved across the room to Teal, then pointed to Felicia and mouthed "she's here?" with an arch expression exaggerated by the query. But everyone acted civilly when they met in the lunch line.

"This place is so beautiful in the summer," Felicia said, sounding surprised, as the three of them headed out to the patio with their trays.

That's right, Teal remembered. Felicia took her annual week at the Ranch in late fall. Teal started to ask Felicia about the change this year when Renee arrived.

"Mind if I join you?" she asked, her tray of sliced yellow tomatoes and black bean soup held above the table.

"Put it down and sit," Teal said. She turned to Carole and Felicia. "You know Renee, don't you?"

"Sure," Felicia said. "You collect Nancy."

"That's where I've seen you," Carole said as she nodded. "You and Teal are old friends?"

She turned her head one to the other.

"More like old adversaries," Renee said.

The group around the table laughed and prepared to eat.

Carole unloaded a three-veggie pita sandwich, fruit, and a dish of cottage cheese from her tray. She tipped her chin at Renee's single soup.

"Your first time at the Ranch, right?"

"Yes," Renee answered.

Carole grinned. "Trust me, you'll starve on that. It can help to ask for more in Spanish—then they aren't so stingy."

"It's a language you speak?" Renee asked.

"Poorly," Carole conceded.

"And let's face it," Teal said. "The whole point of being at the Ranch is to go a little hungry. Loose a few pounds, get in shape—"

"Lay around on the massage table!" Carole laughed.

"Okay, you've got my reason," Teal said and smiled as she set to eating.

Sandra found the table last. Introductions were made all around. Renee looked at Teal under dark brows.

"Thoughts of work remind me—" Renee gestured at Sandra, "your secretary called."

Everyone swiveled to watch Teal.

"Does she want me to call back?" Teal asked.

"No, she gave me the message." Renee concentrated. "The bookbinder called. Nancy came in at about 11:30 A.M. He hopes that helps."

Carole broke the silence.

"Well? Does it?" She narrowed her eyes. "Whatever it is that necessitates a call on your vacation!"

Teal smiled her discomfort and wished Renee had told her privately. Renee's expression registered the same regret. But it was too late.

"Maybe." Teal shrugged. "So, what did everybody do this morning?"

"Wait a minute, Teal. What book?" Felicia asked.

Her voice sounded relaxed, but her hand shook as she raised her glass.

"It had to be her poetry, don't you think, Teal?" Carole said and turned to Renee. "Verse wasn't her forte, not like painting, but she enjoyed sharing her poems with a few of us. Teal and I each received one of her special books—"

"I did, too," Felicia interjected.

That made Felicia the second recipient, Teal realized. The one she hadn't been able to recall. It meant the gallery owner would have understood the bookbinder's message that day in the studio.

"I tried aerobics this morning," Sandra said, oblivious to the tension around the table.

Her innocent comment turned the group to talk of exercise, gossip, and massage. After lunch, Teal walked to the hacienda with Renee.

"Why did you bring up the book?" Teal snapped.

She wanted to like Renee for Nancy's sake, but wasn't sure she could.

Teal wondered if Nancy had held back from going straight to Renee, or if Renee had fought to keep the relationship a secret, whatever the ambitious lawyer now claimed? Either way, the force of such emotions could have provided motive for Renee. Had she had her lover killed? Teal didn't want to think these thoughts of the woman next door to her bed.

"Why did you bring up the book?" she repeated.

"Why?" Renee raised her eyebrows. "My litigator's habit. I wanted to watch the reaction."

"And did you learn anything?"

"Carole doesn't like Felicia. Sandra didn't have a clue. Everyone wonders why I'm here with you," Renee said. "Tell me, what day was this 11:30 A.M. pickup?"

Teal thought back to the calender on the shop counter.

"May seventeenth."

Renee stopped walking and closed her eyes. She shook her head in disagreement.

"Uh-uh. Not May seventeenth."

"What do you mean?" Teal asked although she wanted to forget about the damned book for now.

"May seventeenth at 11:30 A.M. Nancy was with me."

Teal felt her mouth open to protest. Renee reached out to stop her.

"Nancy met me at the Meridian Hotel and we spent the lunch hours in bed, eleven to two. Then I had to hurry back to the partners' monthly meeting. I'd taken the professional risk to prove, I don't know, something to Nancy about her importance to me," Renee said and spread her hands wide. "Trust me, you can ask what we did."

Her eyes sparkled an "I dare you."

Clayborne Whittier used the Meridian Hotel. One partner, who had flown in from the West Coast just for the day, was booked into a deluxe room for a few hours to freshen up before his meeting. But Nancy and her lover? Teal didn't need the details of their use of a hotel room rented by the hour.

"You're upset," Renee said.

Teal tried to grin. "No."

She couldn't explain without sounding jealous. Teal turned her attention from herself. She was missing the point. The point about Nancy not collecting the book of poetry herself.

Felicia's tale about the studio meant Michael knew about Nancy's book. But Teal had missed the obvious— Felicia knew, too. And Felicia had been angry with Nancy's artistic rebellion. What if Felicia had read the journal, could she have decided to distort Nancy's love and call it a perversion for her own purpose?

Could the bookbinder's wife have mistaken Felicia for Nancy?

The puzzle fell together in a different shape.

Here would be a web of betrayal and more betrayal. But who among the players had a motive to kill?

"Teal! Teal!"

Renee shook Teal into the day.

"Your secretary left a second message. Someone named Dan called to tell you Fontane booked a Monday flight to San Diego. His wife died Saturday night. When Dan knows more, he'll call here again."

Felicia lay on the lounge chair with one towel draped over her breasts and another shading the sensitive skin of her face. Otherwise, like Teal beside her, she sunbathed nude.

"Felicia, were you very angry with Nancy about her experiments in a new artistic style?" Teal asked.

She had turned to watch the gallery owner. Felicia did not disappoint. The redhead bolted upright, covers dropping from face and chest, and glared at Teal. Felicia snatched a towel back to her breasts, but not before Teal had seen what Felicia hid.

Felicia's nipples bore the dark stain of pregnancy.

? THIRTY-ONE

The Ranch—Tuesday.

Teal beat the sun on Tuesday and tiptoed out of her bedroom. Renee slept on undisturbed as Teal brushed her teeth and drank the day's first glasses of water in the shared bathroom. She wasn't sure what to believe in the tangled skein of Nancy's life. She tried to remember Felicia's words, her voice shrill with anger yesterday.

"Nancy didn't tell you about my pathetic little affair?" Felicia had snorted as Teal shook her head.

"No? How discreet for such close friends as you two. Not like Nancy and me." Felicia sank back into the chaise and raised glistening eyes to Teal. "I'll tell you what happened. Nancy laughed at me that night on the pier. Watched the fireworks and laughed. I wanted to hurt her as much as her indifference hurt me. But she didn't care about Michael's infidelity. That's when I made up my mind about the pregnancy."

"Michael used you, didn't he?" Teal had asked, feeling brutal. "He never intended more than a fling. Had you actually imagined he would leave Nancy?"

Michael might have misled Felicia into collecting Nancy's book in the North End. Made her promises anyone could have known would be broken. Teal had started to speak.

"Did he—"

"Stop it!" Felicia spit out. Hysterical laughter made her work to continue speaking. "Okay, I was a jerk. Don't you think I regret him? Don't you think I feel humiliated and ashamed? But this is the Ranch, Teal. Lighten up on women's frailties."

Felicia had made Teal squirm.

Teal gentled the hacienda door closed and took a breath of cool morning air. Yesterday, when the group started to make their plans for today, she'd said she wanted to climb the mountain at sunrise. No one, not Carole, Sandra, Felicia, or Renee, pressed to join her. Now she was grateful.

She needed the walk to be early and alone. She needed to regain her perspective. Felicia had a point.

The world glowed like a silver-nitrate photograph in the moon's reflected light. Teal saw her breath form clouds of fog in the cold. She moved faster now to heat up, knowing by the end of the climb the direct sun would have her sweating and hot.

Voices speaking Spanish drifted from the dining building and broke the eerie morning hush. There followed companionable laughter and the purposeful clatter of pots. The cooks and dining staff were up.

Past the first gymnasium, its architecture low and Mexican, around a cluster of haciendas and through the field of grapevine, Teal's remained the only footfall. An occasional light shone from a window. Nearing the base of the mountain, cultivation yielded to a thick grove of old trees. Here Teal left the authorized path to circle to the back of the mountain.

She'd climbed to Skull Rock with Renee yesterday, but that didn't count, not as a pilgrimage, not as it would today.

She began to climb. Coarse earth slid beneath her sneakers. Here and there a desultory tuft of tough grasses sprouted. Bushes of aromatic sage lined a stretch of path. For the most part, the mountain bared an ocher soil cut deep with the gullies of erosion. The ponderous rocks believed to harbor souls stood like families with an occasional rebel separate and alone. The dusty road curled and rose from the base of the mountain.

Teal reached the Ranch's boundary at a fence and gate posted "STOP NO TRESPASS." By-pass steps, meant to save the work of opening a cattle gate, remained. They were like tilted ladders joined at the top. A lone cow eyed Teal with bovine indifference as she descended.

An edge of orange at the horizon brought hot wind as the sun rose to lift the cold of desert night. Beneath her, the monochromatic blur of the Ranch began to assume color and shape. Tiny people walked on the thin paths from where she'd come. Some hurried to join the supervised group which assaulted the mountain daily. Teal quickened her pace. Certain other guests, like her, would choose to avoid the group and ignore the sanctioned route. She wanted her time at Skull alone.

Now full sunlight illuminated the mountain. Fewer jackrabbits thumped across her path. Fewer strange shadows pooled to dim the trail.

The last quarter cut straight up on a narrow track. Teal ached against the demand of one more and one more and one more step. Then the incline, after an acute rise, dipped to a hollow before the path rolled upward to terminate at the face of Skull Rock.

Exhilaration and exhaustion urged Teal's arms around the rock. She leaned her cheek against the sharp grain running across the elemental nose. She contemplated the eroded eye sockets above her head. They winked with the glint of sun on mica. Teal stepped back to bow.

"Greetings, friend," she said and raised her eyes to the

smaller stones balanced on Skull's crown. "I offer you the meditation of my soul."

Had she seen anyone watching, she would have felt a fool. This was not the staid behavior people liked to attribute to a CPA. But she was safe and alone. She trailed her hand along hard black teeth and the immobile jaw circling to Skull's back until she lowered herself to sit at the nape of Skull's neck. The land dropped off like a cliff just three feet in front of her to an open vista of hills and seared brown valleys fading against a deep, blue sky. The distance shimmered with heat.

Teal straightened and crossed her legs. She placed the back of her hands on her knees, forefinger and thumb joined in a circle. She closed her eyes and sought the still center within, but none of the habitual preparation for meditation brought peace. Her mind rioted with emotion, buzzed with disjointed thought and a nightmare image of Felicia dabbing colored marks on a *laMode* as Michael pointed to each letter.

"Craziness," Teal said.

She lifted her spine and worked to focus on breathing. Thoughts raced and lingered and repeated. She was hungry and wondered about breakfast. Would it be muffins or hot cereal?

Teal made herself inhale to a count of four and exhale on four more. She drew her mind to the flow of air past her nostrils, in and out, cool and warm, time and time again. She brought to mind Nancy's mantra.

Peace . . . harmony . . . well-being.

All other sensation, smell and touch and sound, began to fade.

Absorbed in meditation, she did not hear the scrape of stone against stone. She did not notice the rush of air displaced by the stone that cracked against her head. Her spine collapsed and her hands fell from her knees, palms flat to the ground.

———

"Hey, Teal! Teal! Can you hear me?" Renee asked in an urgent voice.

"I think she blinked," Carole said.

"Should I put a shirt or something over her?" Sandra asked the group with an eagerness to fit in.

"I think we need an instructor or someone from the Ranch to help." Felicia sounded angry and nervous.

"So—what were you doing up here, Felicia?" Carole asked.

Felicia straightened from Teal's prone body.

"Resting. What do you think? I didn't see her behind this goddamned stone."

"Well, I think someone did this on purpose," Carole said then.

Renee didn't participate in the sniping, but put a hand to Teal's brow. When Teal didn't show up for breakfast, everyone began to question Renee. Hadn't Teal come down from the mountain?

Renee sighed and looked at Sandra. The associate managed to stick to the group like a burr on tights. She had been the one to convince Carole they should look for Teal. Renee had expressed doubts, but Carole steamrolled past her objections. There was no escaping joining the group's expedition.

Renee wondered if Sandra simply wanted to climb the mountain. Another person and another time, Renee might have understood. The mountain was a part of the Ranch myth. No one had offered to hike with Sandra and she'd been discouraged from walking with the organized morning group. In the end, Renee gave up her objections.

Sandra surprised Renee. Her girth of excess weight made her ascent slow and she struggled to catch her breath, but she never complained. She was no more winded than anyone else at the top. Which, frankly, was quite a bit, Renee realized as they all panted.

They had seen someone in front of the rock from the final rise. The figure hurled first one stone and then a second past Skull's cheek. Renee tried to run, hoping the person had seen Teal.

Carole named the individual first.

"Felicia!" she had yelled.

The woman stopped mid-bend for a missile.

"What are you doing?" Carole asked.

Renee broke in. "Have you seen Teal?"

"Eek!" Sandra had wailed. "She's back here."

Carole undid the water bottle on her belt and laid a wet hand on Teal's temple. Then she drew her fingers to the back of Teal's head.

"Some lump," Carole said and tilted back to look up at Skull. "Could be one of those ridiculous tokens from above."

Carole stared at Felicia.

"Or some fool made one fall," she said, finally.

"Ugh. Unn," Teal groaned.

She opened her eyes and grimaced.

"Hurts?" Renee asked.

Teal couldn't answer for the throbbing pain slicing apart the lobes of her brain.

Between Sandra spelling Felicia and Renee replacing Carole, they managed to half-walk, half-carry Teal down. She tried not to protest the beat of blood engorged in the vessels of her head which accompanied each step. She obsessed over which precise word had shattered when the rock hit.

Was it peace or harmony or well-being?

She refused the group's unanimous recommendation she go to the infirmary. The determination of her "no" silenced each of them. She didn't say she'd always, since a child, loathed the isolation of the school nurse's cramped and hidden bed.

As proof of recovery, Teal sent Renee to hustle up a tray of food. Carole insisted on staying with the patient.

"I'm worried about you, Teal," she said.

"It was pretty stupid of me to sit right under Skull. I know people balance offerings on top."

Teal made an unsuccessful attempt to laugh. Carole didn't join in, but shook her head.

"I can't help it, but I'm worried after what happened to Nancy. If I have to suffer another loss . . . Is there something you're not telling me? Something—" Carole gestured hopelessly, "something about Michael or Nan's lover? And what was Felicia doing up there?"

Carole began to pace.

"I'd do anything to bring back Nancy. You can't understand how much her death feels like a repeat of history. Poor Libby—I can't stand to think she'll grow up without her mummy. It isn't fair, Teal, to Libby or me or you or Nancy's lover."

Teal tried to nod agreement, but the pain cut her head in two. Carole went on.

"Nancy's death wasn't an accident, and now I'm worried about you. Can you think of anything to identify the person who beaned you?"

"It was an unbalanced rock, Carole."

"That hit you square on your head, Teal, *on your head.*"

Carole left the hacienda when Renee returned with a muffin and soft-boiled egg. Teal managed to persuade Renee to go away by promising to sleep after she ate. Alone, Teal could do neither.

Could it be that Felicia had dropped the stone? Known Teal was there? Crisis pregnancies added up to a lot of stress. Felicia had compromised her personal and professional integrity with Michael. She nearly destroyed the gallery by "borrowing" client money. All enough to make her life a colossal mess. And in it all, Felicia had betrayed Nancy, her best artist and the woman she claimed as a friend.

Felicia had reason to deter Teal from nosing around for more.

Teal didn't want to think about it. She didn't want to agree with Carole. She didn't want the pain of the lump on her head. Teal pulled the covers closer but they couldn't hide her suspicions.

She'd call Dan Malley tomorrow.

? THIRTY-TWO

The Ranch—Wednesday.

Teal lay on her stomach on the table and heard Berta's suppressed sigh. Was it weariness with the work? Did it seem like one anxious, skinny Anglo woman after another lay under Berta's hands? Did Berta wonder what lives these strange ladies lived in the North?

As Teal thought about it, she wondered herself.

"I had a little accident yesterday, Berta. You'll need to be careful with the back of my head. Otherwise, every aching muscle needs your healing hands."

"Señorita, you are too kind. I treat you gentle like a baby."

Berta rotated her right palm to apply pressure along the base of Teal's neck.

"Umm," Teal groaned, limp with pleasure.

"You usually come with your tall friend, no? I remember her every year, her feet hang over my table, and she send my youngest a big set of paints. She is very nice."

Berta laughed and kneaded Teal's shoulder.

"You come together how many years?"

Berta dug her knuckles into the hollow beside each vertebrae down Teal's spine. Teal didn't know how to respond.

"Your friend not here this year?"

Teal had no choice.

"No, Berta, not this year," Teal said.

"You are from Boston, yes?" Berta asked.

Teal nodded into the table's padding and marveled at Berta's memory. Berta sat on her stool, then raised Teal's right hand to work on the fingers. She started at Teal's shoulder and ended at her soles.

"Time to turn, please," Berta instructed.

She laid a gentle hand on Teal's back as she raised the sheet to grant her client privacy. Teal wondered about the life Berta lived, married at seventeen, now the mother of five children. Teal refused to consider her own life as she slid into her mid-thirties. Those kinds of thoughts had driven Felicia to behave abominably.

Berta reached Teal's forehead at the close of the hour and smoothed her thumbs over Teal's mostly unlined skin. Finished, she dropped her hands and stepped back from the table. Normally Berta would wish Teal well and leave, but today Teal sensed hesitation. Berta wiped her hands across her uniform dress as she stood in the doorway.

"I hear about the accident on the mountain," Berta said. "Staff talk."

She shrugged without apology.

"You tell me it is you, so now I worry because somebody ask about the mountain in the village, *señorita.* An Anglo. He is looking for the woman from Boston and he wants to know all about the sacred mountain. Now I am scared for you. Teal Stewart, *si?* The only one on the list with Boston. You okay, though?"

"Yes, I am," Teal agreed. "The rock fell. An accident, not on purpose."

"Good," Berta said as though relieved of a duty. *"Buenos días,* my friend."

"Teal, be sensible. You don't know that Michael wasn't already up there waiting for you," Carole said.

She pushed her sneakers into the locker, pulled out a white terry robe, and turned her back to Teal as she peeled off her clothes.

"There," she said as she slipped on the robe. "I'm ready for a facial and scalp treatment. I don't know how you can stand Berta. Her pummeling intimidates me. Does she still leave your breasts uncovered? She's the only one of them that does, you know."

"You're being silly, Carole. Berta is wonderful and I needed her after three days of the weights I've been lifting." Teal flexed a bicep. "Let's forget Berta and get back to the point you were making—you and Sandra and Renee are from Boston. This guy could have wanted any one of you."

Carole pursed her lips and shook her head. "Each of us booked too late to be listed. What else did Berta say?"

"Some man was asking these questions. She doesn't know anything else."

"And what did he speak? English? Spanish? Michael's fluent—that slum where he grew up."

Carole could tell that Teal hadn't asked. Nancy's best friend looked scared for the first time. Were she Teal, Carole would feel the same.

"You may be smart to be a little apprehensive, Teal. If Michael thinks you've learned something you aren't supposed to know—"

"No," Teal said. "I don't."

"Are you sure? Something you might not realize you know?" Carole prompted.

Teal shrugged, but Carole heard her mouth Fontane and Fontanez.

"What are you saying?" she asked, a little too fast.

Teal snapped her mouth shut and shrugged.

Carole's eyes followed a young woman parading naked between the lockers.

"That's some display!" Carole said.

"You're jealous because she looks about twenty. Which she is," Teal said, laughing. "I met her in yoga class yesterday and she's quite nice. You'd behave about the same with that body."

"Phew! Anyway, take my advice and take care, Teal."

"Are you suggesting I worry about the rumor from the village?"

"Not at all." Carole gestured her impatience. "Just don't strike the match, set off something you can't control. Oh, I'm going to be late for my facial. See you at dinner and look—humor me. Be careful."

"Kathy, I tried Dan three times without success. Maybe you'll have better luck. Do you mind?" Teal asked.

"Hey, you're my boss and I'm dying for something to do. This week's been so boring I cleaned out all our old files and now I'm helping Don Clarke's secretary with a few memos."

"Laura?" Teal asked.

Laura Smart was sure to cause Clayborne Whittier trouble, but Kathy didn't need to worry about the secretary's lack of ethics today. Laura had her uses.

"She'll have the results of the partners' vote soon," Kathy said.

"Don't let her tell you," Teal instructed. "Please, Kath, don't get caught in her web."

"If you're not admitted, the partners are bigger jerks than I thought," Kathy said.

She looked across the hall to Teal's office. Gloomy and dark. Kathy refused to make any promises about Laura. Kathy wished she'd taken the week off. All the administrative staff in the office were waving and raising high fives when she walked by. They were rooting for Teal, too.

"Dan calls every night, so I'll be talking with him later," Kathy said.

"Good," Teal said. "Tell Dan I think Albert Fontane has been down here looking for me. He may be after information before he goes for Michael. I want Dan to find Albert and arrange a meeting in San Diego. I think Albert will talk to Dan if I'm there."

"No problem," Kathy agreed.

"Fax the time and place to the Ranch's San Diego fax machine. They'll get it to me down here. Don't bother to try the Baja number."

They both laughed. Teal didn't need to explain about the Mexican phone system to Kathy. She knew all about how bad it was from Teal's earlier annual visits.

"There's something else," Teal said. "You might need to take notes."

Kathy grabbed a pen and listened. The project sounded simple. If a messenger service had made a pickup anywhere in Boston for delivery to Nancy Vandenburg around May seventeenth, Kathy knew she would find it.

"No problem. How is everything else going?" Kathy asked.

She couldn't shake the tension from the week. Dan's mother had been driving her crazy with invitations to supper every day. Kathy hated feeling manipulated but said yes each time and ate the tasteless meatloaf and shriveled peas and listened to an extra dose of self-pity about Dan deserting his mommy for such a pretty, young girl. When Mrs. Malley asked Kathy to delay the wedding, Kathy almost had screamed.

Kathy wanted Dan back to face down his mother. Most of all she wanted Dan back. And she wanted to know about Teal. Partner's secretary, Kathy thought, and crossed her fingers.

"Things are fine, Kath. And with you?" Teal asked.

"Great," Kathy agreed with false energy.

Why burden Teal with Dan's mother? Then she wondered, hanging up the telephone, how truthful Teal's perfunctory affirmation of equanimity had been.

Michael couldn't believe the message passed to him across the hotel's front desk. He stood and stroked his tie with each word he reread.

"Mr. Albert Fontane asks that you return his call."

The clerk had annotated "local exchange" beside the number and checked the box marked "URGENT." Michael folded the note and put it in his breast pocket.

What a hell of a day. The retrospective's prepublicity hadn't been enough for the tight ass at the museum and now this. Michael pulled the message out to read again.

"Mr. Albert Fontane asks that you return his call."

Not just yet, buddy, Michael thought. *Not until I'm good and ready.*

That night the facsimile machine in the Ranch's San Diego office started printing early.

Dan's reply to Teal extruded near midnight. He hadn't found Fontane, but would by Saturday. Dan set the meeting time to surprise Albert at his San Diego hotel on Saturday morning. The single page directed to Renee Maxwell spit out at dawn.

? THIRTY-THREE

The Ranch—Thursday.

Eleven o'clock meant an empty mountain and hot rocks. He'd caught rattlers since he was a kid, earning the tag Snakeman. The whole village used it. Why not? But no one was crazy enough to promise big U.S. dollars for delivery of a live and venomous one until today.

The eighteen-year-old father of two pursed his lips. All Anglos struck him as *loco,* crazy like the ladies that paid the big dollars to starve. He drew air through his teeth knowingly. The Ranch was the village's best employer.

He moved on quiet feet toward the prime basking spots. The warmth of the sun gave a rattler a fair shot. But the deal was alive and today, or no $200.

"You really think it's Michael?"

Renee leaned across the table to stare at Teal.

"You don't have a thing which would hold up in court," she said.

"Not yet, perhaps, but Albert Fontane should change all that," Teal answered.

Renee ran a finger along the weathered, scarred wood.

"How?" she asked and listened to Teal's plan for meeting Dan and Albert in San Diego. "Which will be when?"

"Dan's fax will answer that."

"That reminds me," Renee said. "I'm waiting for a fax myself. Answers on Sandra from my investigator. I wish you'd said something about her sooner. You think Michael wanted Nancy dead, but I could make as good a case for Sandra Moses Jordan. How about obsessed young woman bent to destroy me as she herself felt destroyed? That's motive."

Renee shifted back in her chair and closed her eyes to the sun. Killing time, she mused, before the rest of the group joined them for lunch. Maybe ten minutes remained before the gong would sound.

"Keep going," Teal prompted.

"Means." Renee smacked the table. "Sandra had access to the pathetic letter from my cleaning man and ditto the mail from Italy when she house-sat. Method? Go after my lover. Make me suffer losing someone I love."

"Just like she did," Teal whispered.

"Your crazy Albert admits he was hired. Sandra's as capable as anyone. And remember, Sandra was there the morning Nancy died."

Teal turned her head and Renee followed. Carole waved from the path, pointed to the haciendas, and swept her hand back to them.

"She'll join us after she's changed," Teal decoded. "I wish you'd tell her, or let me."

Renee shook her head. "Not yet, please. I know that's been your plan here, but I'm not ready to deal with Nancy's family. It's not her, it's me."

Teal waved her hand to dismiss her suggestion. "Go on with the Sandra theory."

"If Sandra saw me, she must have seen Nancy in the road. She must have heard the squeal and the thud. But she never came forward, did she?" Renee said.

"Neither did you."

Renee raised her head to look at Teal. Renee knew all

about the importance of eye contact to a jury. She'd given a great deal of thought to what she next said.

"No."

Renee's stomach lurched and turned. Teal was either innocent or stupid. She still didn't see Renee had caused her lover's death.

"But the accident happened virtually in front of you. That's how Sandra described the sequence of events. She admits she saw Nancy, but before Nancy was hit."

Renee felt the stare. Like all cases, Renee thought, conviction came down to the weight of proof, of evidence, eyewitness testimony and confession. Between Sandra and an SGM partner, Renee had the credibility. There was nothing to be gained defending herself to Teal.

"We'll see what Albert Fontane has to say," Teal concluded.

"Yes, we will," Renee agreed.

Sandra finished her last wedge of orange tomato. Orange tomato! Who would believe it. No one at home in Chicago.

She set aside the plate, satisfied. The feeling actually related to eating this week. She looked at her companions. Every one of them was older, every one thin and beautiful and yet—they treated her like a younger friend, without apparent condescension or censure. That was the Ranch ethic. Even Renee ignored the career hierarchy. Sandra narrowed her eyes as Renee rose.

"See you back at the hacienda, Teal?" Renee asked.

"In a few minutes."

The buzz of conversation resumed. Sandra went back to surveying the group. Blonde Carole was stunning for her age, Sandra decided, and always gracious if a little remote, maybe, except with Teal or Felicia. Carole treated Teal like family, but Sandra couldn't describe how Carole acted with Felicia, exactly. Not quite as nice. Sandra liked Felicia best.

Felicia commiserated about fighting to control her weight, although she looked great to Sandra, and always made sure to invite Sandra to join the activities. Teal was more of a cipher, on good terms with every one, but alert to the tensions among them, Sandra realized. She also recognized Teal's concern about her own unexpected appearance. Renee's doing, no doubt. Apprehension surged in Sandra's heart. Had Renee found her out?

Felicia stood next. "Anyone for lounging by the pool?"

"Sure," Sandra said. Her bathing suit didn't cut so deeply beneath her buttocks anymore.

"Great."

Felicia smiled and ran her hand over Sandra's near scalped head in a gesture of affection. Sandra thought of the wiry, straightened black hair that had filled the bathroom wastebasket this morning. Never, ever again, and Felicia seemed to agree.

"Thanks, but no. I'm planning to walk to the gardens this afternoon then take a long soak in the shower," Teal said.

"I took that tour a year ago, and they let you eat while they explain the organic principles. It's sort of fun to do once. Which pool, Felicia?" Carole asked.

"Fussy, fussy. The big one, everybody?"

"See you there," Carole said.

Housekeeping rolled up with the water cart, and the women entered the dining room's kitchen.

"Hey, you wait a minute and I help you," the dishwasher said. He rushed the last stack of plates into the big machine.

The women didn't seem to mind a wait. They sat on the bench and talked. He knew they liked him to do the lifting and to check the pump for pressure. He rolled the first five-gallon jug to the cart and opened the reservoir. He hoisted the jug and turned it over. When the cart filled, he tested the flow.

"I don't know. Not too good," he said in Spanish. "I come along with you today."

This wasn't usual or unusual. The water cart grew older every year and less reliable, but his heart thumped against his throat and his palms sweat. The women smiled, relieved.

"I'll meet you up there," he managed, "after I change."

Now he fumbled off his white pants alone and pulled on jeans. He hurried to the industrial refrigerator and snapped open the door. He hesitated, then bent to remove the wooden box with the woven top from its cold storage.

Nothing to worry about, he told himself. He replayed the words from the telephone.

"Put the snake in a box and the box in the hacienda refrigerator after lunch. The money will be where I promised. Then forget this joke."

The Anglo spoke Spanish okay.

The teenager thought about the $200 and the little adjustment he planned to make. How would the Anglo know? He pulled the box from the shelf.

Teal flopped down on the couch. "Maybe I won't go on that walk. I'm beat with heat."

She leaned back, eyes closed.

Renee came to the door of the bedroom and said, "Take my herbal, then. I don't like them."

"Too hot and claustrophobic, right?" Teal laughed. "You are just like Nancy. I'd be glad to take the appointment if you really mean it."

"God, yes! I'll be happier taking the aerobics class at three."

Teal stopped to greet Carole who lay by the pool.

"Hi. Where's the rest of the crew?"

Carole squinted up. "Late as usual for Felicia, and Sandra's run back for a book. Where's Renee?"

"Damn, I forgot to let her know you all plan to hang out here. I'll run back," Teal said.

Carole shook her head. "Don't bother, you'll be late for the garden walk."

"No. An herbal because Renee gave me her appointment. She'd rather knock herself out in aerobics. How could I refuse?"

"You made the better trade. Observe my level of activity today," Carole joked.

"Well then, loosen up the tension you're holding in your shoulders and enjoy," Teal said, laughing as she walked away.

He bent to open the courtesy refrigerator and froze. Water started running and he turned his head to see what he hadn't noticed. The bathroom door stood closed. He'd come too early. The hacienda should have been empty.

Panic blinded him, but not his fingers. He shoved the box in and yanked the empty water pitcher off the counter. Outside he pumped it full.

"Who is it?" the inhabitant of the bathroom called as he reentered.

"Water delivery." His voice cracked.

"Oh sure—thanks."

Teal dozed under the wrap of hot, herb-soaked sheets, a plastic barrier and layer of large towels tucked and pulled around her body. Sweat trickled between her breasts. The attendant shuffled around the room of bound women to press cool, herb-soaked compresses against their eyes.

The snake, stupid with cold, did not stir. It lay in a box. This was good. The kid had followed instructions, and he hadn't been caught.

The reptile remained lethargic when placed atop the stack of towels on the rack over the bathtub. Now the rattler had only to wait, groggy and dull, until clouds of steam from the shower warmed it into activity.

Dimly, Teal heard the last woman enter. Then came the slap of burning sheets laid over the padded table and the sharp intake of breath in the instant of heat meeting skin. She imagined the attendant swaddling the body, immobilizing arms and feet. These were the sounds of bliss to Teal. She couldn't understand anyone giving up an herbal.

The maid entered the hacienda burdened with broom, mop, bucket, and an armful of linens. Two guests, so-so neat.

She changed the beds, swept the floors to the sliding doors, and whacked the dust pile out to the patio without using up much energy. She pushed the living-room chairs into place, cleared the fireplace grate, and laid a fresh stack of mesquite. In the bathroom, she flipped on the light and turned the tub tap full on hot to fill the bucket. She pulled free the dirty towels hanging from the rack and decided the replacements above looked well supplied.

Disturbed by the rising steam and the jerk, the snake stirred.

The maid slammed the water off and raised the bucket to the floor. She wiped out the sink and stirred a brush around the toilet. She flushed.

The snake uncurled an inch.

The maid tossed scouring powder into the tub and bent with her sponge.

The snake slithered to the rack's front edge.

Below, the maid dunked the mop and wrung it out. She flung the bucket's water to rinse the tub. She damp mopped the floor and snapped off the light. Altogether maybe twenty minutes in the hacienda. She pushed into the next one.

The snake relaxed.

Renee checked in back. She found Teal lounging on the patio with a book.

"Good treatment?" Renee called, coming through the door.

"The best, thanks," Teal said. "I kept dreaming of Nancy. Do you remember that day at Clayborne Whittier? The day she bummed into you at the elevator? I think she almost slipped up and told me then. I wish—"

"She had? Don't you imagine I fantasize one change in my behavior, something I did or said and she'd still be here?" Renee sighed. "Look, I need another shower. Did you take yours at the clubhouse?"

"You've come to know me pretty well," Teal said.

"At least that part. Not why you'd bother to wash before lying in hot, smelly sheets and plastic wrap." Renee made a face. She hadn't expected Teal to use their shower. "I'll be out in—"

"About twenty-plus minutes," Teal finished.

Renee nodded. "You like hanging out in dirty cotton. I prefer long showers."

In the bathroom, Renee slid the curtain closed and twisted on the water. She liked to step into a stream of hot, hot water. It helped purge memory. She pulled her clothes off and let the steam fill the room, before she eased into the tub.

She stood. She washed. She rinsed. She soaked. The burning spray hit her skin with pleasant force.

"Damn," she said, her voice just loud enough to carry to Teal.

"What's the matter?"

"Towels. I swear they were here earlier today."

Renee heard Teal coming.

"What about the extras on top? Shall I grab one since I'm taller?" Teal asked from the doorway.

"Thanks," Renee said as Teal raised her hand blindly over the edge of the shelf.

Renee turned off the water, pushed back the shower curtain, and stepped out.

The snake flew through the air, its pale red and dusty black diamonds ominous against the white tile. It landed in the porcelain tub with a thump. The pit viper coiled and raised its rattler, shaking with instinctual fury. Renee watched, fascinated.

"A red diamondback," she said.

"My God, Renee," Teal screamed.

She grasped Renee's wrist and pulled. Teal slammed the bathroom door and slumped against the wall. Renee stood wrapped in a towel. She listened as Teal's voice rose.

"Snakes! They terrify me. And if you'd taken your herbal, I would have been in there."

Teal stopped. She stared at Renee, then backed away.

"You asked for help with a towel you could have reached."

? THIRTY-FOUR

The Ranch—Friday.

"Now hiss out your breath."

Teal followed the instruction. She heard the rattle. She imagined the coil of the venomous snake poised to strike.

"Now draw in a deep, centering breath, filling the abdomen, the rib cage, the shoulders. H-o-l-d i-t. Wait. Good. Now press it away, shoulders—rib cage—abdomen. Once again now, the three-part breath."

The teacher spoke in low tones, but Teal heard only Renee. "A red diamondback," she'd said.

Renee's voice had been so calm. *She* wasn't afraid of snakes. Teal recalled pulling Nancy's lover from the room. Recalled how close they came to fighting and then Renee's question.

"Do you think that snake was meant for you? Felicia, Carole, Sandra—they all heard your schedule. A walk, a shower."

"No," Teal had corrected. "Not Carole. We spoke on my way to the herbal."

"Felicia or Sandra, then. Or what about the man in the village you told me about? He might not be your Albert, but Michael after Felicia. Think of this—he put her up to

264

getting you out of the way. She *was* on the mountain when the rock fell. She expected you to shower today."

It seemed to Teal Renee had worked harder and harder to narrow Teal's suspicions pointing to Carole, then Felicia.

"You knew I wouldn't be in the shower," Teal had said. "But you called me in, and you aren't afraid of snakes."

"I wasn't talking rattlers, Teal," Renee snapped. "What are you saying?"

Teal remembered shrugging before she answered, "Nothing, really. I guess I could make a case for anyone. Now, don't you want to blame Sandra next?"

"What do you think?" Renee asked, the fury curling the edge of her voice. "That I'm making this up? I killed Nancy and want to get rid of you, too?"

"Maybe you'd just rather the investigation go away," Teal replied.

Renee had stalked off to her room before the Ranch's teenage expert arrived to remove the snake.

"Look," he'd said, working open the rattler's jaw. "It's been milked. Harmless."

He spit on the ground.

Today, Teal remembered Renee's continued anger. Perhaps the anger of the guilty, Teal thought. She closed her eyes and tried to find the still center of meditation.

Teal flinched and tore the hand from her neck. She opened her eyes to see her teacher jump back.

"I'm sorry, Teal. Your spine—it wasn't quite erect."

The yoga teacher looked afraid and Teal felt foolish. She resettled on the mat and sat straight. She tried to follow the rhythm, but the familiar state of meditation eluded her. She shifted her concentration to the present—the afternoon sun warming the room, the cadence of the teacher's voice.

"Good. Let's pause and consider stress before finishing with a visualization. The human animal reacts to changes in the environment with a series of biochemical events experienced as alarm, resistance, and exhaustion. The stress reaction is indiscriminate and occurs in response to major and minor events. Meditation will help control the cycle. Next time you feel stressed, turn to your mantra."

Yesterday, Teal thought, instinct protected me from the strike of the snake. *I made it out of the way. But Nancy didn't. Nancy was overtaken by death.*

Stop dwelling on it, Teal admonished herself.

She clamped her attention on the air streaming in her nose. She attended to her mind's eye. *Peace—harmony—well-being.*

She must find a different peace, a rebalanced harmony, a reborn well-being. She must accept the loss of Nancy. But Teal didn't want to allow her friend to fade to memory. Resistance agitated in Teal's chest.

Her preoccupation broke the thread of visualization, the solace of the instructor's voice. Inhalation and exhalation took on new names. *Husband—sister—friend—lover. Michael—Carole—Felicia—Renee. Sandra? Maybe.*

Teal's tears glazed the mirror's reflection of the mountain to blur. She saw herself through the distortion of fear. She tried to regain the present and listen.

". . . center of Baja, California. The mountain remains a powerful symbol of spiritual growth," the teacher concluded.

Teal thought about her attraction to the mountain, to Baja and all of California, the state she knew to be her spiritual home. California tapped some un-New England facet of her soul. On her last visit to San Francisco, she had paid a girl to read the tarot.

Something about the challenge of a child who lost its mother.

Teal sat up. Libby? Shivers brushed across Teal's back. The teacher interrupted with a final instruction.

"With the next breath, shed an element of your base self on the exhalation. Out. Out. Now open your eyes slowly and return to this world renewed."

Later, Teal understood the child.

Sandra giggled.

"Well? Who has a better nominee?" Felicia demanded as she stood and waved the wine bottle in her left hand. "I give Sandra 'leaving most improved.' How many inches and pounds?"

Sandra shook her head, embarrassed.

"More than any one of us, I'll bet. I propose you accept the honor with grace and reward yourself with something."

Felicia sat back down.

Four heads nodded in unison and turned to Sandra.

"Agreed," they said as one.

"But not chocolates," Carole said.

She flicked her hand in a gesture of deliberate refusal.

"Sex," proposed Teal.

Sandra warmed with an invisible blush.

"But not men," Felicia said. "Jesus, men are bad news."

"You should know, Felicia," Carole said.

Renee spread her arms like an umpire. "Try girls."

Three wine bottles stood empty in the middle of the table.

"Ouch! Who kicked me?" Renee put to the group.

"Girls? No way men are that bad," Felicia revised.

"Shouldn't we leave the choice up to Sandra?" Carole suggested.

Sandra stared at her plate. She wanted to say something funny. She wanted to return to the group as good as it had given to her. Instead, she fell silent.

"Good point, Carole. Isn't it odd the only things we can think of are sex or food?" Teal asked.

"Money," Sandra raised her voice. It wasn't the participation she envisioned, but it would have to do.

"Don't look at me." Renee lifted her eyebrows.

"But of course she should." Carole pointed her index finger. "You're the boss. Well, there must be something wonderful you can do. Hold her to it, Sandra."

Felicia jumped to her feet again.

"Okay, okay. Sandra's won most improved and most motivated. But just like the old Miss America days, we need a Miss Congeniality."

That set the table in hoots and howls.

"Right," Teal agreed. "The girl too pathetic to be considered a real threat to the other contestants. No wonder they voted for her so happily. I'm still upset they axed that prize. Remember watching how the winner struggled to act thrilled? She knew Miss Congeniality spelled l-o-s-e-r."

"The old kiss of death," Carole agreed. "So in that case, why not give it to—"

"You," Felicia said, smiling.

Sandra stared at the women around the table, women who treated her like a friend. Successful, articulate women now acting like teenagers. They watched the Miss America Pageant?

"You really watch that show?" she had to ask.

Four heads swung to face Sandra. Four voices chorused, "Of course."

"You don't?" Felicia asked.

Sandra heard disbelief and read a judgment in the face.

"No," she admitted.

"Deprived childhood," Teal suggested. "Too much

feminism. Come on, Sandra, the show's a riot. My favorite part is the Question."

"Oh God, the Question." Carole giggled and turned to Renee. "And if you had just one message you could bring to the world, what would the message be?"

On cue, Renee lifted her chin and blinked her eyes as if with modesty.

"I'd ask everyone on this wonderful planet, every child and woman and man to work with me to accomplish the goal of peace," she said in a voice like treacle.

"Don't forget to say 'and I want my mom and my dad to know how blessed I have been by their loving support' or something sick-making about backstage parents," Felicia added.

"And that you plan to balance the roles of traditional wife and mother and being a brain surgeon, too," Teal said.

Carole nodded. "I encourage young people everywhere to turn from apathy to achievement. Together we can make the world a better place."

Tears of hysteria streamed down every face but Sandra's. She stared at Carole, usually so composed; at Renee, the dragon lady of SGM; at Teal, the most difficult to catalogue and most insightful; and at Felicia, the most unaffected and warm. This represented adult behavior?

No, Sandra realized. No, this was simply girls, a phase she had missed in hiding from any distinct identity, from any connection with friends or family. Sandra Jordan, brainy and fat and fleeing the ghosts of the past, fleeing, too, all opportunities which threatened intimacy. So, why let herself go now?

Anxiety rose in her throat with the fear that this unexpected sentimentality could distort her objective for the week. The wine had clouded her mind. Sandra wished she'd refused each refill of her glass, but she couldn't refuse to participate in the traditional last-night festivities and no one let her pass. Sandra became more nervous. So few hours remained and she hadn't accomplished what she'd set out to do this week.

"Oh-oh, Sandra's getting bored with our walk down memory lane. I think our age is showing. Let's change the subject," Felicia said.

"Back to men?" Teal offered.

"Well, does anyone have anything either good or new to say about them?"

Five heads shook "no."

"Then I suggest we speculate about that table over there." Carole inclined her head.

"You know," Renee said, "I've wondered about that group all week."

"Such big hair," Carole said and giggled.

"Texas?" Felicia suggested.

Sandra let the conversation pull her in its wake.

Everyone hugged once, twice, and thrice in the chill night air outside the dining room.

"See you all in the morning?" Carole said.

Three voices assented.

"What about you?" Felicia turned to ask.

Teal shifted foot to foot. "Business, I'm afraid. I have to leave early, but I'll see you all back in Boston."

"Business!" Sandra exclaimed. "You sound like you work for the dragon lady, too."

She giggled, then pulled up short. "Oh shit."

Renee grimaced. "Dragon lady? Can't you associates be more original?"

"Business in Boston?" Carole asked. "There isn't a flight until after noon on Saturday."

"No, in San Diego," Teal said. "Aren't you stopping over to work on the retrospective?"

"For a few days. Shall we do lunch?" Carole asked. "L.A. speak."

Teal smiled. "That sounds great, but I should be finished tomorrow and fly out later in the day."

Teal didn't let herself think about the purpose of her business, the hope of answering her questions about Nancy's death. Nor had she shared her relief at finally receiving Dan's fax with Renee. Knowing the meeting was set for tomorrow morning, alone, was best. Anyway, Renee would have been even angrier that her fax had not arrived, even though she asked the Ranch staff about it every day.

Teal looked at Felicia and Renee and Carole and Sandra. Alone was also safer.

"Clients," Renee said, "more demanding than children."

They shared the laughter walking back to their beds.

Much later this Friday night in the predawn silence, the Tecate police found the body, stiff and odoriferous, two days dead.

? Thirty-Five

The Ranch—Saturday.

Teal rose at 4:35 A.M. with a jolt.

She'd slept through her alarm, caught in a dream of returning to Clayborne Whittier to find her office empty, her name no longer on the door. Her security key-card set off an alarm. It rang and rang as she tried to explain to the assembling crowd that she belonged inside the firm. Finally, the sharp beeping penetrated consciousness. Teal vaulted, sweating, from the bed and slapped the clock silent.

She dressed and pressed the last few, random items into her luggage. She considered waking Renee, but to what purpose? Teal decided to let her sleep.

This morning a new moon left the Ranch mysterious in black. A scattering of low lights shed illumination across the major paths. Teal balanced her baggage in one hand and slung her canvas messenger folio over her back. A taxi waited in the dim pull-around at the Ranch gate. Teal slowed with relief when she saw it.

"Stewart?" she called out.

"*Sí, sí.* I come for you."

The driver was fat but not without muscle. He lifted

her suitcase and placed it on the backseat, then ceremoniously helped her through the door.

"To the border, *si?* And the U.S. cab waits there. He promise me," the driver said.

Teal murmured her gratitude.

The short ride took them through the center of town. A pottery barn displayed colorful bowls in a floodlit yard to lure the tourists, otherwise, all the trade appeared to be local. Two bars, a restaurant fronted by large cut-out chickens, and a market met resident needs. The police station stood maybe half a mile from the border. Bright light punctuated its windows and open door.

"Big excitement tonight." The driver turned to face her as he drove. "A body. They say Anglo. Who's missing at the Ranch?"

He laughed at his joke as Teal prayed he would return his eyes to the road. He did as they pulled up to Mexican customs.

"All done," he said. "I carry if you want."

"No, thanks," Teal said.

She paid him with regret. She didn't want to leave the Ranch to return . . . to what? Rumors of a body in Tecate, the anxiety surrounding admission to the partnership, and herself off right now to meet a detective because of another body. Nancy's.

An Anglo. The driver had said an Anglo. Teal spun around, but the Mexican cab was speeding away. The driver gave a cheerful wave. The taillights diminished and disappeared. The Mexican border official shrugged with irritation at her question and waved her through. The U.S. official suggested "drugs" with a knowing shrug.

The formalities of exit and entrance took almost no time so early in the morning. Best of all, her U.S. taxi stood across the line.

"San Diego, right, lady? Hotel on the Bay?"

"That's it," Teal replied.

This cabby seemed disinclined to further conversation. He flipped on the radio, picking up a static buzz as they navigated through the hills. Teal didn't notice. She pulled Dan's fax from her bag.

He had set the hour of their meeting to give them the advantage of surprise. Early, Teal thought, near the hour Nancy died. Tension shallowed Teal's breath to a hollow flutter. She shifted back on the seat and began to fold the paper as though it mattered to be meticulous. She bent and smoothed the paper.

A line of print on top caught her eye. She hadn't read this before. The originating telephone number, time and date headed the page, all data relevant to the transmission, not the message.

She expected the California area code. The time, like in the military, reflected a twenty-four hour clock. The digits read 23:45 beside Wednesday's date. Late Wednesday night, Teal calculated. But she received the fax late Friday. The Ranch's slow pace, no doubt. Renee had never received her awaited dispatch. Renee became so mad she had yelled at her secretary.

He swore he'd transmitted the investigator's information early in the week, then he read the conclusion to her. Sandra Jordan née Moses had attended each day of the Chicago trial. There was nothing to indicate she'd known about Nancy Vandenburg and Renee.

Nancy. Nancy. Nancy.

Teal's heart beat the name. Nancy, why didn't you tell me? Why didn't you trust me to understand? Now I'll never be able to assure you I do. Death took you too soon and left me guilty, Teal realized. She turned to the window, desperate for diversion. The merriment of the last night at the Ranch had faded.

The narrow road climbed hills and snaked down the other side, the country showing sparse and empty in dawn's pale light. Teal sat back in the torn plastic seat and closed her eyes. Albert must hold the key to implicating Nancy's killer. Had to.

Teal contemplated the inevitable confrontation with Michael, and her heart began to skip and hurry beats.

She tried to clear her mind and imagined yesterday's yoga teacher in class.

"Shed an element of your base self," the woman had said.

Teal concentrated. She wanted to shed her obsession with Nancy, her guilt and fear. Her misplaced focus.

Misplaced focus. The thought resonated in her head as the cab pulled up to the front door of the hotel.

Dan waited for her in the lobby.

"He's not here," Teal said before he spoke.

It wasn't a question. Suddenly she understood the lights blazing from the Mexican police station. She knew she could identify the Anglo's body found by the border.

Dan dialed Fontane on the house telephone. The extension rang unanswered. Dan stared at Teal as he dropped the receiver.

"What are you trying to say?" he asked.

Teal couldn't explain. Her panic rose like hot lava. She wanted to be sick. Words cramped and glued to gibberish in her throat.

They found the manager in his office. One look at Dan's badge and he didn't need persuasion. He opened the room and affirmed what she knew. Empty. He shook his head over the records in response to Teal's question.

"No. Michael Britton checked out two days ago."

Teal yanked Dan's arm. "The Ranch. We have to get back before—"

She couldn't finish. It *couldn't* be too late.

Misplaced focus churned through Teal's brain.

Sexual jealousy arose when once the sleeping princess

awakened. How else to understand what had happened to Nancy? Fontane had told Teal, hadn't he? Killing Nancy was a terrible *mistake*. Teal hadn't heard what he said.

Among all the betrayals, who must feel the most betrayed?

There was Michael fearing loss and a divorce. Renee whose entire career could be destroyed. Carole, a sibling facilitating a sister's greater fame and watching her greater joy. Felicia, silly enough to sleep with Nancy's husband and lose the artist. Sandra represented the avenging angel seeking employment with the woman she hated and discovering the secret.

Teal had detailed every one before, even to the child who lost her mother. But she never understood the real betrayal. Until today. This moment.

"God, Dan, I hope—" Teal's jaw froze.

"We're not too late?" Dan offered.

Teal nodded and bent to urge the car forward. Dan didn't waste any time. The automobile raced along the freeway.

Morning light danced through the skylights of the dining hall and played on the heads of those who breakfasted below. Two women spooned yogurt over oatmeal and scooped papaya from its skin. Teal, standing beside them, made a third.

"I need your help," she said.

Dan made it four. They panted, ran, and scrambled up the mountain. Teal could only imagine those ahead. She crossed her fingers. Before the mountain's final rise, before the two groups must all converge, she voiced her plan.

"I'll go first. You both follow while Dan circles in from behind. That won't be so easy off the path."

Teal prayed silently. *Please Lord help this work.*

"Come along as though this is an ordinary morning. Be noisy and chatty. Call out greetings when you see me . . . and them."

Teal contemplated the path before her. The fine hairs along her arms rose. The weight of good and evil stood everywhere massed in the rocks beside the trail. The Ranch's soul, like a woman's, she thought. Like a man's. She started to hike in earnest.

At the crest, two figures stood outlined before Skull Rock, and Teal's spirits soared. No metal flashed. No guns, no noise. Teal began to run, slipping on the incline. Closer, she saw the bound hands and feet, the blood trickling from the temple to the cheek.

Stones littered the ground. But the pile by one figure waited, stacked and neat. That body bent and raised the next, arm lifted to throw.

"Carole! DON'T!" Teal screamed.

❓ THIRTY-SIX

The Mountain—Saturday.

The figure wheeled around to Teal and heaved. The rock caught Teal in the chest, knocked out her wind and took her to her knees.

Felicia and Sandra came around the bend and chorused, "Hi, Renee. Hi, Carole."

Malley was nowhere in sight as Teal regained her feet and saw the glint of sun on steel. Carole balanced the knife blade against Renee's throat.

Keep the focus away from Renee, Teal decided, and she began to talk.

"You had me convinced, Carole. Everything pointed to Michael and I agreed. Then you slipped, but by so very little."

Carole stood, still wild-eyed. Still pressing the blade against Renee.

"I should have figured out you dropped the rock on my head, but you'd staged the accident so well. You even made me suspect Felicia. That got me worried about Renee. I'd shared the route with her the day before. Everyone seemed a better candidate than you. You were clever."

Carole lost all interest in Teal at Renee's name. She

stepped back a foot and snatched a stone from the pile. Still Dan did not appear. Carole limbered her arm in an arc and the rock twirled as Carole wound up the pitch. Teal raised her voice to a scream.

" 'Strike the match,' Carole. You shouldn't have said that in the locker room when we were talking about the village rumors. But you couldn't have known I'd read Nancy's poem. 'Strike the match' was your mistake."

And almost mine for not seeing it right away, Teal didn't say.

She heard Carole's terrible laugh, but Carole's attention held on Renee. Teal needed more. She gambled on the outcome of Kathy's research.

"You were clever to go for the book yourself. The shop thought Nancy had come, a change of mind, just like you hoped. Did you read the poems right away or make a copy before handing it over to the messenger service? Nancy made it easy for you, didn't she, by expecting messenger delivery. But you weren't as smart as you thought. The service recorded the pickup as your address. And your pretending to be Nancy? I realized it was impossible when Renee told me—"

Teal slammed her mouth, but Carole was too fast. She charged over the rock-strewn yards to grab and twist a handful of Renee's dark hair and Renee's head snapped back. Teal understood the images crowding Carole's head and prayed for Malley. Teal began again.

"You heard the bookbinder on Nan's machine. Did you know Felicia inadvertently shielded you? That's funny. She was in the studio that day, hiding as you came up the stairs. She thought Michael was the intruder and later, for reasons of her own, she said she was sure. Lucky for you."

And unlucky for the body at the border. Teal took as deep a breath as she could.

"Did you realize immediately the message referred to a

journal? You must have been relieved. One read and you'd know who Nancy was seeing. She only wrote for special people. Didn't she title your collection 'With a Sister's Love'?"

"And she did love me." Carole spun to face Teal, screaming. *"ME*. I was the woman in her life! She didn't need anybody but me!"

Carole's voice grew more shrill. "I knew something was up when she changed her will, said the word divorce. But I didn't know who."

Carole twirled and heaved the rock. It fell well wide of Renee.

Teal watched Nancy's lover, stoic and alert, and tried to understand Carole's crazed words.

"She asked for my advice. She confided in me, told me about the new trust for Libby, I lied about that to you. I didn't care if she left Michael, but she never hinted she was going to replace *me!* She never said a word about this *bitch!"*

Carole's attention locked on the bound woman. The shift terrified Teal. She needed Dan to appear. Teal shouted across the space to Carole.

"Her journal disappointed you, didn't it? She wrote so many words of love, but never identified the who. You went crazy wondering. Is that why you marked up that *laMode* in streaks of pink and green? Did you hope to make her confide in you? It was clever to send a marked page to yourself."

"It worked," Carole shouted back.

Teal could feel how much Nancy's dependence meant to Carole. How much Carole wanted to believe her sister loved her always and first. Teal hesitated only a second.

"No, it didn't. She told you nothing."

"You're wrong. You're wrong," Carole screamed as her voice cracked with her frenzy. "Sunday night when I showed her what had come to me, she smiled and said, 'I love *her.*' She couldn't take the word back. Then I knew what the journal had made me suspect. But *I* was enough for Nancy—she'd see."

Teal heard Sandra moving on the path and saw Carole stiffen. Nancy's sister launched a rock. It flew past Teal.

"Ouch," Sandra cried.

Carole returned to throwing stones at Renee. One hit cracked against Renee's shin. Teal tried to think.

"You never meant for Nancy to die, but she did. Albert's screwup killed your sister. You blamed him for the murder."

Carole grinned like a maniac. "No, I blamed her!"

The rock hit Renee on the shoulder.

"But you killed Nancy, didn't you, Carole?" Teal said.

"No! I said frighten her, just frighten her. Hurt her so she could see she needed me! Mummy made me responsible for Nancy. Me! Don't you understand Nancy was mine!"

"And reading the journal, you became afraid of losing Nancy."

"No! No! It wasn't that simple. I wasn't sure. I didn't care if Nancy left Michael for another man. I only set it up when I suspected it was a woman—"

"And then you got nervous," Teal said.

"Yes. I told him twice not to go forward. If only Nancy had trusted me over the Fourth. But Sunday, Nancy said, 'I love *her*' and refused to say who. I had to put the plan in motion and *it should have worked.*"

Carole smashed the rock against Skull's face.

"Do you understand? After the accident, I'd have had Nancy all to myself. THIS BITCH WOULDN'T HAVE BEEN ALLOWED IN THE HOSPITAL! She's not family. I never wanted to have to do it. Nancy shouldn't have made me. She should have confided the truth on Libby's birthday."

Carole gasped and mimicked Nancy. " 'I want you to

meet my lover as a person, not just a name. I love her, so will you.' That's how she told me! THAT'S HOW SHE TOLD ME!"

"And it hurt, didn't it?" Teal said.

"Hurt? You think *hurt* says what she did to me? I called in my final instructions the night before the accident. I would have done anything to get her back. Then Michael ruined the plan. I'd said a broken leg or something, not hurt too badly, not my Nancy. But Michael scared her into the road. He made Nancy so unhappy she wanted to leave for *her.*"

Carole wheeled on Renee, the knife flashing.

The depth of the tragedy suffocated Teal. Carole's needs were a perversion of sibling love, confusing identity with control, attachment with obsession. Nancy's move to independence disturbed the balance of Carole's life. And left Nancy dead.

Still no sign of Dan. Teal grasped at straws to prolong the mad dialogue.

"You couldn't scare her from her love. You couldn't destroy her love. You couldn't discover her lover's name. You must have been frightened. And then Nancy was dead! You must have been in terrible pain. You panicked when you thought her estate lawyer was her lover! She would have died for nothing."

Teal realized her mistake. She had brought Carole back to Renee. She had to divert Carole's focus.

"You surprised me at the cemetery. I couldn't understand why you'd booked the Ranch before I asked, but you wanted to keep me and the investigation in sight, didn't you? Were you afraid I'd find you out before you had time to find her lover? What a mess, Carole. I wanted the killer. You wanted the lover—"

Teal stopped. How had Carole identified Renee?

Carole must have suspected Teal's roommate at the Ranch. Here was a woman lawyer, collector of Nancy's art, mourner at Nancy's funeral, with Nancy's best friend. But what made Carole know for sure?

Teal fingered the fax folded in her pocket, delivered so late. She considered Renee's inquiries about Sandra. Sandra wasn't the story here. The story was, Carole must have stolen Renee's missing fax from the Ranch message board. Renee's interest in Sandra vis-à-vis Nancy proved what Carole had begun to suspect. Renee must be Nan's lover.

"The fax—that's when you were sure," Teal cried out.

Carole grinned. Teal could see how close Carole was to having what she wanted. Had she grinned at Michael this way?

Poor Michael. Albert Fontane had followed him to California and what Michael began to suspect sent him to Mexico looking for Carole with ideas for rapprochment with his sister-in-law far beyond the arm-twisting he'd tried after Nancy's death. Teal imagined he'd made the inquiries in the village Berta reported. Did Carole laugh when he threatened blackmail on the mountain? Poor Michael.

Carole hadn't cared about the money he demanded or Nancy's estate. She wanted time. She'd bought it from Teal by casting suspicion on Michael and blaming Felicia for the rock Carole had dropped on Teal's head to loosen Teal's tongue. Michael's role in her search was over before he started. His knowledge came at the price of death.

The rattler had been a stroke of impulse. And Teal made it easy for Carole to change her plan. Even though the fax hadn't settled her doubt, she targeted Renee. But the snake failed to strike. She didn't realize it had been neutered anyway.

Time had narrowed for Carole to this hike on the mountain. She must believe nothing could stop her now.

"I think you should drop the knife," Teal said. "Detective Malley is behind you with a gun."

Carole wheeled around blind with hate. The knife flew from her hand, but did not hit her target. He came for her and she kicked at his balls.

She saw Teal beside Renee, cutting the ropes with the knife.

"NO!" Carole screamed and her kick connected with Dan's thigh, and he had her foot twisting in his hand.

Her "NO!" echoed in the hills as she crashed to the ground. She tried to claw out his eyes, but he had a knee in her back while he clicked the pair of cuffs around her wrists. Spit was the only weapon left and Felicia got it in the eye.

She made them drag her down the mountainside.

They sat on hard plastic seats in the airport lounge. Four handsome, intelligent women in a silent row.

Sandra turned to Renee.

"Hate motivated me through school. My sole goal was to be in a position to hurt you as you'd hurt me. When I found those letters, I thought I knew all about your hypocrisy. I watched you on the Cape, not knowing who she was to you. I thought I'd caught you out. Then I realized I was no better as an officer of the court. We both drove away from a woman's death."

Renee nodded as Sandra talked on.

"When I heard you tell your secretary about coming here, I decided to come, too. Hatred had consumed my life, but I wondered what was right after the Cape. I don't know. I learned things at the Ranch. All of you treated me like a friend. I lost weight. I guess I want to say I don't expect the past to own my future."

Felicia sat in a daze. Nancy, her rival, if Felicia could

claim that stature in so pathetic an affair—but Nancy, Christ, a lesbian! What a laugh on Michael! Poor dead bastard.

Felicia realized she'd been a fool. Almost bankrupting the gallery in her mania, spending borrowed money to meet him in Italy, indulging him in weekends at the Plaza. He never even loved her. How pathetic.

"Did you have a D & C, Felicia?" Teal asked.

Felicia nodded.

"That weekend, I just wanted to tell her, maybe she'd have let him go . . . as if he wanted me."

Felicia began to laugh and to cry.

"I cancelled the procedure at least three times thinking maybe. Maybe he would leave her. Marry me. That night on the Cape, when I looked into his eyes—he didn't want me. I rescheduled from their house and had the abortion Monday morning. The morning she died."

A chaos of emotion gripped Renee.

The revelations of the day had left her paralyzed. She would have welcomed Carole's success. Why not be dead?

The ravages of possessive love, the horrors of its pain—her head ached. She'd wanted to possess Nancy in her own way, on her terms and had driven to the Cape, heedless of Nancy's request she stay away. She had killed Nancy, at least that's what she believed until this week.

Had she surprised Nancy into running to the middle of that road? She would never know. Renee dropped her head into her hands.

Teal asked Nancy's forgiveness. *I suspected the wrong woman,* she admitted as she turned to look at Renee. *I suspected almost everyone.* Teal observed the pride with which Sandra held her head. Beside Sandra, Felicia fussed with her ticket, a single, Michael ever out of the picture. Renee wiped tears away. No life had escaped untouched.

I suspected almost everyone, Teal thought, *until only Carole remained, crazy with a sister's distorted lust.*

❓ AfterWord

Monday, One Week Later.

Teal stood motionless at her office window and stared, sightless, at the street below. She had been back in Boston for a week.

A year ago in San Francisco, the tarot reader predicted "a child would challenge." Not Libby, Teal realized now, but Carole Anne Vandenburg's needy inner child. Carole, who never intended Nancy to die and who could not accept the blame, awaited extradition to the United States from her Mexican jail.

And what had become of the others touched by Carole's crime?

Albert Fontane returned from Mexico to give himself up to the custody of the Shell Bay police.

Dan Malley lingered in Tecate, caught in Mexican red-tape. His mother's possessive love continued unabated. Kathy bemoaned the invitation to dinner every night, but grinned and ate.

Michael's ashes lay for eternity beside Nancy in Mount Auburn cemetery.

Sandra Jordan planned to leave SGM for a position with the district attorney in Chicago.

Felicia and her new partner, John, began to benefit

from the publicity as Vandenburg's commanded record prices.

Teal shifted her attention to the book open in her hands, the book she'd been reading for the last hour. Renee had pressed it on her when the plane landed.

"Please, read it again. I want you to see," Renee said.

And Teal did. She saw that "Robert's place" referred to home in Robert Frost's "The Death of the Hired Man." She saw how Nancy's new love had stunned her friend.

"But if it comes to a question of preference," Nancy had written in closing, "I prefer to be true to myself and leave the safety of convention for love of you."

Renee already was fighting for custody of Libby. Teal wondered how the courts could presume to define true family. The genetic tie of Carole and Nancy? Renee's desire to assume care and responsibility for her lover's child? The wisdom of Solomon again would be put to the test.

Teal closed the book and the artifacts of her life came into focus. A red pen lay beside a set of draft financial statements. The top telephone message read "Urgent! Call with comments on the 10-K ASAP!"

"Urgent!" Teal laughed, tears blurring her eyes.

And there was Nancy's painting. The half-rendered professional woman and the scenes of life below. Teal sighed. Her own questions of preference remained. Isn't that what Hunt had meant last night?

"And if they offer you a partnership tomorrow, Teal, is that what you want?" he had asked before he told her he expected to return to Boston. "I'll enjoy watching you find your way in the partnership community—if you say yes, of course."

Teal tapped her heel to the floor. Patience had never

been her strong suit. She swung around at the first knock.

Don Clarke stuck his head through the door.

"The partners agree," he said. "Congratulations!"

Please turn the page for an
exciting sneak preview of
J. Dayne Lamb's newest Teal Stewart mystery
UNQUESTIONED LOYALTY
on sale now
wherever hardcover mysteries are sold!

One

? ONE

Monday

The woman with the bright hair rolled a tissue across the smear of red lipstick glistening on her lips. She crumpled the stained paper to a ball and let it drop on the sidewalk as she watched the revolving door spin. *Someone else working the weekend?* She felt like she'd been losing time and tried to think. *Could it be early Monday? Before the sun rise?* The disorganized buzzing in her head stopped long enough for her to blink and recognize the face as she raised her pale eyes. She extended her cup and grinned. Time to collect.

Teal Stewart stepped across a drift of magnolia petals curled with heat and brown at the edges and walked rapidly across Beacon Street. Long legs powered her forward as she cut every corner of the path meandering through the Public Garden. The frill of cherry blossoms arching over her head failed to delight this morning. She checked her watch for the fourth time, but the possibility she would arrive late did not change. Her pace hurried into a trot.

Hope, habit or loyalty pounded through her mind on a three count beat in time with each footfall.

Hope?

Surely not. She as good as hated Hunt for expecting her to jump at his invitation to meet him for breakfast, no matter the tension separating them for the past months. She hated herself for moving the trot to a run.

Sweat soaked full around her waist by the time she crossed from Winter to Summer. Boston could change seasons that quickly, in the interval of a bisecting street. Winter to Summer, Milk to Water—the patchwork of cow paths turned into roadways made drivers crazy and left tourists queuing for the security of fake trolley buses. Teal slowed, sure in her direction and now close enough to see her destination.

The First New England Bank building punctured the skyline, pressing out and down to straddle a block of prime city ground in Hunt's controversial design. Teal's watch showed one minute to seven on a morning which promised a scorcher of a spring day. The cherry blossoms would drop by tonight.

Teal leaned against a light pole and fished her office shoes from her briefcase. This was as good a place as she'd get this morning to make the exchange. Comfort for torture. Sense for vanity. Keds for spikes. Most days, she used the privacy of her office, but not today; she couldn't afford the time. Teal smiled at the irony since Hunt was the one of them to always arrive late, if he turned up at all. But something in his voice had assured her he planned to break their natural order. He would be there first, and impatient.

She had intended to refuse the invitation in the same cool voice with which she had refused all the others following their disastrous breakfast last summer. That meal had been intended to celebrate her admission to the Clayborne Whittier partnership and his return to Boston from Chicago. She still blamed him for picking the fight.

So, why had she agreed to meet him today?

Habit? Teal groaned. Huntington Erin Houston, famous architect, once lover, now friend, had intertwined her life since she arrived new to Boston from graduate school too many years ago. They had lived together for a few years, and, when the wounds of breaking apart faded, meals at the private Ivy Club on top of the FNEB building replaced the eat-in kitchen of their old apartment. Breakfast remained the favorite until a different separation further deteriorated their relationship.

The wedge of Teal's career ambition had made Hunt crazy.

Loyalty? Was it loyalty that set her in motion, hurrying across the street? Hunt hardly would agree. Their last conversation across the plates of Ivy eggs and cups of special-blend tea circled through her mind.

Hunt had raised black eyebrows in a blacker judgment. "You think Frank Sweeny is a jerk! You've always thought he was a jerk. Why offer to be his second partner on—"

"His one client big enough to get Clayborne Whittier in trouble? Figure it out Hunt," she'd snapped.

"Unweaning loyalty to the firm? Is that why they made you a partner—to cover up for Frank? Why should you correct their admission mistake?"

"Because now I am a *they.* And Frank has his uses."

"Like what?" Hunt had laid sturdy hands flat on the table as he leaned forward. *"You* partners could fire him."

"Firing partners is not in the Clayborne Whittier culture."

Teal remembered Hunt's snicker. His mouth tight with disapproval.

"What's happened to you?" he had asked later, as they stood. "The new partner drugs getting to you?"

The old barb hurt, turned against her. Hunt had come up with the quip years before, when Teal described the behavior of a once reasonable human being turn monstrous after admission to the partnership. "Must be a mandatory course of personality-altering drugs comes with the big office," had been Hunt's observation. The running joke held less humor when Hunt refused to let the subject of her complicity on Frank drop.

"So, the great firm can't admit they goofed—but you're talking to me, Teal. Be honest. Why should you help keep Frank from facing his mistakes?"

"Because he's my partner," she had explained, hearing the defensive edge on her voice.

"Oh, l-o-y-a-l-t-y to the great firm. They wouldn't thank you," Hunt had concluded.

Hunt had had a way of hitting the target. Clayborne Whittier wouldn't thank her and acknowledge their mistake.

"Damn," Teal muttered. She rammed her sneakers into her briefcase.

Hope. She could feel the signs. See hope in her outfit this morning. How long had she searched the closet to find the red linen dress Hunt loved? When was the last time she had used his favorite perfume? She was crazy—and late.

She sprinted for the FNEB revolving door, hand raised to push. She wasn't paying attention to the ventilation grate. When her heel caught, she went down before she could be afraid. The pedestrians hurrying along the sidewalk kept their momentum, troubled only long enough to swing wide of her fall.

Temper and relief rose in a measure equal to Teal's vanity as her hands braced to absorb the shock, landed on something soft.

The homeless woman who cushioned the drop did not shake Teal's grasp from her shoulder. She did not ask for spare change although her hand held a lipstick-stained

Dunkin Donuts cup as if extended for a donation. Two quarters rested in a curdle of cream in the bottom.

"I am sorry," Teal said. She saw the woman better as she straightened.

The woman's dress was arranged in a swirl around her curled legs. A little pillbox hat perched on tarnished hair smoothed into a french twist. Teal realized that under the patina of hard wear, the woman could be near her own age, over thirty, less than forty. Teal knew her as a part of the FNEB scenery many people chose to ignore. Usually a cigarette burned between the carefully painted lips from which she flung foul or gracious appeals for money, depending on inexplicable whim. Right now the woman gazed at Teal with her lips turned down.

"Sorry." Teal held up her battered shoe. "Stupid of me."

The woman stared with wide eyes. Teal stared back, the smile contracting off her face. A less self-centered and preoccupied morning, and she would have recognized the truth at once. Kneeling at the woman's side did not change what Teal did not want to recognize.

Death had provided the woman with a permanent home.

"I didn't see a thing, Dan. Really," Teal repeated.

She clenched a fist behind her back, rolling newly polished nails into her palm before she shook her fingers free. First one hand, then the other, the tension spilling from her shoulder and down her arm. Detective Daniel Malley could not be hurried. Her right hand curled back into a fist.

Why had she called him from the FNEB lobby? Someone else would have noticed soon enough. Someone else would have summoned the Boston police. Someone else would have been answering Dan Malley's questions.

Or she could have taken just a minute to stop upstairs in her office to ask Kathy to make the report.

No. Kathy might love her job, but Teal's secretary was not available for this duty. Not now that Kathy had become Mrs. Daniel Malley.

"The thing is, her hat," Teal had said to Malley on the phone to explain her calling homicide. "It's all soaked with blood in back."

Detective Malley confirmed her worst guess as the hour set to meet Hunt at Ivy receded.

"Her head is b-b-bashed in," he said.

Teal squeezed her eyes shut. "I didn't see anything. Really, nothing. She's been around town, I don't know, on and off for years, I think. Sometimes she's at International Place, sometimes 75 State. Sometimes here, in front of the FNEB. The guards asked her to leave and tried to make her uncomfortable, but she understands her civil liberties. Understood," Teal amended.

She shifted her weight one foot to the other and wanted to get going, leave this sudden death to Malley.

"Must be she died sometime late in the night or early this morning—"

"So what did you expect me to see?" Teal cut in, irritated.

Dan shrugged. "Something that didn't strike you as right."

His tan eyes squinted against the glare off the FNEB facade as he scrutinized the woman.

"She's not going to be anyone's priority," he said and spread his palms open like a benediction.

Teal heard defeat in his voice.

"No. I'm sorry, Dan. It's just—" *just what,* Teal wondered. "She had nothing to do with me. You'll do better with the guard."

Dan eased his head up and down. The youngest, smartest detective on Boston's force, Teal thought. Conscientious to a fault. He would make the homeless woman his problem. But she wasn't Teal's, not this time, not like when Dan and Teal had worked together before.

"If I think of anything, I'll call," Teal said, restless to be on the elevator, to see Hunt. *It was hope, damn it.*

Teal spun through the door into the FNEB lobby. He might have waited, she thought.

"Teal!" Roger Singer grabbed her arm as she stepped inside. "You aren't going to believe this—Frank is going off to Funsters. Right now."

Roger's voice betrayed sly pleasure.

"He showed me a letter, honestly, with *Funsters An Action Oriented Meeting Place* at the top. He doesn't know, and I wasn't about to tell him."

"Letter?" Teal said, stupidly. She could not believe Boston's oldest and most notorious gay bar had a motto.

"It's got to be a joke off some PC!" Glee shook Roger's shoulders.

Teal couldn't decide if Roger was reverting to his former, more whimsical self, or was simply hysterical. The transition to partner had failed to bring out Roger's best, or hers, according to Hunt. The thought made Teal uneasy.

"Did you send it?" she asked.

"Are you nuts?" Roger's grin dropped. "Someone pulled our prank."

She and Roger hadn't been the only Clayborne Whittier managers to consider Frank Sweeny an ass. Frank had crafted a career out of the behavior of a sycophant. A zealous, thoughtless loyalty to the great firm had been his admission ticket.

He chased after any prospective client, no matter how misdirected his effort. Most of those he brought in were inappropriate to the practice of an international accounting firm. Roger and Teal each had worked on more than one of Frank's dogs as staff. Teal had enjoyed coming up with the unkind hoax.

"Funsters," she had suggested to Roger. "We'll send him a phony letter asking him to propose on the Funsters audit."

"Funsters is audited?" Roger had asked.

Teal couldn't believe Roger could be so dense. "Of course not, but what will Frank think?"

"Practice development!" Roger yelped.

"Can you imagine Frank walking through Funster's door?"

They had taken a second to savor the image, the malice in the humor, before both had shaken their heads. And that had ended Funsters three years ago.

Roger was back to grasping her arm.

"I'm not kidding. Frank waved the letter as he climbed into his car. I can't wait to ask him how the proposal is going—"

"Roger, this isn't really funny," Teal said.

Actually, it was, sort of, and they both knew it.

"If you didn't send it and I didn't send it. . . ."

"Who did? Right?" Roger suggested. His concentration brightened. "Probably your Amy."

Teal's chuckle of dismissal caught in her throat. Amy Firestone, her best senior manager. Clayborne Whittier's best senior manager. Teal hoped Roger guessed wrong.

"You told her the story," Roger persisted. "You admitted you told her."

Teal grimaced.

"I never told any one," Roger finished.

Of course he hadn't, Teal thought, just like he hadn't come up with the idea in the first place. Roger was another exemplification of what the partners thought they wanted, someone willing to cede his imagination and autonomy. That's what she used to think in her least kind moments in the year between his promotion and her own.

"Frank'll be back soon. He's only going to Cambridge Street," Roger said as if Teal did not know.

She got the message. Frank had been sent on a tasteless practical joke to her part of town. Funsters was located on the commercial street which separated the West End from her neighborhood, Beacon Hill. This could look bad, except no one would imagine one partner could want to humiliate another. Leaving Amy as the best suspect. Damn, Teal thought.

She made a show of checking her watch.

"Roger, I've got to run. Going up?"

"No." Roger squirmed. "Across the street—"

"To sign your jumbo mortgage?" Teal asked, glad to be off the subject of Funsters.

Roger evaded her direct gaze. Teal knew Barbara Singer, not her husband, had decided she wanted to move into a big, big house. Barbara could outspend Imelda Marcos. No wonder Roger looked trapped.

"You think it's safe?" Teal asked.

Roger pinched a wrinkle into his lapel. "I hear two years in the same office means you're safe from a transfer."

"Hum." Teal wasn't as sure.

"Well, I have to go," Roger said.

The elevator sped express to forty. Ten slow stops brought Teal to the Ivy Club at the top on forty-nine.

Walter spotted her scanning the dining room.

"Mr. Huntington has left, Ms. Stewart." The maitre 'd compressed his lips as if to say what could she expect from Hunt.

Teal flushed with a prickly heat of dashed hope.

"Perhaps he stopped by your office," Walter suggested.

"Of course." Teal kept her smile until she left the club.

———

Kathy raised a blank face when Teal mentioned the architect.

"I haven't seen Hunt in ages, Teal." Kathy said. "Can I talk to you about something?"

"My office?" Teal offered. She swallowed her disappointment.

"I don't know if I should tell you this, but since you are friends . . ." Kathy shut the door behind them, but did not sit.

Teal stiffened. If it was going to be about that stupid Funsters joke and Amy—

"Laura saw the list," Kathy finished.

Teal stopped thinking about Amy. Laura Smart worked for Boston's partner in charge, Don Clarke. Laura was his secretary, among other rumored things.

Teal had heard the talk. Had planned to tell Hunt this morning. Frank Sweeny could get fired, after all. Clayborne Whittier's management committee was adopting a long-term strategy to *transition out* under-performing partners. The decision ended a ninety-year history of protecting partners from termination. All the talk in the firm in the last month centered on speculation about the names on the list. Nothing had leaked from a good source until this.

"Who?" Teal asked, alert with curiosity.

"I don't understand, Teal." Kathy's heart-shaped face suffered with confusion. "Roger."

"Roger Singer?" Teal's voice rose. Mr. Competent? Mr. Safety? About to be canned? And not Frank Sweeny? Roger had worried about a transfer like any partner, but termination?

"That's who Laura said. And she flashed the memo at me." Kathy lifted her shoulders and let them drop.

Teal stepped for the door. "I'd better stop him."

"Stop him?" Kathy's emerald eyes blinked in confusion.

"He's about to sign a huge mortgage. If I warn him—"

"That's the other thing I don't understand. Laura acts like he already knows."

"He knows?" Teal repeated. "You could have fooled me when I saw him a minute ago."

Kathy squirmed.

"There's more?" Teal stiffened.

Ever since Kathy and Laura Smart had become friends, Kathy knew details about the partnership hidden from Teal. The shift had its discomfiting moments.

"The reason." Kathy bit her teeth together.

"I'm not sure I should hear this," Teal said, and she wasn't.

"But it's because of Emma Browne." Kathy's mouth contorted to a frown.

Then Teal understood. Kathy was warning her if she wasn't careful, she would be next.

WHO DUNNIT? JUST TRY AND FIGURE IT OUT!

THE MYSTERIES OF MARY ROBERTS RINEHART

THE AFTER HOUSE	(2821-0, $3.50/$4.50)
THE ALBUM	(2334-0, $3.50/$4.50)
ALIBI FOR ISRAEL AND OTHER STORIES	(2764-8, $3.50/$4.50)
THE BAT	(2627-7, $3.50/$4.50)
THE CASE OF JENNIE BRICE	(2193-3, $2.95/$3.95)
THE CIRCULAR STAIRCASE	(3528-4, $3.95/$4.95)
THE CONFESSION AND SIGHT UNSEEN	(2707-9, $3.50/$4.50)
THE DOOR	(1895-5, $3.50/$4.50)
EPISODE OF THE WANDERING KNIFE	(2874-1, $3.50/$4.50)
THE FRIGHTENED WIFE	(3494-6, $3.95/$4.95)
THE GREAT MISTAKE	(2122-4, $3.50/$4.50)
THE HAUNTED LADY	(3680-9, $3.95/$4.95)
A LIGHT IN THE WINDOW	(1952-1, $3.50/$4.50)
LOST ECSTASY	(1791-X, $3.50/$4.50)
THE MAN IN LOWER TEN	(3104-1, $3.50/$4.50)
MISS PINKERTON	(1847-9, $3.50/$4.50)
THE RED LAMP	(2017-1, $3.50/$4.95)
THE STATE V. ELINOR NORTON	(2412-6, $3.50/$4.50)
THE SWIMMING POOL	(3679-5, $3.95/$4.95)
THE WALL	(2560-2, $3.50/$4.50)
THE YELLOW ROOM	(3493-8, $3.95/$4.95)

Available wherever paperbacks are sold, or order direct from the Publisher. Send cover price plus 50¢ per copy for mailing and handling to Penguin USA, P.O. BOX 999, c/o Dept. 17109, Bergenfield, NJ 07621. Residents of New York and Tennessee must include sales tax. DO NOT SEND CASH.